D0455415

NO PLACE
to FALL

JAYE ROBIN BROWN

NO PLACE to FALL

HARPER
TEEN

No Place to Fall

Copyright © 2014 by J. K. Robinson

For information address HarperCollins Children's Books, a division
of HarperCollins Publishers, 195 Broadway, New York, NY 10007.

www.harpercollinschildrens.com

Library of Congress Cataloging-in-Publication Data

Brown, Jaye Robin.

No place to fall / by Jaye Robin Brown. — First edition.

pages   cm

Summary: Sixteen-year-old Amber Vaughn dreams of attend-
ing the North Carolina School of the Arts to gain confidence in
using her amazing singing voice, but her family is falling apart and
she is torn between two boys.

ISBN 978-0-06-227099-3 (harcover)

[1.   Singers—Fiction.   2.   Family   problems—Fiction.
3. Dating (Social customs)—Fiction.   4. High schools—Fiction.
5. Schools—Fiction.   6. North Carolina—Fiction.]   I. Title.

PZ7.B814197No   2014   2013051284

[Fic]—dc23   CIP

                                                                          AC

Typography by Alicia Mikles

14 15 16 17 18   LP/RRDH   10 9 8 7 6 5 4 3 2 1

❖

First Edition

For all the small-town girls,
and for Raven,
who showed me how to fly

NO PLACE to FALL

CHAPTER ONE

The man talking on the local news has it out for me. Through the screen door, I watch Mama, remote control in hand, mouth gasping like a banked fish with each new tale of murder and woe. Every single day, morning and evening, she convinces herself the world beyond our doorstep is a Very Bad Place. I've managed to sneak off in plain sight all summer long, but I never know when she might decide an ax murderer is lurking in the woods and keep me home.

Devon's Jeep barrels around the curve in the road. I stand up, wiping the dust off my jean shorts. He parks and makes his way across our overgrown yard, guitar slung over his shoulder, foil-wrapped plate in his hand.

1

"Ready?" I say. "Mama's working herself into a scare."

He peers past me into the house. "Hey, Mrs. Vaughn."

"Hello, young'un."

I groan as Mama walks toward the screen door.

"You've got your cell phones? You won't be out too late now, will you?" Mama has her hand on the door pull but doesn't open it. "Devon, you look after Amber. Sometimes there are hikers from who knows where out on those trails." She looks at the plate and his guitar. "What? No salamander hunting today? Y'all meeting somebody?"

"No, ma'am," I lie. "Just us, going to go sing up on the overlook, and we may try and find us a hellbender or two."

That's been our story. That we're on the hunt for the elusive hellbender salamander. That we spend our long teenage hours in the woods, alone, digging under rocks, trying to find a slimy amphibian. The reality is we're headed to the hiker barn. Again.

A twinge of guilt burbles in my gut. If Mama knew what I was up to it'd destroy her. But the thing is, Mama only sees what she wants to see. Even when I come home, lips swollen, with stars in my eyes and a hickey on my neck, she'll look at me all maternal and say, "Did you have a nice time, sugar?" She's as clueless about me as she is about my sister, Whitney, and her drug-dealing husband.

Or about Daddy and his *overtime.* I wonder if the faithful are meant to be so blind.

Devon and I tell her good-bye, assuring her six ways to Sunday we'll call if we run into trouble, and cut across the back pasture toward the trail.

We traipse past Whitney's faded gray trailer and head for the tree line. Sammy, my sister's husband, is outside washing their car, his shirt off, his pale blond hair long on his back.

"Hey." Sammy leers at me and starts playing air guitar on the garden hose.

"What?" I spit the word at him. Whitney may still be in love with him, but I see him for what he is. A low-life loser who'd rather sell oxy than do what it takes to make an honest living. He's a total idiot, but he *can* play the guitar.

Sammy sticks the hose between his legs, spraying water in our direction. "Have a good time—salamander hunting."

I flip him the bird. "Go to hell, Sammy."

Devon ignores him and whistles his favorite Lady Gaga song, keeping his eyes straight ahead until Sammy's hidden by the trees.

Devon's funny. Smart. He moved to town at the start of ninth grade, right around when Whitney abandoned me for Sammy, and we clung to each other like rabbits in a storm. Unfortunately, despite what Sammy may think, Devon's not into girls. It's a crying shame, too, because he's dark-haired, boy-band cute, and although our taste in music runs toward polar opposites—me, bluegrass and ballads; him, Lady Gaga and pop divas—he loves playing the guitar and singing as much as I do.

But most of all, he gets me. Devon understands my burning desire to get the hell out of Sevenmile, North Carolina, which is a seemingly impossible prospect, given my mama's stalwart belief that her flock should settle within a couple of hundred feet of her back door. But Devon's willing to help me try to figure it out.

He jumps into the middle of the trail, tall stickweed shuddering as his guitar hits the leafy branches, and puts his hands on my shoulders. "This is it, Amber Plain and Small, our last night of reckless endangerment."

I hate the nickname. Devon says he's doing me a favor to distinguish me from the other two Ambers in our grade. The two we lovingly refer to as Cheerleader Amber and Amber-o-zia.

Devon ignores my look. "We are going to make the most of this bonfire night with the through-hikers, a final salute to the bad girl that lurks inside of you. Or maybe, might you find . . ." He mock gasps. "Love?"

A part of me bristles as he says it. I mean, yes, he's right. I guess on some level love *is* what I'm looking for. Not necessarily the love of someone, but of *something*. The something that will help me rise above, make me special, make me feel like somebody. Like singing at a music festival or auditioning for one of those television music shows. What would it be like to go somewhere, to do something big? Hell, just to have the guts to sing in front of people besides Devon, my family, and my church. But I can't tell him. He'd tease the hell out of me.

Devon hits a chord and starts singing, "You're beautiful. . . ."

I roll my eyes and turn as he serenades me. We're walking in the middle of an overgrown logging road back behind Pastor Early's farm. The road takes us to the Appalachian Trail and then to the hiker barn. Our destination. The place where I've entertained myself all summer long with interesting boys who don't know my family's reputation.

I've met hikers from as far away as Europe and as close as Johnson City, Tennessee. I'm marking the towns on the map in my bedroom. I know on a certain level that meeting all these people doesn't really count as having been to the places they come from, but it's the closest I've ever gotten. I heard about a jazz festival in New Orleans. A bluegrass festival in Telluride. I even heard from a Tennessee boy about a big festival outside of Wilkesboro where you can camp and play music all weekend long.

This summer has been different that way. The magic of the hiker barn lets me fly as far as I want in my imagination.

Whitney is the one who showed the barn to me first.

She'd taken me there the spring of her junior year, my last year of middle school, before she started dating Sammy. I'd noticed the carvings right away. On every board were names and dates and places. They said things like "Wooly Bear, passing through, June 2002" and "Mark and Joni, honeymoon hikers, Boston to Maine to Georgia, 1997." I'd pored over those carvings, imagining what it would be like to be the kind of person who could pick up and walk away from home like that.

"Through-hikers, from all over the place," Whitney had said. At the question on my face, she'd explained, "The Appalachian Trail is just up that path. There's a sign pointing the hikers to this barn. The property owners let them use this place as an overnight shelter."

I remember thinking my sister was wiser than Jesus. Like she'd opened my eyes and the door to the rest of the world was right here, practically in my own backyard.

CHAPTER TWO

- -

I hold up my hand. Devon stops behind me.

We creep up the spur trail. The big barn is just around the bend.

I can already hear the murmur of voices and bursts of laughter. The smell of camp smoke swirls on the breeze.

We sneak closer and I see sleeping bags hanging out on lines. A hose has been rigged from the creek to wash the hikers' stuff and the tail end of a bright August sun is drying earth-colored clothing.

I feel Devon at my right shoulder. "Are you ready?" he asks.

I see a group of dreadlocked hikers, two guys, one girl.

Another guy, a little older.

There are more bags on the line. That means more hikers. Either in the barn or down at the creek.

"Ready," I say. "The dread guys are kind of cute." It's still hard to believe how easy this has been. Sliding in by the campfire, talking, singing. The first time we showed up I was nervous, but each visit since has been easier. Especially since they've all been so nice, and so eager to hang out with anyone new and different.

Devon purses his lips and gives me his best Marilyn Monroe. "All right, darling, let's go find us a man."

We walk into the clearing. The dreadlocked cluster looks up. The older guy is more suspicious, glancing at us sideways. I sigh under my breath so only Devon hears. He knocks me with his elbow and whispers, "Say your greetings."

"Hi, how you'uns doing?" My voice sounds extra tangy with a side of hillbilly as it bounces down the path.

Devon elbows me again.

"I mean, how are y'all doing?"

"Tired." The boy with the dark dreadlocks smiles up at me, but the girl, super-pretty despite being fresh off the trail, instinctively wraps her arm snug around his waist. I guess hippies get jealous, too.

"Long day on the trail?" I look at the blond dread-locked boy. He raises his arms behind him, cradling his head as he leans against the barn's exterior. His eyes linger on my face before doing a quick trip up and down the rest of me. I don't really mind. He's definitely hiker cute.

"Yeah." He pauses, a wry grin settling at the corner of his lips. "Long day. Y'all just sightseeing or did you actually bring a little trail magic for some tired hikers?"

The dread girl speaks up. "Basil, be nice. Anybody that arrives at camp with a guitar and something in foil wrapping is all right by me." She smiles at me. "What's in there?"

Devon points to the tray. "Brownies. Plain or Secret Ingredient."

The girl smiles and turns to Basil. "See, Basil. Secret Ingredient brownies, your favorite."

The older guy speaks up. His voice is nasal and his words are clipped. Yankee. "You two live around here?"

I nod.

"Curious or Good Samaritans?"

I figure honesty is the best policy. "Both. We've met people from all over the place this summer."

He smiles and even though he's bound to be at least twenty-eight, he has kind eyes. "Well, pull up a log. We've got a little stone soup cooking. My buddies hitched a ride to the store for some supplies." He looks at Devon. "Can you play?"

Devon sits down and pulls the guitar around. He starts with "Blackbird" by the Beatles.

"Righteous." The dread girl's boyfriend lays out long on the dirt and pulls her in to his side. Basil comes and sits next to me. He smells like he's been in the woods for days.

"How old are you?" he asks.

"Eighteen," I lie and unwrap the foil. I point to the ones that Devon's older brother, Will, baked. "I think you might want one of those."

Devon says Will's in an experimental phase, one that's intended to piss their judge daddy off. But Will claims his dad won't find out and besides, his pot-infused butter is worth it. Better than smoking. Not that I do much imbibing of any sort during the school year. It's too big of a risk. The whole town's already seen my sister's fall. All I need is everyone assuming I'm headed down the same path.

The foil crinkles as the hikers gather around and take brownies. The girl reminds them to save a few for the guys who hitched to the store. I notice the older guy takes a plain old sugar-and-butter variety.

Devon finishes his song. "So, what are your trail names? Where are you from?"

I take a bite of one of Will's brownies—it is the last hurrah of summer after all—and wait to hear the answers.

Dread girl says her trail name is Whiskers, something

to do with a rogue hair that sprouts when she doesn't have a mirror to pluck it. She, her boyfriend, and Basil are all from Athens, Georgia.

The Yankee guy laughs. "Mine's Cheese Steak. Because I'm from Philadelphia. But most folks on the trail just call me Philly."

"What would our trail names be?" Devon asks them. It's a question we've asked every group of hikers.

Philly laughs and the sound is more melodious than his speaking voice. It makes me wonder if he can sing. Basil edges closer to me.

Philly points at Devon. "We've only just met, but let's see. I think we'll call you the Picker."

Devon rolls his eyes. "I *do* hope you're referring to my guitar."

"And her," Philly says, winking at me, "we'll call her Pixie, because of that haircut and her impish grin."

I giggle, the brownie already taking effect.

Basil is close enough I feel the warmth of his leg on mine. I glance sideways at him. He might be really handsome without all that nappy hair. I wonder if he's in college, taking the summer off to hike the AT. He shifts slightly, the hair on his arm brushing mine. I look down as a shiver rises on my skin. When I look up, he's staring at me.

Basil arches one eyebrow and stretches his leg out long

so that it nudges me in the process.

I look away but feel the flare rise to my cheeks and a tickle jump in my belly.

Philly throws logs on the fire and Devon cranks up his guitar again, slipping into Johnny Cash mode. He plays "Jackson" and I sing the June Carter Cash parts. Basil, Whiskers, and her boyfriend all squeeze in on me as we raise our voices. Then, Devon switches to "Poker Face" and we're laughing and singing and making crazy faces at each other, the brownies a good half hour into our system. Philly watches us with laughter in his eyes. I'm definitely stoned, but tonight I don't care.

A group of guys walks up the logging road from the direction of the old Whitson house. Hikers, two who look like they belong with Philly, and one younger, surprisingly clean, loner. They're loaded down with bags of groceries and a case of beer.

"Beer!" Basil jumps up from his spot next to me and rushes the approaching hikers. He grabs two bottles and returns, twisting the caps, then passes one my way. "Here you go, Pixie." He loops his arm over my shoulder. I should move out from under it—he's probably too old for me and I've just met him. But it's not like I'm ever going to see these people again.

"You know, you've got a great voice." Basil's voice is

low and conspiratorial, like he's telling me a secret.

I take a sip, the rim of the bottle cold on my lips. "You think?" My heart rate picks up a beat or two, and I fight the urge to move out from the heat of his arm across my shoulder.

"I do," he says. "Come on, I want to hear you sing something else." His arm drops but he grabs my hand instead.

I let him pull me back toward the campfire.

CHAPTER THREE

The new hikers settle around the fire. Two sit near Philly, and the loner guy sits next to Devon, across from me and Basil.

"Hey, man." He holds out his hand to Devon. "I'm Kush."

"Devon." Devon grabs the guy's hand and pumps the hell out of his forearm.

I try not to laugh.

Kush retrieves his hand. "Whoa, some grip. Y'all from around here?" His glance skips between us. He sounds close enough to be local, but he doesn't look like anybody I know. Shoulder-length black hair. Big sleepy eyes the color of goldenrod in the fall. Bronze skin. I think he must be part Indian. *India* Indian, not Native American.

Devon's gone all tongue-tied. "Right here in Seven-mile," I say, speaking for him.

Kush nods like he already guessed. He points at the foil in Devon's hands. "Can I have one?"

"Oh, right, sure." Devon recovers and squares his shoulders. His voice drops an octave. "Here you go." He doesn't point out there are two varieties, and Kush takes one of Will's doctored delights.

Basil casually slides his arm behind me before nodding at Kush. "They do things different here than in Georgia. Am I right?"

"You can say that again. There is nothing out there." Kush points beyond the trees.

I guess Kush is from Athens, too. It surprises me they're hiking together. Basil and his other friends seem granola crunchy compared to Kush, but what do I know?

Philly and one of his friends leave our circle and start seasoning burgers over by the charcoal grill.

Basil leans in. "So, you going to sing for us, or what?" The thumb that had been casually touching the side of my thigh lifts up and explores the hem of my shorts.

Devon inclines his chin so slightly in my direction I almost miss it. Then he purses his lips.

I shrug. He knows, like I know, that after this week, our fun is over. It's back to school and homework and life as usual. But I also know Devon won't judge me. What happens at the hiker barn stays at the hiker barn. And so what if I hook up with Basil? It's not like I'm going to marry him or have his baby. I'm not Whitney.

"Well, what do you want to hear?" I clutch the beer bottle in my hands.

Basil leans closer. "Sing something hot."

Kush snort laughs. Then Devon starts giggling. Pretty soon we're all laughing and Basil's taken his hand off of me and is waving it in the air for us to stop. "All right, all right. I get it." He nudges me. "Sing what you're good at."

"Play 'Amazing Grace,'" I say.

Devon pulls his guitar around and hits a chord. His eyelids are hanging low and he's wearing this goofy sort of half smile. I wonder if I look as stoned as he does.

He starts strumming the guitar and I pretend I'm in our family pew at my church, Evermore Fundamental. It's the place I feel safe singing it loud. My voice rises up. I open my mouth and the notes fly to the trees and swoop up and down and around our little party. It's almost like I can see them up there, glistening with promise. Tiny sound bursts that sparkle and fall. When I finish, everyone is silent. Basil has his eyes shut and he's smiling.

Devon strums absently on the guitar.

Kush stands and stretches out his legs. He pushes his

hair back from his face and shakes his head. "Man, that was a downer. That's seriously what you like to sing?" He runs his hand down the sides of his mouth, and then reaches for a beer.

Basil puts his hand protectively around my shoulder. "Dude, don't. That was tight."

Kush shakes his head. "Church music. It's what all these people up here are into. That and country."

Blood rushes into my face, and I press my lips to keep from calling him an asshole. I'm about ready to walk on home when Philly calls out from the grill. "One more song and dinner's ready."

Devon nudges Kush's foot with his own. "So what do *you* want to hear?"

"Can you play anything real?"

Devon hits the opening chords for "Smells Like Teen Spirit."

One night last year, we were messing around and came up with a bluegrass version of it. Even Will, who usually never has time for us, joined in on his banjo. It sounded great. For real, great, and I've been wanting to play it again like that ever since.

But tonight Devon plays it regular, and I go ahead and sing, growling out the lines. I'll show this city boy church music. I'm high enough that I grab someone's walking stick, turning it into a make-believe microphone. I even swing my beer bottle in my other hand, taking swigs when Devon plays guitar solos.

When I finish, I bow and let Basil pull me toward him in a hug. "Girl, you ripped that."

It's then that I get a little self-conscious. What do these people see when they see me? A country girl with a twang and no future, or do they see me as someone who really might be able to fly?

Philly calls us to dinner. His buddies pass out plates and we all fall silent. I eat another one of Will's brownies and say yes to the second beer Basil hands me.

Philly's friends spin tales about the trail. They crack us up with their interpretation of the speed hikers and the crazy hermits that shun the company of others out in the woods.

Devon starts playing good old James Taylor sing-alongs and even Kush doesn't complain.

Basil is next to me again, and I notice he leans in when we laugh, and gives me a little nudge with his arm. It doesn't feel all that bad.

"So, Kush?" Devon asks. "You're from Athens, too?"

"Atlanta," Kush says. "The city. Nothing like this place." The way he rolls his eyes and tilts his head in the vague direction of town puts me off.

I remember when Devon first moved here from Raleigh. He'd do the same thing. Roll his eyes. Make fun of us. Like if you weren't from a city, you couldn't possibly be a worthy human being.

Philly's friend, Larry, yawns and starts gathering up the pots and pans, mumbling about an early start and cleaning up. It's a good break, so I jump up to help.

"Hey, man," Basil says to Larry. "We got that. Go on to bed. I'll leave your things by your pack." Basil smiles and walks over next to me, piling dishes in his arms.

What's the harm? It's just dishes, after all. Isn't this why I'm here? To meet new people?

Basil sings along to the song Devon is playing as we traipse down the skinny track through the woods.

He slows until I'm walking next to him. "So, Pixie, you ever think of taking off up that trail? Why don't you come with us?"

Because I'm barely sixteen, my mama's a fundamental Baptist, and my daddy has a thirty-aught-six rifle. Though lately, he hasn't seemed to care too much about what I'm up to.

What I say is, "Not this year."

"Too bad." He hip-checks me. "Gets sort of lonely out

there, when you're hiking with a couple."

Before I know what's happened, he's leaned in and kissed me, real quick.

"Uh, I've gotta pee."

"That's not usually the effect I have on girls." He laughs.

We reach the stream and I put down the dishes I'm carrying. "No, really. Be back in a sec."

From the woods, I can hear him singing and washing dishes. I squat and realize just how buzzed I am and place my hand on a tree trunk to steady myself. What am I doing? I'm acting like Whitney. But what does it matter? They'll all be down the trail in the morning anyway, and with school starting next week, it's back to plain old me. I stand and pull my shorts up.

Basil smiles as I walk back. We wash the remaining dishes while I hum the tune to "Pretty Saro." It's my favorite old Appalachian ballad.

When we're done, Basil takes my hand and leads me to a grassy spot near the bank. "Will you sing that? For me?" He pulls me to sit next to him. I recognize where this is going and picture my map, with a new thumbtack stuck on Athens, Georgia.

I take a deep breath and feel the notes resonate in my

belly. I close my eyes, then press my hand against the dirt to steady myself, before bringing up the first words.

*"Down in some low valley in some
lonesome place,*

*Where small birds to whistle their
notes do increase . . ."*

I keep singing with my eyes closed, only catching my breath when I feel Basil's fingers tickling the skin on the back of my neck.

When I finish, I open my eyes and he's there, waiting for me with a kiss. I turn so I'm facing him and put my hand on his shoulder. We kiss for a minute and then he pulls back. "You know, you're really good." Basil pushes short wisps of hair behind my ears.

"Thanks."

"No, I mean, like, *really* good. You should let somebody record you."

I shake my head and blush. "No, it's only for church and hanging out with my friends."

Basil moves his hand down to the side of my neck. His expression is earnest. "I'm not punking you, Pixie. I don't know that much about it, but I'd guess you have near perfect pitch. You ever watch *American Idol*?"

I giggle at his suggestion. Singing in front of crowds is my dream—and my biggest fear. But I'll never get to that level. I'm just a girl who sings at church and around a campfire.

His eyes focus in on mine, and then he pulls my mouth to his. At first, he's real gentle.

But his kisses get more urgent, and he parts my mouth with his tongue.

He tastes like chocolate and beer. My head buzzes but my tongue meets his, circling and tasting. His lips press harder against mine and I kiss him back.

I could tell him to stop and head back to the rest of the group. But I don't.

A groan escapes his lips and he leans against me, his arms easing me toward the ground.

I lie back getting lost in the feeling of his mouth on mine.

His hand eventually works its way under my tank top, unhooking my bra. "You're so beautiful," he whispers. "One day, when I see you singing at some amphitheater, I'm going to remember this night, my brush with fame." He kisses down my stomach.

I gasp as every feeling in my body settles between my

legs. I'd come prepared for something like this. Devon and I'd planned all summer about what it'd be like to hook up for real—the ultimate hookup. It'd been easy to get a condom. All I had to do was rummage deep in the glove box of Daddy's truck. Tonight could be it. Basil could be the one. Lord knows I wouldn't let it happen with someone from here. Sevenmile's gossip train has a loud whistle.

Basil's dreads scratch my skin, as he reaches to push down my shorts.

"Wait." I put my hands on his arms.

"No, baby," he moans.

I hold his arms tight.

"Seriously, wait." I move my hands to his head and lift his face up.

His eyes meet mine and I guess he sees I'm serious about stopping. "No fucking way." He groans and rolls off of me. He lies there for a minute before getting up and gathering dishes.

"Sorry," I say.

He shrugs and waves me off.

As he disappears up the trail, I look through the leaves at the stars.

American Idol. Now that'd be something.

CHAPTER FOUR

Sunday morning and Mama is yelling at
me to hurry up. "We're gonna be late to church, Amber
Delaine!"

I grab my church skirt and blouse out of the closet and
slip them on. Good enough. It's not like there's going to be
anyone at church to make a fuss for anyway.

Downstairs, Coby is in his high chair, his bib covered
with Cheerios.

"Hey, buddy, you finished?" I ask him.

"BerBer." My nephew grins and waves his chubby fists.

Mama waddles into the farmhouse's kitchen and
I jump out of the way. Daddy says she's two ax handles
worth of love. That means her rear end is as wide as two

ax handles. I hate when he says it, but Mama acts like she doesn't care.

You don't want to get in Mama's way on church day. "Well, don't just stand there. Get that baby out of his chair and clean him up."

"Where's Whitney?" I huff as I say it, but I know the answer. Running late because she and Sammy were out till God knows when. But my sister knows better than to skip church, even if it means showing up halfway through the sermon looking like death warmed over.

I get Coby cleaned up and head out to the yard.

Fog is settled into the folds of the valley and I hear Daddy walking over from the cow barn. "August fog means . . ."

"A snowy day this winter," I say.

Daddy sheds his coveralls to reveal his Sunday slacks and shirt. I've never seen him in a tie, ever. But that doesn't stop half the women in Sevenmile from noticing him. Coby toddles over and holds up his hands. Daddy obliges, hoisting him onto his hip.

Daddy looks me over. "Amber, girl, I don't know why you don't let your hair grow long. Wear some nice heels. You might be as pretty as Whitney if you did. Might even get yourself a boyfriend."

My mind flashes to the hiker barn. Girls don't need to

look like Whitney to get guys to notice them. Basil didn't seem to care that my hair's short and I don't wear fancy clothes. He thought I was interesting. He liked to hear me sing. I roll my knuckles against my thigh and ignore Daddy.

The porch railing creaks as Mama grabs it and takes the three stairs down to the yard. "You haven't started that truck yet, Herman?"

"Hold your britches. I'm going."

Daddy cranks the engine while Mama pulls herself up into the passenger seat. I strap Coby into his car seat in the back.

At church, Pastor Early stands on the front stoop greeting the early parishioners. We are always there first. Mama thinks it will somehow make up for our sins.

I take Coby to the toddler room in the parish hall and linger. Deana May, the babysitter, goes to my school. Even though she's right up there with Mama on the devout-o-meter, I've always liked her.

She comes through the door leading the youngest of her five siblings. "Hey, Amber," she says when she sees me. "You going to sing today?"

"Hey, Deana May. Yeah, Mrs. Early expects me to. Ready to start junior year?"

She shrugs and tightens her ponytail. "I guess. I'm in the baby class this fall."

I laugh. "You'll definitely get an A, then." The baby class is this stupid class where the teacher assigns everybody a robot baby. If you manage not to kill it from neglect or shaken baby syndrome, you get an A. With five younger siblings, it'll be a cakewalk for Deana May.

"Hey, did you hear?" Her pretty blue eyes go wide.

"No, what?"

"Some new family's moved in and they have sons. High school age."

"Really? Where'd they come from?"

Deana May leans in because if there's one thing about her, she loves a good story. "I'm not sure. But the father is a Whitson. My papa knew his father. Said the family moved off for work but now the son is moving back in to reclaim the old property."

The hiker barn sits at the edge of the Whitson land. Is that the property she's talking about?

The church bell rings and I say good-bye to Deana May before heading inside the sanctuary to our family pew.

Sammy and Whitney show up late and squeeze in. Sammy lets his legs splay open, so he's pressing against me. It's embarrassing, but it used to give me a thrill when he'd notice I was around. He was the ultimate bad boy, a musician, and I was only one degree of separation away, being

Whitney's little sister. But now it's just annoying. And weird. I scoot closer to Mama, but there's not a lot of room.

Pastor Early starts preaching and at first he holds my attention with talk of family and community. But then the slender beam of sunlight illuminating the pulpit's crimson carpet disappears and he switches gears. Before long I'm tuning him out. Blah, blah, blah, sinner. Blah, blah, blah, darkness. I slink down the wooden pew so my head rests on the back of it.

Mama hisses at me. "Sit up, girl."

Mrs. Early, the preacher's wife, the choir director, and my high school's guidance counselor, smiles a sweet-tea smile at me from her place up front and motions for me to stand. She raises her arms and hums the opening notes of "River of Jordan." As I sing my solo, I don't think about Pastor Early's condemnations, or the way that hiker, Kush, curled his lip at me. All I think about are the notes and how they purify me. Make me whole and wash me clean of anything but the sound of my voice.

"I'm on my way to the River of Jordan,
Gonna walk right in, in the rushing waters,
I'm going down to the River of Jordan,
And let the cool waters cleanse my soul."

The folks in our congregation, no more than a hundred, look up and nod when I'm finished. They're the only audience I've ever really had, besides Devon, sometimes his brother, my family, and the hikers this summer.

Mrs. Early motions for me to sit down on the last note with a smile.

When I sing, I'm free.

Sammy decides it's a good time to drape his arm across the back of the pew and lean over. I smell the strange mix of his wintergreen Skoal and my sister's sour apple shampoo. "I need to talk to you."

I glare at him and put my finger to my lips. "Shhh."

Whitney leans forward and stares at us, then latches on to Sammy's arm.

I flip open the prayer book and bow my head, praying loud, ignoring the pressure from Sammy's leg. Mama pats my other leg and whispers, "That's right, honey, give it all to the Lord."

If only it were that simple.

After church, Sammy follows me to the nursery to get Coby, while Whitney helps Mama set up refreshments in the fellowship hall.

Before we get there he pulls me into a darkened Sunday school room.

"Sammy, what are you doing?"

"Listen." He pulls the door shut behind him and I look around for a light switch. He takes a step closer. I back up, bumping a wooden chair onto the floor.

He laughs. "Careful. You might bruise something."

I find the switch and flick it on. "You're being weird. What do you want?"

Sammy gathers his hair, still damp from a shower, and flips it onto his back. "Don't be like that. Aren't I still your favorite guitar player?"

"Please, the only place you play anymore is around the console of your Guitar Wars game." Sammy's guitar's been gone for months. Whitney told me they'd pawned it to invest in their "business."

Sammy licks his finger, presses it against his forearm, and makes a sizzling sound. "That burned, baby sister."

"So? Truth hurts."

"But, see, that's what I have you in here for. I'm thinking of forming a new band. I met a drummer and another dude who plays bass."

"Great." I try to push past him toward the door, but he grabs my arm.

"Not so fast, I'm not finished." Sammy pulls me close enough that I feel uncomfortable.

"Then finish. Coby's waiting for us."

Outside in the hallway, I hear the sound of children's voices as parents gather them up for Sunday lunch.

"Please, Sammy, hurry up. What do you want?"

"I want you to be our backup singer."

My head snaps up and I meet his eyes. "What?"

"You heard me. I know you've got a rock singer in there somewhere. Besides, if you're in on it, then Whitney won't give me grief."

I'm stunned. Two years ago, I would have given the moon for Sammy to ask me to play in his band. But now, he's a burnout and a drug dealer and there's no telling who his other so-called band members are. Sure, I want to sing, but with Sammy? He's got to be kidding.

"No way."

"Aw, come on."

"Forget it, Sammy." I push past him and fling open the door. "Deal with Whitney yourself."

As I hurry down the hall, curiosity sneaks around the edges of my thoughts. The first band Sammy played in was pretty good. The old drummer moved to Nashville and picked up session gigs. He isn't famous, but he's living a real music life. Maybe this could be the start of something.

Inside the nursery, Coby's rolling a truck across the

windowsill. He looks up and grins at me. "Ber."

No. That drummer made it on his own. He didn't need Sammy. Sammy can't even pick up his own kid from the nursery without thinking of himself first.

That's not my dream. It's not my music. No matter how bad I want an audience.

CHAPTER FIVE

Thank God for school starting and thank God for Devon's daddy.

That's all I can think as I hear the horn beep out front and appreciate that Devon has the Jeep. Which means I don't have to take the bus on the days Daddy can't drive me. I give myself one more glance before heading out the door. First-day attire: fitted Carolina T-shirt, baggy overalls with perfectly placed knee holes, a black crocheted pair of Toms shoes—Mama about had a cow when I told her I wanted fifty-dollar shoes that we had to order off the internet, but Daddy said yes, since they were feminine—and black hoop earrings. Devon had fought me on the overalls, but they *are* my trademark.

I give Mama a kiss and grab a package of Pop-Tarts and a bottle of water. "Bye, Mama, love you."

She shifts in her seat and waves her hands at me, like she's conducting a symphony. She gets all misty, her first-day-of-school ritual, and I wait for it. "Come give me a hug."

I wrap my arms around her. People may make fun of fat people, but I like having a squishy mama. She's comfortable.

"I can't believe you're a junior. Lord, two short years and you'll be graduating. I hope you won't be in a hurry to grow up as fast as your sister did."

I cringe. Mama doesn't get it. Though I might like to go out and have fun like my sister, I don't plan on getting pregnant, or picking a guy anything like Sammy. I want to travel, hike the trail, and maybe even go to college.

"I gotta go, Mama."

She hangs on tighter. "You be a good girl."

"Yes, Mama."

Devon honks again.

"Mama, I gotta go."

She releases me and wipes a tear from her eye. "Have a good day, sugar."

I fly out the front door and down the steps. Devon is beaming from the front seat of his Jeep. I slide into the passenger seat. A plush soccer ball dangles from the rearview mirror. Devon's our team's goalie and he's pretty good for a mountain kid. Most boys around here are into football or baseball. But then again, he's a hybrid, what with his mama being from off and his daddy, the judge, only returning with his family two years ago when he got a wild hair to run for a district court seat. I still marvel that Devon picked me to hang out with.

Devon lowers the rim of his aviator glasses, checking me out from head to toe. "You know, Amber P & S, you could work it a little more."

I shake my feet for him. "I've got cool shoes. Ordered them online."

He smiles at my feet. "I can't believe you talked *your* parents into putting their credit card number into a computer."

"Right? Daddy's got an eBay addiction now. Hunting up old Clinchfield Railroad stuff."

Devon laughs hard and backs out of the yard.

It takes about ten minutes to drive to Mountain High and park.

Devon loops his arm through mine after we get out of the Jeep. "You ready to kill this year?"

"Let's kill it," I say. But there isn't any of the excitement I felt this summer, when Devon and I hit the hiker barn.

We trudge up the hill from the parking lot and slide into Mountain High's commons. Groups of kids are already forming, and there's nothing new, except the clothes and haircuts.

I glance around to see if I can spy the new boys Deana May told me about. "Did you hear about the new kids?" I ask.

Devon's Adam's apple bobs. "Oh, yeah, about that."

"About what?"

Will, Devon's brother, interrupts us. "Hello, young subjects," he crows, throwing his arm over Devon's shoulder. Will and Devon are the same height, even though Will's a year older. Today, he looks effortlessly cool in his loose "My Grass Is Blue" T-shirt, a pair of hiking shorts, and faded trail runners. It's sweet, I guess, the way Will's always hovering, making sure nothing bad happens to Devon. He doesn't usually pay much attention to me, but when he does, my palms sweat a little.

"Hey, Will. I like your shirt," I say, looking up at him. I stand with my hands by my sides, then in my pockets, then back by my sides.

It's stupid how nervous I get around him, but there are reasons. One, Will's as cute as Devon, but straight. Two, he hangs out with the cool seniors, and by that I don't mean the cheerleaders and jocks. I mean the artsy kids—once they're gone, they're going to have a life. Three, hanging out with Will involves the likelihood of getting suspended—he's irreverent. And four, I always feels like he's making fun of me. Like he knows that if it weren't for me being friends with Devon, I'd just be some random girl at his school.

"You are looking fashionably unfashionable as always." Will raises one brow and grins at me. "And I mean that in the best way possible."

Then I hear the voice of Amber Rose Slagle. Amber-o-zia. "Will. *There* you are."

Amber-o-zia is our school fashion plate. She's part Cherokee and has perpetually tan skin, long, gorgeous dark hair, always wears makeup, and, according to Devon, hooked up with Will two weeks ago at a party out on the lake.

"Dahling . . ." Will, suave even when he's kidding, turns and holds out his arms, and Amber-o-zia tucks into them. He kisses her right there in the commons. I see Amber-o-zia's hand slip into the back pocket of his jeans. Territory established. An odd couple—Amber-o-zia's about as straight arrow as Deana May—but she and Will look good together.

I wipe my hands on my overalls.

"Come on." Devon pulls me toward the double doors

and the soccer crowd. "There's someone we need to say hello to."

"Amber. Devon. Hey! Wait up!" Cheerleader Amber, or C.A., untangles herself from a cluster of burgundy-ribboned girls decked out for the opening-day pep rally. "I need y'all to do me a favor."

"C.A., we're right here." Devon pokes his fingers in his ears.

"Sure. Whatever." C.A. directs her request to me. "We need juniors to win opening-day spirit. Can you get them to yell a little louder?" C.A.'s hands are on her hips, her face serious.

"Sure, C.A.," I say.

"Thanks!" She clasps her hands and bobs her head like she's just finished a cheer. She turns to go, then stops and speaks to me. "You taking art, again, Amber?"

"Yep, Devon's in, too. You?"

Last year, C.A. and I forged a surprising friendship over silk screen prints. Devon had been in a different block, but this year we'd be together.

"Yeah, but I hear the new teacher is a bitch."

Before I can respond, C.A.'s friends have pulled her back into the squad and Devon's tugging on my arm. "Amber, I need you to listen to me."

"What?" I look at my cell phone. Bell's about to ring for opening assembly.

"You know we had our first soccer practice a couple of days ago."

"Yeah . . ."

"Well, we've got a new player."

I see Principal Hedges walking in our general direction and I quickly slip my phone in my pocket.

"That's great. Is he any good?" Mountain High's soccer record is abysmal.

We're walking in the direction of the soccer team and the girls that hang out with them.

"No, it's not about that, it's . . ."

"Shit." I stop dead in my tracks. Ahead of me, surrounded by the team and soccer groupies, is Kush, the guy from the campfire. Why did I assume he was a through-hiker? He must be one of the new boys Deana May was talking about.

I can feel Devon's crush energy radiating off of him. Me, all I feel is mortal embarrassment. I acted like Whitney out there. Making out with Basil, getting high. All I need is for the new guy to start spreading rumors about me and for them to get back to Mama and everyone else in Sevenmile.

And then he's standing across from us, shouldering a first-day book bag.

Devon's practically giddy. "Amber, you remember Kush? Kush Whitson? He moved here. From Atlanta. Isn't it awesome?"

I look at Devon, look at Kush, then look at my feet. "Hey," I mumble. I'm torn between feeling sorry for the guy, and feeling a little freaked out he's going to run his mouth. And now he's hanging out with us?

The bell rings and the shuffle starts toward the gym.

I grab Devon's arm. "Um, sorry, Devon, I forgot I told Deana May I'd sit with her for assembly."

"Wait, what . . ."

But I ignore him, and push my way into the crowd, leaving him, and Kush, behind.

I never do find Deana May in the gym, but instead, I settle smack dab in the middle of the burnout crowd.

"Hey, Amber."

"Hey, Frog."

Anthony Speller has been Frog as long as I can remember. He's actually sort of cute in a moppy hair, stoner sort of way.

"You met Sean yet?" Frog asks me.

I look past Frog and see another new boy. His hair is a light brown razor-cut mess, sticking up in the back. His eyes, which are a pretty blue, seem hidden behind clouds.

Sean lifts his chin. "What's up?"

"Hey. Are you new?"

"Yeah, me and my cousin." He points several rows below us at the soccer team. "The dark-haired dude down there."

"Oh."

So, *this* is the other Whitson. Sean looks nothing like Kush. And it's weird they're not hanging out on the first day. If I were at a new school, I'd be clinging tight to the people I knew.

"Where's your homeboy?" Frog asks me.

I point in the same direction Sean had. Devon's sitting next to Kush and waving his hands while he talks.

Sean glances my way. "Your boyfriend?"

"No. He's my best friend, though."

"I never have understood why you two don't date, Amber." Frog tilts his head.

Frog is clueless, but so is most of Mountain High.

"I don't know. We make better friends."

"Friends are good," Sean says quietly.

I glance over at him and see him twisting the bottom of his T-shirt. I hear my mama's voice expounding on the virtues of being welcoming and generous.

"Do you play?" I ask.

"What?" Sean asks.

"Your shirt. It says 'Fender.' Do you play the guitar?"

Sean pulls out the shirt and looks down at it. It takes a minute for him to answer. "I got it at a thrift store. Thought it was cool."

"Oh." I slump back against the bleachers.

Cheerleader Amber, newly promoted to cocaptain of the squad, bounces out on the gym floor and tries to whip the junior section into a frenzy.

"Come on, y'all." I stand up halfheartedly, remembering my promise to help bring on the spirit.

C.A.'s nodding her head in little choppy up-and-down movements in time to the clapping of her hands. Her mascaraed eyes twinkle. She points at me and gives me a thumbs-up.

I watch Devon get the whole soccer team and their friends up, even Kush, and pretty soon they're screaming and fist pumping and chest flailing. I turn to my ragtag section of the bleachers. "Spirit, y'all. Come on. Get up."

Frog groans and stands, pulling Sean to his feet. A few more kids stand and clap limply.

I look down and see that Devon has the soccer team doing the wave.

My group is pathetic. I elbow Frog and whisper, "Mountain High *high*, y'all," and air toke. He grins and holds out a fist. I bump mine against his and he takes over for me. Frog gets the section laughing, and soon they're all on their feet screaming, "Mountain High *high*, y'all."

Soon, Principal Hedges comes out onto the center of the gym floor and tries to settle us down, but he's laughing as he does it. Seniors win spirit, of course. They always do. Then, Vice Principal Smoker (no joke) comes out for her yearly lecture on how to be a model Mountain High citizen. She plays bad cop to Principal Hedges's good cop, and just as we're wondering why we even bothered coming back to school, she switches gears and gets all sparkly like she loves us so much, and throws MHHS pencils into the crowd.

I watch Kush grab a pencil in flight. Devon must pick up on my vibe because he turns, searching the bleachers till he finds me. He looks at who I'm standing with and asks a question with his raised eyebrow. I shrug. I know he'll tell me I'm being paranoid, and I am, but the last thing I need is a new kid telling people how hard I was partying this summer.

After the assembly, I push down the stairs, elbowing past a group of huddled, wide-eyed freshmen. The surge of the student body pushes me out into the commons and I start looking for Devon.

He finds me first. I see his hand shoot up from near the windows, waving me over. I cut through the crowd to him.

"Who's the new guy?" Devon asks in a low voice, nodding past my shoulder.

I turn around and Sean's right behind me. I'm surprised Devon doesn't know who he is yet. I grab Sean's elbow and pull him into the conversation.

"Um. Kush's cousin? Sean? You haven't met?"

"No." Devon looks sideways at Kush as he joins us. "Hey, man, why'd you leave your cousin hanging? You should've brought him out to practice." He turns to Sean. "I'm Devon, by the way."

Sean stuffs his hands into his pockets. "It's okay. I'm not so into sports. Besides, I'm only a sophomore."

Devon rolls his eyes. "Like that matters? We'll take any live body." He looks again at Sean. "I'm surprised, though. I would have guessed you for older."

Kush pushes a strand of hair behind his ear. "He *is* older. He should be a junior."

Sean doesn't say anything, just looks away from us.

"Hey," I say. "Come on, Sean. I can show you where your classes are. Let's see your schedule."

His eyes meet mine and he exhales. "Thanks."

I turn to Devon. "See you in art?" I don't bother saying good-bye to Kush.

CHAPTER SIX

After I show Sean his locker and his class-rooms, I catch up to C.A. on our way to art. She links her arm through mine. "So, Amber Vaughn, tell me all about that bed-headed boy you were showing around. And how'd you get to him so fast?" She licks her glossed lips for emphasis.

"You did not just lick your lips."

"Yes, I did. He looks like he could use a scrub behind the ears, but he's cute, and he was all eyes on you."

"Only because I was being nice to him."

She bumps me with her hip. "All I'm saying is he's cute. Go for it, girl."

Devon catches up to us in the hall. "Go for who?"

"Bed-head boy," C.A. says, turning to look at Sean again.

"She means Sean," I clarify for him. "Anyway," I say to C.A. "I've got my main man right here." I pat Devon's hand. We've never directly said that we're together, but it never hurts that some people jump to conclusions. Let them believe what they want to believe.

C.A.'s not fooled for a minute, though. "Right. Uh-huh."

We walk into the art room and sit at the same table we did last year, but everything's totally different. Gone are the piles of old canvases and plastic toys for still lifes. Instead, the room is tidy and neat, with bright arrangements of fresh flowers in place. My favorite box of crumpled acrylic tubes has been replaced with neat plastic watercolor trays. I'm not sure I like the change.

The bell rings and Ms. Thomas, the new teacher, starts taking attendance. She's interrupted by Vice Principal Smoker leading Kush in. "I found you a lost little lamb, hon. Don't mark him tardy. He's new."

Kush does look sheepish. "Sorry," he mumbles, and sits near the door.

C.A. whispers, "Cherokee Boy's pretty damn cute, too."

I glance over at Kush again. She's right. Cute, really

cute. But Mama always says, pretty is as pretty does. And so far this Kush boy may have Devon fooled into thinking he's some big-city wunderkind, but I'm not convinced.

"I'm pretty sure someone in his family is from India. You know, the country?" I say.

"*Ohh.* But his last name's Whitson?" C.A. peers behind me to get a better look.

Devon leans in to whisper to me and C.A. "His mom is, indeed, Indian. But she grew up in Atlanta." He sounds so smug when he says it I stick out my tongue.

Ms. Thomas shushes us and hands out the syllabus for Art II.

No way. Drawing. Pen and ink. Watercolor.

Where's the recycled sculpture, the printmaking, and the mud painting? Where's the fun stuff?

It doesn't take long to figure out that, for me, Art II is not going to be fun. We will do a watercolor landscape. We will draw from the right sides of our brain. We will create the perfect contrast of positive and negative.

What we won't be doing is exploring our inner land-scape like we did with our old art teacher, Mr. Cottrell.

"Fuck," I say under my breath, but still louder than I should.

"Did you say something, Miss Vaughn?" Ms. Thomas asks me, meeting my eyes.

"No, ma'am." Surely she couldn't hear me.

"I'm pretty sure you did." Ms. Thomas leans over and scrawls on the top of a familiar pink pad of paper. She rips the slip off the top and hands it to me. "Go see Vice Principal Smoker. Explain it to her."

Did I just get written up in my first class on the first day of school for dropping an F bomb under my breath? Apparently, I did, because Ms. Thomas is standing with her hand on her hip, pointing to the door.

C.A. mouths, "Good luck."

I hate new teachers.

Smoker keeps me waiting for my lecture till right before lunch. Apparently, I have been chosen as the poster child for how not to behave this school year, because I get a day of in-school suspension. I am the beacon, the first-day warning for the entire student body.

When she finally sends me on my way, I slam through the office doors and head for the lawn outside the cafeteria. My eyes burn with held tears. Mama's going to kill me.

Devon sees me first. "What happened?"

"Smoker gave me a day of ISS."

"*No* way." He gives me a hug. "You going to tell Donna?"

"I guess I have to. Save me a spot, will you?" On pretty

days we always eat outside on the lawn.

The cafeteria line snakes around one wall and it's moving slow. People don't have their accounts set up yet and the lunch ladies have to make change. I stand in the line for a second, before I say screw it and head for the vending machines.

I have to pass by the it-girl table, where Will's sitting with Amber-o-zia. I wonder how many wine coolers it took to make *that* happen. Not that he's the kind of guy who gets a girl drunk to hook up. Or that he's not hot. But I don't get it—they seem so different.

At the vending machine I fumble with my dollar bill and try to ignore the laughter from Amber-o-zia's table. I hit G-5 and watch as a package of strawberry Pop-Tarts drop. Nothing like a breakfast do-over.

"You tried the cinnamon roll flavor?"

I look behind me. It's Sean, holding a tray of food, hair still sticking up. He's biting at the corner of his lip, but his bright eyes make him look happier than they did at assembly. His nervousness is almost as cute as his smile.

"No. My mom always buys frosted blueberry. Are they good?" Are we really talking about Pop-Tart flavors?

Sean nods. "Yeah. My mom used to buy them sometimes."

"You want to sit with us outside?" I point out the

window to where Devon and the other soccer players, Kush included, gather under the trees.

"Nah, it's okay. But I wanted to tell you something."

Sean talks so deliberately that you have to really listen. I wait, trying not to be impatient. Finally, I say, "Okay?"

He blushes and nods down to his shirt. "I play. Wish I could play more, but I had to sell my guitar."

I can hear it in his voice—the sound I hear my heart make when I think about not being able to sing. I look out the window. Devon's thrown his head back, laughing, and Kush gestures wildly beside him. They seem fine without me.

I hold up my lunch in one hand and point toward the door. "Hey, why don't we go sit out back, by the band room? It's quiet there. I'd love to hear about your playing."

Sean's eyes meet mine. They're Carolina blue with a few flecks of gray. "Really?"

I glance back at Will. He's pinching tots from Amber-o-zia's lunch tray. When he sees me looking at him, he grins and sticks out his tongue, a tot balanced on the tip.

I turn my head quickly, not sure if I should laugh or blush.

Sean's still waiting for my answer.

"Yeah, really," I say.

CHAPTER SEVEN

That afternoon, I walk out to the parking lot to look for Devon. I hadn't seen him again since lunch. But it's Will who finds me, zipping up to the curb in his black Honda. The window rolls down and Will leans over it, grinning at me. "Amber Vaughn, as I live and breathe! Devon asked if I'd give you a ride. He's got soccer practice." Will's hair's grown out over the summer, and it flops over his eyebrows. He brushes it away and unlocks the door.

I quickly shut my mouth before it drops all the way open, and try and play it cool.

"Yeah. Sure, thanks." I open the door and climb in next to him. I notice that the seats are leather, with that new car smell. The McKinneys aren't mansion-rich, but they do well enough for two brothers to have their own cars even though they go to the same school.

I drop my book bag onto the floor at my feet. Will's got an Avett Brothers sticker on his dashboard. "You like them?" I ask, rubbing my fingers across the gloss of the decal.

Will checks his mirrors and pulls out of the parking lot onto the road. "Yeah. Got to see them earlier in the summer."

"Really?" I ask with a lilt in my voice that I hope doesn't sound like jealousy.

Will looks over at me. "You like them?" He sounds surprised. "I thought you were into the music Devon likes. That's all y'all are ever playing when I'm around."

I'm a little disappointed he doesn't remember our front porch Nirvana bluegrass session last year. But Devon does pretty much take over when it comes to the music we play, for the most part. "No. I'm into a lot of different kinds of music."

Will looks at me a little longer this time, and then turns his eyes back toward the road. "Cool. I didn't know. Hey, Devon said you got called down today."

"Yeah. The new art teacher. It was like she needed to piss on some trees or something."

Will laughs and slows the car down a little. "You ready to go home?"

I groan. "*No.* I dread telling my mama about the suspension."

Will zips past the turnoff for the long country road where my house is and heads north.

"Um, where are we going?" I ask, peering over at him.

Will's eyes follow the turns in the road, but there's a wry smile crinkling around their edges. "You said you weren't ready to go home. I figured we could go burn one up on the bald. Got to admit, it's a gorgeous day."

It's true. I'm not ready to go home. I look over at Will. His fingers tap on the steering wheel in time to the song blasting from his speakers. He has the same thick, dark eyelashes over liquid brown eyes that Devon does, but Will's face is sharp and lean where Devon's is softer. A tiny scar slices across Will's cheek, and I wonder how he got it.

He shifts gears and slows down a bit, looking over at me. "Do you need to go home? Can you hang out?"

"No, I don't have to go home. But, why?"

"Why, what?"

"Why do you want to hang out with me?"

We pass the Franklin house. Mr. Franklin is out front mowing, and the dirt-tangy smell of fresh-cut grass blows in through the window.

Will cuts his eyes toward me. "What, my brother is good enough to hang out with you, but I'm not?"

I shake my head. "I, it's . . ." That's not it at all, but I lose my words, and Will doesn't wait for my answer. He just guns his car around the curve and turns up the music.

This is strange, but after today, I'm ready to take it as it comes. I relax into the leather seat and turn my face toward the wind. The iPod switches to a local Southern rock band, Flat Trucker, and I sing along.

"Those guys would kill to have you in their band," Will says loudly over the music.

I blush. "No way."

Will's car hums around the curves. "No. Seriously, you're really good. I can't believe you're not already in a band, or at least in the chorus or something."

I didn't think Will knew I even existed, other than being the girl who's always taking up half the sofa in his family's TV room, eating his parents' popcorn, and singing his brother's favorite songs on command.

"It doesn't matter. My mama would never let me be in a band. She thinks singing's only for church and baking."

"What do you think?"

"I don't know. I don't think about it much." I'm surprised at my own answer. I mean, of course I've thought about it. I thought about it Sunday when Sammy asked me to be in his band. I thought about it down by the creek when Basil was talking about *American Idol*. I think about it all the time.

I glance at him. "I think I'd be too scared to sing in front of crowds like that."

He opens his mouth and scoffs, then nudges my shoulder with the flat of his hand. "I bet you'd get over it."

Will's taking the switchbacks at close to thirty miles an hour, way too fast, but I'm not scared. He's a good driver. I've got my hand out the window making swimming motions against the wind.

We come around the next curve and almost kiss headlights with a faded burgundy Ford truck.

"Whoa!" Will corrects the car but doesn't slow down.

Whoa is right. That was my daddy's truck. I twist around to see if he noticed me. My answer to what he's doing way out here is in the wink of red taillights and a flounce of blonde hair right up next to my daddy. I pull my hand out of the open window and cross my arms over my chest, squeezing.

"Wasn't that your dad's truck?"

"Yeah. So?" I press my fingers into my sides.

"Doesn't he work for the railroad?"

My reply is fast. "Yeah, he does." Then I lie. "But he promised to pick up his foreman's wife for an appointment. I heard them on the phone last night."

I don't know who was in his truck, but it wasn't my mama. My mama's at the house, probably making home-made corn bread for his supper. I've known about Daddy's "habit" for a couple of years, but I still don't like seeing it. That woman was as far from the passenger side as she could get, and from the look of it, practically in Daddy's lap.

I scrunch down into the seat. I take a shovel and open up my heart and pour in load after load of grief and anger until everything is level and I can plant nice pretty green grass on top.

When the pain is good and buried, I pull my knees to my chest and clear my throat. "Where'd you get the scar?"

Will's voice is perfectly even as he says, "Fight with an alligator."

I crack up and smile out at the road.

Will parks at the turnoff, shuts off the car, and jumps out, grabbing his banjo from the hatchback. I follow him, and we walk out among the rhododendrons, their blooms long since gone, and head up off trail to a rock outcropping. From up here, we can see the whole valley. It is beautiful—every color of green mixed with a tinge of blue here, a tinge of gold there. Red and gray barns stamp the sides of silver snaking roads. If I looked long enough, I could find the roof of my own house hidden under the big sugar maples. It's easy for lies to get buried when you're surrounded by so much beauty.

Will settles into the grass at the edge of the rock and lights up a pipe. The burnt-sugar smell of green drifts on the air. "So, Amber Vaughn, you like the new kid?"

I fold cross-legged into the grass next to him. "Which one?"

"I don't know. Either."

"I guess they're nice enough."

"You know what I mean." Will pokes me with his foot.

Of course I know, but why does he care? "Does it matter?" I ask.

He passes me the pipe. "It doesn't, particularly. Just making small talk."

I take a small hit, despite my only-for-summer rules. When the smoke clears my lungs, I exhale and cough a little. "I think Kush might be sort of stuck-up."

"He's all right."

"How do you know him?"

"He's come over and hung out with Devon a few times this past week."

Devon and I have talked. We've texted. Why didn't he mention Kush was Kush *Whitson*, and not a hiker, until I was standing in the hall staring at him?

"Devon likes him." I say it out loud to justify why Devon might not have told me everything.

"I doubt that will ripen." Will knows all about Devon. "I think Kush is a ladies' man."

I take another hit when Will hands me the pipe. I ignore the voice telling me to lay off and the smoke settles in my chest.

I can't believe Devon. We talk about everything. I press my knees to my chest and lean against the big rock.

Will picks up the banjo and starts plucking aimless patterns. The sun is blazing, so I unhook the top part of my overalls and roll up the legs and lay back on the rock, soaking it in. I hum the melody to the song we were listening to in the car. Will finds the tune and plays along. No sense in wasting the afternoon. Summer days like this fade as quick as they come in the mountains.

"What about you? And Amber-o-zia?" I ask, during a pause.

Will shrugs and puts down the banjo. He takes off his shirt, wadding it up under his head for a pillow, and lies down in the sun. "She's good-looking. Nice enough." He shades his eyes with his hand and looks at me.

Will is miles above the high school scene. Cool and self-assured. Funny and nice, but always a bit removed. I can't imagine him ever settling for one of us. Before I can stop myself, I ask him, "But not good enough for you?"

Will rolls over to face me. My eyes wander to where his hip bones jut out above his shorts. He's slender, and looks like one of the guys on the Appalachian Trail with his Columbia shorts and trail runners. I resist the urge to reach out and touch his hip.

"What does *that* mean?" His eyes narrow.

"Come on, Will." Some boldness within me takes over. "You know you're biding your time till you can leave all of us behind. Go out and follow in your judge daddy's footsteps. Move to Raleigh or somewhere big. I think I know what you think of us from-heres."

Will flashes a goofy smile and props his head up on his elbow. "I'm not like that."

"Yes, you are." But then I smile and without thinking, reach out to touch the scar on his face before rolling over onto my back again and staring at the sky and trees above us.

We lie there, not talking, listening to the wind and the sound of the birds, taking in the smell of rich earth and summer hanging in the air. Far off in the distance I can hear the sound of cars.

I can also feel the energy from Will's arm, parallel to mine. Will starts humming the tune to a country song about a city girl and a country boy that the radio plays all the time. After a minute, I join in with the words, quietly at first. And then I sing a little louder, belting it to the clouds. Will's humming is in perfect tune.

Just before the song ends, I feel Will move his hand to touch mine, tracing circles with his fingertips onto my skin. And I think to myself, Will has a girlfriend, sort of. Will is Devon's brother, definitely.

But I don't pull my hand away. I don't know why, but I can't. Instead, I turn to face him when we finish the song. He's staring at me, and I break our sudden eye contact to notice the way his upper lip forms a perfect cupid's bow. Will leans forward and places his lips on mine. A worried voice tells me I might be making a mistake, but I silence it. I hear his hesitant intake of breath. I answer with my tongue.

A new melody starts to circle in my brain and I let it stay as I explore Will's mouth and his lips with mine. A fine spray of stubble wraps the edge of his jawline, and I let my thumb rub against it. Will's hand slides over my hips and he softly pulls me toward him as our legs spaghetti through each other's. He sighs and moves his hand underneath the back of my shirt. I like the way he fits. I move my hand to his shoulder blade to pull him closer. He kisses my face, my eyelids, the corners of my mouth.

Every now and then I think, I'm kissing Will

McKinney. Will McKinney is making me feel this way. It doesn't matter, though, because I'm reading sheet music. Will's jawline, Will's ear, the hollow of Will's throat. The song I'm singing silently doesn't want to fade. Its chorus grows so loud I take off my shirt so I can feel Will's warm skin against mine. Will's lips trace the pattern of my ribs and raise goose bumps on the surface of my summer-tanned stomach. Once, a voice of reason tries to insert itself into my song, one that says *stop right now*, but it fades away as I let the melody soar to the top of my range.

"Are you sure?" Will whispers, his eyes even with mine. But his hands and his mouth play a different tune, and I don't let him stop.

Somewhere far overhead a hawk circles and screams. I can smell the crush of earth and rock beneath us. Then it's nothing but song and skin and the warmth of a boy against me and it's all I can think about. Will's all I want to think about. And then, almost as soon as we started, it seems like it's over.

Will lies down close to me and traces the tip of my ear with his finger, his eyes bright. "Wow."

I hide my face in his chest.

The ultimate hookup. It wasn't exactly what I expected. Or how I expected it to happen. Definitely not with who I thought it would be. My best friend's older brother.

He lifts up my chin. "Are you okay?"

"You've got a girlfriend." I put my hand on his chest and hope he's going to tell me it's just a rumor or that, as of right now, it's over.

Instead he just sighs. "Yeah."

He doesn't try to say anything else, and I bite back my disappointment. "And you're Devon's brother."

"Yeah."

He's acting so nonchalant that I figure I should act that way, too. "So, I guess that's out of the way," I say with a smile. The joy I'd been feeling only moments before gets replaced by something else. Something that feels kind of like grief.

"Yeah." Will laughs and searches my face for something. I guess he finds what he's looking for when, after a few seconds, he kisses me again. "You're cooler than I thought, Amber Vaughn."

No. I am not cool.

I am an idiot.

On the ride home, I sink into the passenger seat. Will's drumming on the steering wheel like it's a normal school day afternoon for him, and I pull my knees up to my chest. "Nobody can know, Will."

"Right. Girlfriend, remember." Will looks over at me

and smiles, but I notice his knuckles go white as he grips the steering wheel.

"Right." But it hurts a little when he says it.

Will turns onto my road and after a mile or so, we pass the Whitsons' place. Kush and Sean's house.

"So, do you think they're going to keep letting the hikers stay in their barn?" he asks.

I tense and glance his way. Will's biting on his lower lip.

"What do you mean?" I ask.

"I mean, from what I heard from Kush and Devon, sounds like it was a nonstop party out there this summer. It'd be a shame for it to end."

My knuckles dig into the side of my thigh, twisting against my overalls. What had Devon told him? I am so stupid. I should have known when he just happened to be carrying condoms. How he only hesitated one second before he decided to have sex with me. And I can't decide who I'm madder at. Devon, for spilling our secrets. Will, for taking advantage of knowing them. Or me, for letting it happen.

But I don't have time to dwell on it, because as Will corners the curve before my house, we're greeted with the flashing blue lights of a sheriff's cruiser, parked right between our big maples.

Will slams on the brakes and slows to a crawl.

In the front yard, in fading daylight, a cop guides my sister into the backseat of his police car. It looks like Sammy's already in there. Mama's on the porch holding a crying Coby, his face bunched in a tight knot, talking to some lady with a clipboard and a skirt. Daddy's not around.

Will stares at the crime scene in my front yard. "How about I let you out right here."

"How about," I say and step out onto the weed-choked lawn.

CHAPTER EIGHT

I've got Coby in my lap, trying to get him to eat applesauce. He's sensitive, always picking up on our feelings. It's hard for anyone to stay calm with Mama pacing the kitchen.

Daddy shows up around six, coated with grime from his job fixing and checking the train tracks for CSX. The blonde must have been a late lunch break.

"Herman, did you not get my messages?" Mama's holding back a shriek so the sound comes out funny, like a bleating calf. I watch, waiting for my daddy's response. For the lie.

"Donna, don't get your panties in a wad. Left my phone in the truck and the battery died. Nothing more than that." Daddy heads straight for the jug of sweet tea in the fridge. I watch his face, looking for a tell, a tic in his cheek, anything that might indicate he held a sliver of guilt. But there's nothing more than my normal daddy at the end of a long day of work.

"My panties are *not* in a wad, but our daughter *is* in jail." Mama's mottled red cheeks give away her anger.

Daddy's hand stops mid-reach. Then he goes ahead and pulls out the glass jug, and gets a glass from the cupboard. I watch the amber liquid fall from one container to another. When he rights the jug, the painted lemons on the side of the glass look brighter.

He drains the glass in one long draw and sets it down on the counter. Mama taps her foot and waits.

Finally, he speaks. "Whitney's in jail."

He doesn't even say it like a question. We've all pestered, lectured, and fussed, hoping Whitney would see what Sammy was doing to her, to us, to himself. But nothing's changed. And this arrest? I suppose it's the thing we've all been waiting for.

Mama spills over, talking so fast you'd think the devil was after her words. "The sheriff was here. Said they'd set up some sting operation, undercover or some such, and Sammy and Whitney are suspected of selling prescription medications. Not only that, Sheriff Cliff says he's out to prove they've been breaking into houses to get the drugs. Possession, intent to distribute, breaking and entering. Good Lord, he was naming off charges so fast my head was spinning. They could get up to ten years in prison. And if that weren't enough, some woman from Social Services shows up here in the midst of it all to see about Coby. Started talking some nonsense about taking him from the home when his grandparents and aunt are right here to take care of him just fine and . . ."

Daddy clears his throat. "You say someone from Social Services was here?"

"Yes, that's what I said, but I gave her a earful and sent her packing. Poor Coby was in hysterics with all the goings-on. And the neighbors, Herman. All out in their yards, or driving by real slow. I imagine tongues are already wagging all over Sevenmile. I'm surprised Pastor Early hasn't shown up on our doorstep already to see about us."

Daddy walks to me and takes Coby, then settles in his recliner in the kitchen nook. "I don't know what happened to your mama, little fellow. She was the prettiest girl." Coby tries to grab the CSX pen from Daddy's pocket, but Daddy takes it back and keeps talking. "Kept that honey hair of hers long to her waist. Boys flocked around my Whitney. She could have had her pick. And now . . ." His voice trails off as he stares out to the trailer at the back of the yard.

"Well, what are we going to do, Herman?" Mama is shrieking now.

"Call old Bud Phillips. Guess she's gonna need a lawyer. He'll help us figure out bail. I ain't worried about Sammy. Let his own folks figure him out."

I cook up some Hamburger Helper and mash some potatoes. There's a little coleslaw left over in the fridge so I put that on the table, too. When I reach up to scratch my face, I catch the lingering smell of Will, pipe smoke, and the dirt scent of granite. Up there, the air felt clean. I felt free, like it didn't matter who I was or what I did. I was like a current in the air, flying, swirling, traveling. From up there, this place looked beautiful, but from down here . . .

"Sugar, aren't you sweet." Mama steps through the doorway and kisses me on the cheek.

Daddy piles his plate high and leaves for the big television in the den. I watch him walk away, fighting the urge to run after him, punching. If I were him, I'd be out back loading Sammy's crap into a pickup truck and driving it somewhere two or three states away. Instead, it's like he lets Whitney get dragged down.

Mama sits down with a heavy sigh at the kitchen table and picks at her plate.

"I'm sorry, Mama." And I mean it. Sorry I don't have the guts to tell her what I know about Daddy, sorry that Whitney's life is such a mess.

But I'm not sorry Sammy's been arrested. Maybe it'll knock some sense into him. Or better yet, maybe Whitney will divorce him.

Mama hugs me. "Lord, child, this ain't your fault. Your big sister's just looking for something in all the wrong places. She wanted to find herself but found Sammy instead. She'll figure herself out. Jesus is going to help her."

I wish I had Mama's faith. It's not that I'm a non-believer or even a doubter, but I like to put my hands on the steering wheel. Mama believes Jesus will take the wheel for us.

"Did Coby go to sleep?"

"Yes, the day wore him out. He's up in your bed. Hope you don't mind."

I picture Coby, his golden curls, lighter than mine or Whitney's, curled up in bed, his sweet-bread smell filling my room. "That's fine."

Mama eats another bite or two, then snaps her head up. "Oh, sugar, I am so sorry. In all this I've plumb forgotten to ask you how your first day of school went."

Now there is a loaded question.

I could say, *Fine, Mama. This boy I thought was a*

through-hiker is really a local. Which would be no big deal, except I acted kind of wild in front of him. Oh wait, maybe I am wild now? Because, after school, I had sex for the first time with Will McKinney—you know, Devon's brother. But it's not like he's going to be my boyfriend or anything. He already has a girlfriend. Oh, and on that note, I also saw Daddy riding around town with some blonde in his lap. And I almost forgot, I got written up for swearing and have a day of in-school suspension. So all in all, I'd say it was a blue ribbon day.

Instead I smile and say, "Better than yours, Mama."

She smiles a weak smile. "That's good, sweetheart."

My phone buzzes in my pocket. Devon.

—Is it true?

Shit. Is he talking about Whitney? Or Will? I don't answer, and in a few seconds, Devon texts again.

—Is Whitney really in jail?

—What's it to you? Plan on spreading it around?

So maybe I'm crazy pants for thinking he'd tell every-thing to Will. But Will and I had *never* hung out before without Devon, and hardly ever hung out when Devon *was* there. The worst part is, I can't tell Devon what happened today. There's no one I can talk to about it.

—???? What's with the 'tude?

I text back.

—Look, never mind. It's true about Whit. I've got to take
care of Coby. TTYL

Around ten, I hear Daddy's truck in the driveway. A little
later on, Whitney comes into my room and crawls into bed
with Coby and me. She smells like cigarettes and her hair
looks lank and clumped, like she hasn't washed it in days.
But I don't say anything, just scoot closer and wrap my
arms around her while Coby nestles between us.

"I love you, Whit."

She doesn't answer, but I can feel her tears as they hit
my arm. I hope they're going to lock her husband up for a
good long time.

CHAPTER NINE

Turns out Whitney being arrested has given me a perfect cover for acting weird in front of Devon. Normally, he'd notice my silence and my nervous fingers and be all over me. "What's wrong, something's up, what are you not telling me?" But today, he just figures it's because my sister got arrested.

When we walk into the commons, Will is laughing and talking with a cluster of the cool seniors. Amber-o-zia's standing next to him, hand in his back pocket. Typically, Devon always acknowledges Will and vice versa. I wonder if today will be different.

Will's playing it cool, though. "Greetings, earthlings," he says, leaning over to us just as Devon and I walk past.

He looks at me and I look at him, and if there's anything different that passes between us, I sure don't see it, so I doubt anyone else does either.

Is that how hooking up works? You just do it and then things go right back to the way they were before? I look around at the other girls in the commons. How many other not-special looks have been passed today?

I stand up as tall as I can and walk past him without shame. So I was definitely impulsive, maybe stupid, but I don't have to fold in on myself.

I stop and turn and cock my hip. "Hey, Will?"

His shoulders stiffen, like he's worried I'm about to blow his cover with Amber-o-zia. "Yeah?" His smile hovers, waiting.

"May the Force be with you."

His smile cracks and he starts to laugh. "May the Force be with you, Amber Plain and Small." Then he winks.

Now I can walk away and hold my head up. Because while he may have used me, maybe I used him, too.

"You are such a geek," Devon says, grabbing my arm and hurrying me away toward our morning hangout down the hall.

"Whatever." I've told Devon nearly everything for two years, and me and Will falls into the giant news category. Everything about not telling him feels wrong.

So when Kush comes walking up to us, I use it as an excuse to slip away.

"Hey, Devon." I nudge him and point toward Kush. "I'll see you later for that program?"

Every year, the first week of school, colleges come and set up tables for the juniors and seniors in the gym. It's our first year to attend and I'm excited, not only to get a free tote bag and a water bottle, but to see for myself what opportunities are out there that I don't know about.

Devon swallows and whispers, "Really, you don't mind?"

"No. It's cool. I'll see if I can find C.A." I push him toward Kush. "Talk to the boy."

While I'm standing there watching Devon walk away with Kush, Sean walks up.

"Hi, Amber." He's wearing a guitar pick on a leather cord around his neck like a necklace.

"Hey, Sean."

He nods in the direction of Devon. "You going to their game Thursday?"

"Yeah, probably. I try to go to all the home games. You?"

"Yeah. No choice. My aunt Aneeta said I have to stay, she's going out shopping that afternoon."

"You can't go home on the bus?"

Sean looks away, then looks at the floor. "She doesn't want us home alone unless someone else is there."

I wait for him to say more. Like why his aunt won't let them be at home alone. When he doesn't, I start to head toward class.

He clears his throat. "So, um, maybe I could sit with you?"

"Oh, I have an assembly today, it messes up lunch schedule for juniors and seniors."

"No. Not at lunch." He scratches his head. One crazy sprig of hair flops over like a broken cornstalk. "I meant at the game."

Behind me, I hear Will's laugh. I want to turn around and find him, but I don't.

Sean slips his hands into his jeans pockets waiting for my answer.

"Yeah. Sure."

Sean's smile is shy and sweet. "See you then."

On the way to art, I hear a few snickers from a group of girls walking out of the girls' bathroom. It's Lila Cliff and her posse. Lila's only a freshman, but she's the sheriff's daughter. She catches my eye and arches her brows. "Hey. Got any oxy?" Then she whispers to her friends and they break into peals of laughter.

This town is too damn small. Everyone thinks they

know who you are now and who you're going to be down the road. I don't want any of these girls thinking they can get to me, but they do.

Just then, I feel a hand on my arm.

Cheerleader Amber. "Come on, biscuit. Don't let the gossip girls get you down."

"*You're* a gossip girl," I say, nudging her with my arm.

"Yes, but I'm one that's made out of fairy dust and unicorn fur."

When we step into the art room, the first thing I see is Kush at our table. In my chair.

"Who's made out of unicorn fur?" Devon asks, lifting his head up.

C.A. twirls. "Why, *me*." She puts her hand on her heart, then points to me. "And this Amber, she's made out of sugar and spice and everything nice."

"You're in my chair," I say to Kush. But Kush is slung back in my seat like he owns it.

Kush pushes the chair back on two legs, balancing against the wall behind him. "And?"

I stare at him, then at Devon. Devon swallows and looks away.

Ms. Thomas interrupts us. "Class, settle down. I need to take quick attendance, then we're headed to the gym for College Access Day."

I keep glaring at them, but slump into the chair next to C.A.

Ms. Thomas's pencil bumps against air as she points, then marks in her book. I have to hand it to her, she's nailed our names on the second day. When she's done, she has us line up at the door like elementary school students.

"Really?" I turn to Devon ready to mock her, but he and Kush are talking about last year's World Cup playoffs and line up like ducklings.

C.A. bounces from flip-flop to flip-flop. Her toenails sport hot pink polish with a Hello Kitty painted on each big toe. "College boys. I can't *wait* to go to college."

"Do you know where you want to go already?" I ask.

"Of course. East Carolina. Cheer squad and an hour from the beach. What could be better?"

I think about it. I'd like to study music. Maybe learn to play an instrument. But neither Mama nor Daddy went to college. I've never even been on a real college campus.

Ms. Thomas leads us down the hallway and into the gym. It's a propaganda center for a bunch of local colleges and universities, from Chapel Hill to NC State, full of tables covered with pamphlets, peppermints, and free stuff that everyone's scooping into recycled tote bags. It's unlikely I'll go anywhere other than the local community college, if that, but I'll talk to them. Dreaming is free.

C.A. runs off to the ECU table and Kush drags Devon away to the table for a private liberal arts college that he claims has a top-rated soccer team. I wander around until I find a table for a nearby technical college that has vet tech information. I nab some brochures for Whitney. She'll probably just throw them in the trash, but it's worth a try.

Across the gym and the crowd of students, I see Will at the East Tennessee State table in animated conversation with a grizzled-looking guy who reminds me of Daddy's second-favorite country singer, Willie Nelson, Johnny Cash being the first. Amber-o-zia's by his side, looking bored as she holds up strands of her hair and inspects the ends.

I feel a twinge of guilt. Amber-o-zia's never done anything to me. I could have stopped things yesterday, but I didn't. If I'm honest with myself, I'd sort of hoped hooking up with Will like that might have knocked Amber-o-zia out of the picture. But is that what Daddy's blonde thinks about my mama? I put my hands over my eyes and press.

Just as I'm about to sink, C.A. appears at my side. "Come on, I found the goods."

She drags me to a booth manned by a blue-haired guy with a lip ring. Kush is standing with him, chatting like they're old friends.

"Here." C.A. winks at Blue Hair and scoops up a handful of drawing pencils, sliding them into my bag. "These are free, and *this* is Troy."

Kush rolls his eyes at C.A.

"How do you two know each other?" I ask, tilting my head toward Troy and Kush.

Troy goes into sales mode, gathering school literature as he talks. "I used to intern for Kush's dad when I was in high school. Before I started working for North Carolina School of the Arts."

"Intern?" C.A. asks.

"Yep. Y'all didn't know Kush's dad is a famous potter? Eric Whitson?"

C.A. and I both shake our heads.

"Kush, my man." Troy mock punches Kush's shoulder. "You've been holding back key information from the ladies."

"Troy, the stuff these ladies *don't* know would fill a lecture hall at NCSA. I don't have that kind of time."

"Seems like you have as much time as the rest of us now." I cross my arms over my chest, tired already of Kush's digs.

Troy clears his throat.

C.A. grabs my hand. "Amber, you rocked at clay in

Art I! Maybe Kush's dad would let you intern for him." She glares at Kush. "Then maybe she'd be at the *front* of a lecture hall at NCSA one day."

I want to hug her.

Troy clears his throat and holds out canvas-covered sketchbooks for us. "Are either of you considering a future in the arts?"

C.A. immediately grabs the sketchbook. "Maybe."

"She's really talented," I add.

"Are you seniors?" Troy asks.

"Juniors," we say in unison.

"Well, here." He digs under his table and pulls out a glossy folder filled with papers. "Do you know about NC-Arts, our feeder school?" He's still awkwardly holding out my sketchbook.

We shake our heads.

"It's a public school, just like this one, but focused on the arts. It's in Winston-Salem."

C.A. plants her hand on her hip. "Do they have a football team to cheer for?"

"No." Troy laughs. "But they have an awesome show choir that's always looking for dancers. It's a boarding school for talented students in dance, theater, music, along with visual arts, of course."

I edge closer to the table. A high school where I could focus on music?

He stops and flips through the pages, his finger tracing down the text. "The next portfolio deadline is October first, and if you know any musicians, dancers, or drama geeks, the closest auditions are in Boone, in about a month."

"No thanks, but thanks for this." C.A. takes the sketchbook he's been holding out for me and tucks it under her arm.

But I take the folder he's holding in his other hand. As I slide it into my bag, my chest fills with nerves. But not the kind that make me want to gasp for air. These feel like anticipation and birthday surprises. Like the opening notes of a hymn I've been waiting for too many Sundays to sing.

Kush says, "Right. You're a singer."

"Oh, yeah?" Troy asks, suddenly interested in me.

"Yeah," Kush says. "She's a real gospel girl." The corners of Kush's lips turn up slightly. "Sean says she has big dreams."

What he's saying isn't all that bad. But the way he's saying it, smirky and all-knowing, drawing out Sean's name, pisses me off. We had a common language, that's all. It's Kush who's suddenly turning it into something more.

I'm about to tell him to shut the hell up when Devon walks up behind us and grabs the glossy folder out of my tote bag.

"What's this?" He props his elbow on Kush's shoulder and casually flips through the pages. Kush crosses his arms and looks with him.

C.A. nudges me and grins. "Only the beginning of Amber Vaughn's singing career."

Devon looks at the cover and peers over it at me. "Are you going to apply?"

I shove my hands in my pockets, twirling a piece of loose string around my index finger. "I don't know. It's probably stupid."

I don't want to talk about it in front of Kush. If I open my mouth, I'm worried butterflies are going to fly out.

"What do you mean? Can't you at least audition?" C.A. asks me.

I shrug and take back the brochure from Devon, sliding it carefully into the bag. "My mama would never let me go to a boarding school so far away from here."

C.A. looks at Devon. "Can *you* talk some sense into her?"

Devon glances at me and answers her. "Mama Vaughn is pretty protective of Amber."

"So? I bet we can convince her." C.A. claps her hands. "I am *awesome* with mothers."

That's when Will and Amber-o-zia walk up to us. Will looks around and asks, "Convince who of what?"

I open my mouth to say something, but all that comes out is a lone butterfly only I can see. On its wings I see the word *sing*.

CHAPTER TEN

- -

Thursday afternoon, Sean meets me on the path leading up to the soccer fields. He's sitting on a low cement wall, staring off at the mountains.

"You ready?" I ask.

He flinches like I caught him off guard. "Yeah. Hey." He hops down and drags his book bag to his shoulder.

"Dang. What are you taking?" His bag is solid and stretched to full-size.

Sean blushes. "Nothing special." Pause. "The library here . . . is better than my old school's."

I'm glad I've had a lifetime of listening to my slow-talking great-uncle Jim. I've learned sometimes, you have to slow down and listen hard to find out what you want to know.

Sean drops the pack to the road and unzips it. Inside is what looks like every graphic novel on our library shelves. "See?" he says.

"I'm not a huge reader," I say. "But let me know if one of those is really good, and I'll read it."

"Okay." Pause. "Sure."

Mrs. Early's manning the ticket booth today.

"How's your mama, Amber?" Mrs. Early's wearing a MHHS polo over crisp guidance counselor khakis. On Sundays, she tends to go for floral patterns.

I appreciate her not coming out with the details of the question she's really asking. "A little overwhelmed right now," I answer.

She nods and tears off tickets when we hand her our money. "Tell her to stop in if she needs a friendly ear."

"I will."

Mrs. Early looks at Sean. "Young man, how are your first couple of days going?"

Sean tugs at the hem of his shirt. "Pretty good, I guess," he says quietly, and looks at the ticket counter.

Mrs. Early sizes him up. When she notices the guitar pick around his neck, she asks him, "Do you sing? I could always use more boys for chorus." She pivots her head toward me and taps her index finger on the counter. "And more girls."

It's been a sore point between us. I'll sing for her at church, but hanging out with my preacher's wife at school is a whole different kind of inbred. You start bringing all your friends and acquaintances together into every part of your life and soon you've gone all cross-eyed and you can't breathe. Plus, it's an extra hour and a half of school every day.

Sean hunches his shoulders. "No, ma'am. I can't carry a tune. I just play the guitar."

"Well, band, then?" Mrs. Early asks.

"Yes, ma'am, I'm taking it."

She smiles, and I notice that this time, Mrs. Early has Sean's attention. "Good. I'm glad to hear it."

As Sean and I walk toward the stands, I see Will sitting with Amber-o-zia out of the corner of my eye. I try not to look at him, but I can't help it. He's sprawled out against the risers, arms spread wide. His hair's falling in his eyes and he's laughing, like always. Amber-o-zia turns around to say something to him with her hands waving and he lifts his chin and smiles at her. What does she have that makes her good enough to be Will's real girlfriend?

C.A.'s waiting for us in the stands, and I'm surprised to see her sitting with Frog.

"Hey, girl!" C.A. pats the bleacher seat next to her. Then her voice softens slightly. "Hey, Sean."

"Hey," he mumbles. But he never looks at her directly.

"Sit here," I say, and point next to C.A. I sit on the other side of him.

C.A. shakes her head no and I shake my head yes. Sean seems clueless and sits down where I pointed.

"Are y'all watching this?" Frog says as he stares at the field.

Devon's in the goal box, his hands on his knees, waiting. I'm kind of surprised, because normally he's always swarmed with the other team. He has to work hard to make up for the lack of defense out on the field. But today it's different. It's the away team's goalie who's working overtime and it's Kush who's handling the ball like a pro.

"Damn. Would you look at that?" I sit up.

"I know, right?" C.A. starts cheer clapping. "If they keep it up, we may just need a soccer squad." Her eyes light up. "I know. You could cheer this year!"

I roll my eyes. "Not going to happen, C.A."

"You don't want to be a cheerleader?" Sean asks.

I start to explain that I'm sort of a klutz when I hear Amber-o-zia laughing loudly at something. I look her way to see Will leaning in, whispering something in her ear.

"Booyah!" Frog yells, and starts jumping up and down.

We all turn to look at the game unfolding on the field. Kush runs away from the opponent's goal box, his hands over his head. The other guys on the MHHS team are jumping and slapping his hands. Unbelievable. Our soccer team scored a goal. Devon's doing an Egyptian strut and screaming something about "doing it right" on the far end of the field.

At halftime, Devon comes up to where we're sitting, high in the stands. "Oh my God, can you believe it?" He stretches his calf muscles on the concrete benches and points at the scoreboard.

Kush climbs up behind Devon, then Will comes over to us, loudly humming the theme to *The Beverly Hillbillies*. He throws his arm around his brother's shoulders and croons,

> *"Come and listen to a story about*
> *a team that was dead,*
> *Barely had the strength to kick the ball*
> *above the other players' heads,*
> *But then one day they met this dude named Kush,*
> *Who hit the goalie's net with a great big whoosh.*
> *City boy, soccer star!"*

Sean smiles down at the ground.

Kush rolls his eyes and looks around at us. "Seriously?"

Will, still hanging onto Devon, lifts his brows and

smiles. "Yeah, what's wrong with it? That was a sick tune."

Kush shrugs. "You'd be laughed off stage with that rhyme in Atlanta."

"What? Are you our poet laureate now or something?" Will's laughing, but it's awkward.

Sean laughs under his breath.

Kush starts to run in place, snapping his knees to his hands, and glares at Sean. "I might pen a rhyme or two, punch out a rap," he says, breaths coming unevenly.

"Oh?" Will asks.

Devon punches Will and stands taller, shaking Will's arm off his shoulders. "What's wrong with rap?" Then he looks at Kush and nods his head like a dashboard bobble head. "Rap's cool."

I look at Will and raise my eyebrows. Devon's got it bad. Will flutters three fingers over his heart and I try to keep from laughing, too. The moment feels almost normal, like Monday afternoon never happened.

"Coach is signaling for us. You coming?" Kush looks over at Devon.

"Yeah, man," Devon says.

I watch them barrel down the stairs to the field.

C.A. stands up. "I've got to give Frog a ride home, and Mom will kill me if I don't get home soon. Thursday is our movie night and she rented *Sleepless in Seattle*." She crooks her finger to motion for me to come closer, then whispers in my ear, "He likes you. Not me. I see what you're trying to do."

I glance over my shoulder. Will and Sean are laughing, coming up with another *Beverly Hillbillies* rhyme. Maybe I should tell C.A. the truth. That I slept with Will. That I think I like him, not Sean. Lord knows, I'm dying to tell somebody.

But then, Amber-o-zia climbs the stairs. "Will, come with me to the concession stand." She flips her hair and smiles at us. "Hi, Ambers." Around Amber-o-zia's neck is a gold *A* on a delicate chain. She's wearing a fitted orange camisole, skinny jeans, and three-inch wedge heels that make her already long legs look even longer. She's the kind of girl Will can take home as his girlfriend.

"Yeah, we're going, too. I have to get home. We'll walk with you." C.A. motions for Frog and they all take off, leaving me with Sean alone on the bleachers.

I'm tempted to fill the silence, but I don't. Eventually Sean speaks. "Kush isn't as bad as he seems."

I can't help myself and snort.

Sean smiles. "Yeah. I know."

We sit for another minute. "So, what's your story? Why are you living with your aunt and uncle? If you don't mind sharing." I cross my legs.

Sean rubs his knees. "No. I don't mind. It's a simple story."

It's probably the longest thing I've heard him string together without pausing. I wait.

Sean clears his throat and runs his hands through his messy hair. "My mom left Georgia when she was seventeen and pregnant. She tried to make an honest life and failed." He tucks his fingers under the riser and leans forward before adding in a quiet voice, "She's in jail right now for possession and solicitation."

I put my hand on his forearm. "It's okay, you don't have to tell me anything else. And you don't have to worry about me gossiping. My family's pretty messed up, too."

Sean takes his arm out from under my hand. "No, I want to tell you."

He looks at the field. The soccer players are filing back out, high-fiving, ready to start the second half. "Our neighbors saved my life."

"What do you mean?" I ask.

Now I see Sean's fingers dancing on his knee and I realize he's playing it, like a guitar.

"They lived in the apartment down the hall. Arthur and his wife, Virginia, fed me, took me in when I left the apartment scared shitless because of whatever guy my mom had brought home that day." Sean looks up at the sky, then at me. "Arthur was the one who taught me to play. Found me my guitar and made me do stuff like take out the garbage to pay him back. Virginia made sure I never went hungry."

"They sound like great neighbors," I say.

He swallows hard. "I'd hoped I could live with them, but the state couldn't look beyond the difference in our skin color, and Arthur had a felony from when he was in his twenties. Then they moved to Florida." He pauses. "But I had my guitar. Playing it was my lifeline. Let me block out the pain." He picks a fleck of paint off the riser and flicks it down a row. "And the sound." Sean looks up and meets my gaze. His mouth settles into a line and his eyes narrow. "Then my mom sold it. Not long afterward, she got locked up." There's something hollow in his voice. A gaping hole left by his lost instrument.

Tears well up in my eyes. "Wow, Sean. I'm so sorry."

He shrugs and glances skyward. "Arthur died last year. Cancer."

I feel the punch in my gut. A tear rolls down my cheek. I wipe it off before Sean notices.

We sit and watch the game silently.

"Sorry to lay all that on you," Sean says after a bit.

I want to wrap my arms around him and hug him, pull his head to my shoulder and stroke that crazy hair, tell him everything's going to be all right. Instead I grab his hand and squeeze it.

Sean looks down at my hand on his and smiles.

"Thanks," he says and tentatively squeezes back.

I let go when I see Will and Amber-o-zia return to their seats. Sean leans forward with his elbows on his knees and taps his fingers together. We watch the game for a while in silence, and then Sean starts to fidget.

"Do you smoke?" he asks me.

"What?"

"Cigarettes. I really need one. Is there someplace I can smoke without getting caught?"

I look around. There are a few teachers down near the field, but they seem occupied by the game. I'm not in a big hurry to get caught in the smoke hole, but after the way Sean opened up, I figure I can at least help him out.

"Come on, I'll show you."

We slip down the stairs, past the concession stand, behind the concrete bleachers. There's a little nook hidden by bushes in front of the maintenance room door.

Sean lights up and takes a long draw. I take a step back away from the smoke. He takes a few more draws, then throws the cigarette to the ground. Before he can stomp it out with his foot, I hear a familiar voice.

"Who's back there? I can smell you." Vice Principal

Smoker. Where the hell did she come from?

"Shit," Sean says. "My aunt's going to crucify me."

I look at him and see terror in his eyes. Like he's going to get way more than a week of being grounded.

Smoker's face pops into view over the bushes. "Miss Vaughn. Mr. Whitson." She looks down and the cigarette lies between us, a curl of smoke rising up in the air. "Do you care to explain yourselves?"

Sean starts to open his mouth but I take my arm and whack it across him like Daddy used to do to me when he came to a stoplight. "I'm sorry, Mrs. Smoker. I tried to wait till I got home but I couldn't. Sean was only keeping me company."

Mrs. Smoker looks at me over the bridge of her glasses, weighing my words. "Miss Vaughn. This seems to be a new development over the summer. Your in-school suspension for Friday is now out-of-school. This is a tobacco-free campus, young lady. I'll be calling your mother." She lifts her nose and gives Sean the inquisition eye. "And I'll be keeping an eye out on you."

Sean stands next to me with his mouth hanging open and edges closer.

"Do you have a way to get home?" Mrs. Smoker asks me.

"I'll give her a ride," Sean says.

"Good." Smoker glances between us once more. "I think it's time for both of you to leave campus."

"Yes, ma'am," we say together.

She follows us out from behind the bleachers. A real executioner's march. Sean excuses himself to jog over to the fence where the team waits to go on the field. I see the coach call time-out and Kush runs off the field to the fence.

Sean says something to him and Kush's face goes even redder than it already is from playing. He says something back, his hands gesturing like he's telling Sean off. Then he looks in my direction.

I don't meet his eyes. When I look up, Kush is fishing keys out of his gym bag. He throws them to Sean before running back onto the field.

The shrill cry of the coach's whistle cuts across the evening.

Sean pulls up to the front of my house and three points the car around so he's facing back in the direction of his aunt and uncle's house.

"I still don't understand why you did that for me." His hand rests on the top of the steering wheel.

Sean's uncle's truck is cluttered like my dad's. But instead of smelling like a stranger's perfume, it just smells like dirt. Streaks of clay mark the vinyl on the interior doors. It's an old one, with roll-down windows and hand-operated locks. It suits Sean.

"Me neither." I look toward the lights in the house. I sigh. "I'll be okay, though. Mama will for sure ground me for the F bomb, but she'll probably cut me some slack for helping you. She knows I don't smoke and you'll get a free pass."

"I don't want her not to like me. We're neighbors."

I reach for the handle. "You don't know my mama. She's the world's most forgiving person." I turn to push the door open and let out a yelp when Sammy's head appears in the window.

"Hey, baby sister." He smells like he wallowed in a still. "Who's this?"

I groan. Sammy's family must have figured out a way to pay his bail. "You're out. Great."

He pushes his arm in the truck, reaching across me to shake Sean's hand. "Hey, man. I'm Sammy." Then he notices Sean's shirt. "Guns N' Roses. Hell, yeah." He stumbles back a step and starts ripping the air, playing an imaginary guitar, then straightens.

Sean nods. "Yeah. Rock and roll, man."

Sammy leans back in. "Did you know this little girl has one of the sweetest singing voices in all of Sevenmile?" He opens the car door and sits on the edge of the seat, making me scoot over closer to Sean. "Come on, Amber, sing with me. Show your new boyfriend what you can do."

"Sammy, stop, you're being an ass."

"I'm not moving till you sing for him. I want to see his face when he hears you. I want you to see it so you know what it'll be like when all those boys line up to hear our band and hear your sweet voice." Sammy burps.

"Sammy, I told you no."

"You think I listened? I need you, Amber, and you know we'll be great."

Sean nudges me. "I wouldn't mind hearing you sing."

Sammy's resting his chin on my right shoulder, whispering, "Sing."

"Fine." I lean forward and flip through a box of cassette tapes on the floor.

Sammy reaches past me and grabs one of the tapes. "Play that one." He hands the cassette to Sean, who shoves it in the player.

I drop my forehead into my hands and tilt my head toward the house. Hasn't someone in there heard the truck idling out front?

Sean turns up the volume and I hear the intake of breath on the tape, then the slow guitar start. I sing along, and when I fade off from the first chorus and the guitar solo starts I feel like I'm trapped between bumper cars.

They're both jamming, their fingers crawling across invisible frets. I reach forward and hit stop on the tape. "Enough. Sammy, let me out."

Sean's laughing. "Sorry, Amber. But he's right. You do have an amazing voice."

That softens me for a second. "Thanks."

"So y'all are starting a band?" Sean asks.

At the same time Sammy says yes, I say no.

I reach across Sammy, push open the door, and then push him out. He falls onto the grass. From his prone position, he yells up to Sean. "Yeah, man. A band. You should play with us."

I get out, careful to avoid stepping on Sammy. "See you, Sean. Thanks for the ride."

Sean leans over and says, "No problem. And thank you. Again."

He drives away, and I walk toward the house. I'm halfway there when Whitney's Chihuahua mix, Giant, meets me. My sister has a thing for wounded and stray animals. Giant's no exception, his leg crippled from a long-ago fight with somebody bigger and tougher. "Hey, buddy." I lean down and scoop him up. "What are you doing out of your fence?"

Sammy catches up to us and grabs me from behind. "Amber, go get Whitney for me."

I manage to get Giant to the ground without dropping

him, but Sammy ends up knocking me down. He's so drunk he can barely stand.

I try to get up but he flops down next to me and grabs my hand.

"Sammy, get up. You're freaking me out."

He starts giggling like a madman and looks at my face. Then he pushes my hair off my forehead.

"Jesus, Sammy." I squirm away from him and sit up.

Sammy lunges for my wrist, holding it tight before letting it go. "Tell your parents to send my *wife* and *child* back out to our house."

I pick up Giant, my arms trembling, and clatter up the stairs. Maybe Daddy will come to the door and send Sammy off with a shotgun greeting.

But it's Whitney who meets me on the porch, with eyes red-rimmed from crying. I can hear Mama and Daddy screaming in the kitchen.

"What happened?" I ask shakily.

"Phone," she says, with a shrug. "Got cut off."

Well, that's one thing that's gone my way. We won't get a call from the school now about my suspension tomorrow.

"What's Giant doing out?" Whitney starts to take him out of my arms and I move to block the open door, but it's too late.

"Sammy," Whitney whispers. "Oh, baby, you're home."

Her voice cracks and her hands fly to her heart, then she pushes me out of the way. She runs down the stairs into the yard and throws herself into Sammy's arms.

I can hear Mama shrieking about money and Daddy telling her to shut her yap, that he's working his ass off and why doesn't she go and get a job. Coby toddles over from the den, where he was watching *Blue's Clues*, and grabs my leg. "BerBer," he says and reaches up.

I put down Giant and swing Coby to my hip.

In the front yard, Sammy and Whitney are on their knees, hugging and crying. I can hear him apologizing, then Whitney's, "It's okay, baby. It's okay."

"Come on, Coby." He buries his face into my neck. I whistle for Giant. He may as well escape with us, too. The stairs creak as I climb to the bedroom Whitney and I used to share. I shut the door, waiting for the click, then turn on the public radio station to classical music.

The three of us—me, Coby, and tiny Giant—huddle under the blankets, blocking out the sounds from downstairs. I make up a story about a singer who rides a magical bird and performs for kingdoms far and wide.

As we fly out of the window and up into the night sky, my voice stops working.

Because, honestly, I can't see how I'm going to get out of here.

CHAPTER ELEVEN

The first thing I think about when I wake up the next morning is Sean. I've never even heard him play, but I know, from the sound of his voice, from the look in his eyes, that the guitar is the thing that keeps him together. My instrument is part of me, and I'll never lose it. Nobody can sell it out from under me.

The smell of bacon floats up the stairs. Mama's downstairs frying up eggs and pouring juice. I roll over on my pillow, not yet ready to open my eyes. I could fake sick. I could meet Devon like normal, then have him drop me off somewhere for the day.

I open one eye and stare at the map on the wall. Winston-Salem jumps off the paper in bold print, like a warning. If Mama catches me in a lie, I'll be in way worse trouble than just coming out with the truth. The folder from NC-Arts lies on my bedside table. All I've been able to bring myself to do is stare at the cover. It's a dream. Opening it and figuring out the requirements for getting in, that's reality. And right now, the dream's as real as it gets.

I sit up and jam my feet into the slippers Whitney and Coby bought me for my birthday. Coby loves them. He claps and screams, "Boo feet!" when he sees me wearing them.

I pick up my phone and text Devon.

—Suspended. Don't need a ride.

—I heard. Sucks. Talk later?

—Game?

—Won! 4–1

—!!!

I tug the belt of my robe tight around my nightshirt and head for the stairs. Better get this over with.

Downstairs, Daddy sits in the recliner drinking a cup of coffee. "Morning, caboose."

I sit on the couch across from him and tuck my feet underneath me. He's staring at the television. His profile is handsome. His hair is still thick and only a little darker than mine and Whitney's. There's a little gray shining from the stubble of his beard. He rubs his face, then holds out his coffee cup. "Get me another cup, will you?"

Get him another damn cup of coffee? Is that all we are to him? How *dare* he cheat on Mama?

When I don't immediately take the cup, he turns and looks at me. "Is there a problem?"

I don't say anything, just look at him.

"Is this about the phone? Not you, too. I paid the bill online last night, and it should be coming on any second."

Sure enough, the phone jangles on the table next to him like it was waiting for the word.

"Hello?" Daddy cradles the phone against his ear.

My anger drains as it rises on Daddy's face. He's saying "Uh-huh," and "Is that right?" and staring at me all the while. I sink back into the sofa cushions. When he hangs up, he yells, "Donna, get in here!"

Mama trundles through the doorway from the kitchen holding the pot of coffee. "Who was on the phone?"

Daddy holds out the cup. Mama fills it. Daddy takes a sip before answering.

"That was the school. Seems our Whitney's not the only one kicking up some dust."

After my parents' explosion, the dust settles around my feet. I can clearly see a week of purgatory. No Friday night at Devon's. No hiking. No television. No cell phone. I am at school, at home, or at church. End of story.

Even though Mama believed me about the smoking, both of my parents are convinced I was taking advantage of the phone being cut off. They're madder than hornets they had to find out from a phone call from the school and not from me, no matter how much I protest I really was about to tell them.

"Can I at least talk to Devon about tonight? It'd be rude for me not to show up at his house when he's expecting me."

By this time, Daddy's gathering up his keys and his tool bag.

"Herman?" Mama's voice is a question.

Daddy looks at me. "The McKinney boy?"

I nod.

Both Mama and Daddy like our friendship. They think me being in with the judge's son is good for our family. He nods at Mama.

"One phone call," she says.

I wonder if this is how Whitney felt in jail.

I shut the door to my room and pull the quilt over me. It's raining outside, which makes me feel less dreary about being stuck inside. The North Carolina School of the Arts brochure's slick surface shines from the lamplight spilling over it. One piece of paper sticks out a tiny bit. I can see the words *Admissions Requirements* at the top. I turn on the radio to the local AM station as a distraction.

Sandwiched between the swap and shop listings and the lost pet announcements, the station plays beautiful gospel, ballads, and the bluegrass I love. I was raised on this music and it feels as soothing to me as a piece of Mama's spice cake. I like other music, but these songs, they are my heart.

I sing along as the rain falls out my window. Drops of water gather on the windowpanes like a shimmering audience. I play with my voice, testing out my range, creating new sounds, trying to both imitate the radio singers and to be myself. Finally, I can't stand it anymore. I roll over and grab the folder.

The list of requirements is long. Transcripts. A long application. Two letters of recommendation, at least one from someone who has been your instructor in your art form. An artist's statement. An audition. The applicant must perform three pieces from the following list. My eyes scan the options. I push the paper back in the folder and shove the whole thing under the bed. I don't even know what half of that music is. I ball the quilt up under my chin and scoot deeper under the sheets. Mama would never have let me go anyway.

. . .

That afternoon Mama gives me my cell phone so I can call Devon. "Hey," I say.

"Hey." He sounds breathless.

"I won't be coming over tonight." I wait for Devon's dramatic outburst, knowing it will make me feel better. Instead, he just says, "Okay."

I hang on the line, waiting for more. Finally I say, "Okay?"

"Well, you know you're grounded and all."

"You don't sound disappointed." I hear Whitney's and Coby's voices downstairs.

"I . . ." Devon hesitates. "Of course, I'm upset, but it might be better this way."

Panic beats in my chest. "Better?" I ask. Did he find out about me and Will?

"Yeah. Look, I'm sorry I didn't talk to you first, but last night, after the game, I gave Kush a ride home, and I might have suggested he come over so we could work on some beats."

My panic turns into something red. "You invited Kush! Friday nights are *our* nights and you don't even like rap."

There's silence on the other end of the line. Then Devon speaks low into the phone. "People can change, Amber. I don't appreciate you putting me, or Kush, in a box."

"Wow. Okay." My hand starts to tremble. I've never had a fight with Devon before. "Sorry, Devon, I just . . . I'm surprised, that's all. Do you really like him?"

Devon exhales and sounds more like himself again. "Enough to try to write some sick rhymes. Plain and Small, don't be mad. We have room to expand, right?"

"I'm not mad," I say, then pause. "Devon?"

"Yeah?"

"Why'd you tell Will about the hiker barn this summer? He made a crack about it when he dropped me off on Monday. Did you tell him how wild I was all summer?"

"Amber. God! Of course not."

"Did you tell Kush?"

"No."

"Are you sure?" I squeeze the phone tight in my hands.

"Why would I *do* that?" Devon asks. He sounds innocent. But Will knew about the hiker barn. And Kush is everything the rest of us aren't. Worldly. Different. Interesting. New. Devon might be glad to have someone new to swap stories with.

"Sorry. I'll see you Monday." Then, "Have fun, Busta Rhymes."

Devon laughs and the phone goes dead, beginning my weekend of exile.

CHAPTER TWELVE

Whitney opens the door to my room after lunch on Saturday. "Daddy says you need to go scrub the water troughs."

"Why me? All I did was get suspended for cursing. Seems like you're the one who should be getting hard labor."

Whitney rolls her eyes. She looks like shit. Actually, she looks high.

"What are you on?" I ask.

She walks over and flops backward on my bed. "What do you mean?"

"You know what I mean."

She rolls over on her stomach and reaches her hands

down to the floor. "I took half a Valium. Want the other half?"

"Whitney."

"God, don't get all preachy on me. I'm really stressed out."

I pull on my work jeans and an old T-shirt and don't say anything.

"Hey, what's this?" Whitney pulls the NC-Arts folder out from under the bed.

"Nothing. Give that to me." I try to grab the papers from her. She rolls across the bed, holding it out of my reach, and reads the cover. "North Carolina High School of the Arts." She rolls back and stares at me. "Have you shown this to Mama?"

"No. I told you, it's nothing. Are you done?"

She sits up cross-legged and flips through the folder. "Are you going to apply?"

I fall onto the bed. "No."

"Why not?"

"Because." I shove the audition page into her hands. "This." I point at the list of audition choices and name a few off. "An aria from the seventeenth or eighteenth century, an English art song, and a German lied, sung in German! Do you know what any of this is?"

"No." She lies back on the bed and reaches her fingers

up to the ceiling. "But I bet Mrs. Early does." Then Whitney starts laughing. "Look at you, Miss Dreamy Face. Do you really think a place like that would take someone like us?" She closes her eyes and starts humming.

I shove the paper in the folder.

Then I pull it back out.

The next morning, Mama doesn't let up until she gets everybody ready for church. It's the six of us, spit-shined and polished, showing up at the doors of Evermore Fundamental. I can feel eyes looking at us every way I turn.

Today's opening hymn is "Amazing Grace." The organ swells in my chest and I breathe deep into my diaphragm. If I'm really going to try to audition for NC-Arts, I better get used to folks watching me. I leave our pew and walk to the front of the sanctuary and turn to face my family and our neighbors. They quiet down, their expressions expectant.

"Amazing Grace, how sweet the sound,
That saved a wretch like me."

It's a song I never get tired of. The sanctuary reverberates with sound and I close my eyes. As I sing, I don't have time to daydream. But when I finish, in those seconds before I return to our pew, I picture myself on the stage of a mega-church like you see on TV. There are thousands of parishioners and their hands are all waving back and forth. I feel larger than life, larger than the sum of my family, larger than Sevenmile.

In the receiving line after the service, I watch Mrs. Early purse her lips as I approach.

"I understand school got a little rocky this week." She clasps my hands.

"Maybe," I mumble. I want to ask Mrs. Early about the songs on the NC-Arts audition list, but I don't want Mama to hear. "Mrs. Early?" My voice is a whisper. "Do you know what an oratorio aria is?"

"I do," she says. She smiles and I smell peppermint on her breath. "Why do you ask?"

"I was hoping you might have some sheet music," I say.

"Why don't you join my after-school chorus? That way your mama won't have to worry about you hanging around with the wrong friends, getting into trouble, and I can teach you all about arias."

I look up at this. "Sean's not trouble."

I hear Pastor Early say his final "We'll pray for you, hon," and Mama is standing next to me.

"Donna, dear, how are you? Amber and I were just discussing my after-school chorus."

"Oh?" Mama's voice is hopeful. She's bugged me to

join since I started high school.

I talk fast. "I'm sure it's too late. My schedule's all set." Which I know is lame—chorus won't affect my other classes at all. The thing is, I do want Mrs. Early's help, just not in front of other kids. The ones who will think it's a joke I'm even trying to get into an arts magnet school by auditioning.

Mrs. Early pats my hands. "It's no problem. I'll get you added tomorrow morning, first thing." She looks at Mama. "We even have a chorus bus, if pick-up is a problem."

Mama is radiant. "Amber?" Mama looks at me, her eyes full of light.

I don't say anything, but shrug my shoulders.

Mama kisses my cheek, then wipes off the smudge of her Sundays-only primrose pink lipstick. She grabs Mrs. Early's hand. "Oh, thank you. I don't know how you finally convinced her, but there's nothing like hearing my baby sing."

I sure hope she keeps smiling once I tell her why I'm joining.

CHAPTER THIRTEEN

Devon picks me up Monday morning.

"I've missed you," he says, and holds out a travel mug of mocha his mom made using the McKinneys' new espresso machine.

I take a sip. "Oh, delicious goodness. Why can't Seven-mile even have a coffee place?" I ask lightly, trying to tread carefully, "How was your date?"

Devon shrugs. "Okay." Devon sighs. "I can't read his meter. I think I was wrong."

"Are you going to give up?" I try to keep my voice from sounding hopeful.

"I dropped some boy-on-boy hints into our stupid rhymes and he didn't react. But it could just be because he's from the city and his dad's an artist."

"Devon. You should tell him how you feel."

"I can't. What if he starts talking? I need to live under the radar here."

I hold the travel mug up as Devon navigates his Jeep around the pothole they refuse to fix in front of our house. "What if you, I don't know, have a party or something? Get him a little drunk."

Devon starts laughing. Then he turns to me and asks, "What if you got C.A. to kiss him?"

"What?"

"It's the perfect solution. Boys who like girls *like* her."

"Ouch," I say.

"Oh, come on. I didn't mean it like that."

"Uh-huh."

Devon blows out an exasperated sigh. "Stop. You're beautiful."

"But not enough for a guy to want to kiss."

"Really?" Devon asks, throwing his head back in mock irritation. "Are we going there? Because I have an entire summer I can catalog for you. Besides, you can't stand Kush. But if you want to be the one, go for it."

I laugh. "True."

"So? Will you ask her?"

I look down at my feet. "I'll ask, but Devon, I don't

think she's going to agree to it. And if she does, and he kisses her back, then what are you going to do?"

"Then I can stop wondering. The mystery is making me crazy."

In the commons, I'm surprised to find Sean and Kush standing together.

When we join them, Sean reaches into his backpack and hands me a mix CD. "Sorry you got grounded. I thought you might like these songs."

Kush blows out a breath of irritation before I can thank Sean. "What?" I ask. "I did get him out of trouble, didn't I?"

"Yeah. You did," Kush says. "Everybody's always saving Sean." He looks at Devon. "I promised Coach I'd stop by his office. Are you coming?"

"What? You're captain now?" I ask him.

"Yes." Kush slings his backpack onto one shoulder and looks down at me with his catlike eyes. "You got a problem with that, too?"

I hold up my hands. "No. I'm just surprised, that's all."

"Why? Because I'm not from here?"

I glance at Devon. I've stepped into something deep and I'm not sure what it is. Devon shrugs.

"Sorry, Kush. I didn't mean anything by it."

Devon leans over and grabs my arm. "See you in art, okay?"

"Yeah, okay." I watch them walk away together, heads close in conversation, and I wonder if I've been as much of a jerk to Kush as I think he's been to me.

Sean steps closer and says, "He's spoiled." His voice is so quiet I barely hear him. "He was an only child, until I moved in a year ago. He's still learning how to share."

"His friends?" I ask, with a small smile.

Sean shakes his head. "It's more complicated than that."

Just as I'm about to ask what Sean means, C.A. bounces up to us. "So, are y'all coming to the game Friday night?" Though the question's directed to both of us, she's looking right at Sean.

Sean stutters. "I, um, football's not my thing."

She slugs him. "Not for the football, silly. For the dance. They're actually kind of fun." Her eyes go wide. "*I* know. You two could go together."

"Um," I sputter. I've thought more than once about C.A.'s suggestion, but I'm still not sure I'm ready to make a move. Or that it's the right one.

"You *never* come to any dances, Amber." C.A. taps her foot. "And I want you both there."

"I usually go to Devon's on Fridays."

Devon reappears with Kush right before the bell and sticks his head into our little conversation. "What are y'all talking about?"

"Friday night," I answer—and then I think of a plan, for me, and for Devon. "C.A., can you drive me home on Friday?"

"Well, I have to get ready before the game, but yeah, I can come over for a little while."

"Great. I need you to help me. You know, with the thing."

She clasps her hands and nods. "Oh." She draws it out. "The *thing*."

"The *thing*?" Devon asks.

I know what he's asking—is the *thing* the *kiss*. The thing is actually C.A. helping me convince my mom to let me audition. But I say, "Yes, the thing," because Friday after school will be as good a time as any to talk to C.A. about Devon's favor.

Devon flushes.

"Then we'll come to your house, Devon. We can have a pre-party before the football game and the dance." Daddy has a stash of apple brandy out in the barn I can bring. Kush won't miss a chance to brag to his friends back in Atlanta that the country kids he's hanging out with really do drink moonshine. And once that's fired up Kush's system, Devon might be able to find out what he's dying to know.

Will chooses that moment to walk over, sans Amber-o-zia, to ask us, "Did I hear *party*?"

"At your house," C.A. answers, swiping the baseball cap off his head and handing it to him with a flourish. "Before the game."

Will looks to Devon. "What say you, bro?"

Devon pumps his fist. "I say par-*ty*, yo!"

The bell sounds in agreement.

At the end of the school day, I head to chorus, still riding the high of my plan from this morning. Mrs. Early greets me with a clap of her hands. "Amber, *so* nice to see you!"

The list of audition song options is tucked inside my book bag, but I figure I'll wait to talk to Mrs. Early about them until Mama's on board.

She points me to a chair in the soprano section. A motley assortment of students filters in. Chorus seems to be a combination of the devout, church-singing crowd and fringe kids who play in bands or want to.

Then, Will McKinney walks through the door. His dark hair flops over his forehead and now that it's afternoon, I can tell he didn't shave this morning. I watch him walk across the room in his faded Levi's, a vintage plaid shirt, and red Converse. All that's missing is his banjo.

He sees me and pauses before walking toward the bass section. As he passes me, he whispers, "How's it going, oh Forceful one?"

A slice of hot lightning bolts straight to a point below my belly button. I shift in my chair. I can't let him see how he gets to me. "It's going *nowhere*, Will."

He ducks his head, but not before I see a flash of color on his cheeks. "Too bad. I'd be more than happy to give you another ride home."

But I can't find the words for a snappy comeback, because when I look up at him, his eyes look open and sincere.

Mrs. Early claps twice and I'm startled out of my thoughts. "Ladies and gentlemen, let's get started. As you can see, we have a couple of new additions to the chorus." She gestures toward me, then Will.

I lean over my book bag as an excuse to sneak a glance in his direction. Will's all focused on Mrs. Early. I'd even venture to say he looks excited. For some reason, seeing his face so open, like he's waiting to be filled, fills *me* with happiness. Like I don't care if he knew what I was up to this summer, or if the moment between us never happens again. Because what I care about is singing, and I liked singing with Will.

Mrs. Early passes out sheet music. The song they've been working on is called "Shenandoah."

I figured school chorus would be an extension of church music, but I can already tell that I was wrong. The song is hard. So is working with a group of kids all trying to sing together. But Mrs. Early is good at what she does, and by halfway through the hour and a half, we're at least all coming in on the right parts.

After chorus is over, I rush out of the room. It's Will's voice I couldn't stop hearing over the others' in there. Will I imagined singing with onstage. I've got to get him out of my head.

Outside, on the circle, a car horn honks.

I look. Whitney's there in her dented Chevy Cavalier. Coby's sleeping in his car seat.

I slide into the front.

"You dating that guy?" she asks me.

"What? Who?"

"That one." She points.

I look over to see Will standing on the curb, waving his sheet music at me.

"*No.*" I say it too quickly.

Whitney smiles. Even under her new pallor of popping pills and stress, my sister is still beautiful to me. "Too bad.

He's hot." She starts the car. "You know, I gave you all those old clothes of mine. You ought to work it more. You *are* pretty."

"Thanks." It feels good to hear Whitney say it, even if I don't always believe I am, compared to her.

Whitney drives down Main Street and turns on Reserve Road.

Maybe she's visiting a friend. Or maybe she's picking up something for Coby. But everyone in town knows Reserve Road is a hangout for users. "Where are we going?" I try to keep the panic out of my voice.

Coby wakes up in his car seat and starts fussing.

"Just give him his sippy cup and don't worry about what I'm doing."

"Whitney, they'll revoke your bond if you get caught dealing. Mama and Daddy had to put a lien on the house to get you out."

Whitney pulls up to a dirty white trailer in Reservoir Hills. An old trampoline frame stands guard next to a Toyota truck up on blocks, its tires long gone. I hear the yapping of small dogs.

"Look." She turns toward me, eyes exhausted. "I need to do this. Sammy needs the money."

My sister is out of the car before I can ask why. She

glances around, then climbs the rickety wooden steps. Her long hair is tied up, and her T-shirt hangs out over old sweatpants.

The door cracks and I see a weathered, dark-haired woman peek her head out. Whitney disappears into the trailer.

The apple juice is perking Coby up and I'm torn between making faces at him and keeping an eye on the door Whitney vanished behind. I look around for the law. They cruise this place regularly. I know because Frog lives over here and he tells stories. And the sheriff is bound to know Whitney and Sammy's car now.

Finally, Whitney reappears, tucking bills into her shirt.

She gets in the car and turns around. "Hey, baby boy."

Coby reaches out his hands to his mama and Whitney leans over and grabs them, kissing his fingers.

How can she do this? How can she think that she can sell pills, get caught, and still keep selling pills, and not have Coby taken away from her?

"I've got to run to the store. Sammy needs a six-pack and Coby needs diapers." Whitney's voice is I've-got-a-bra-full-of-cash bright.

It's out before I stop myself. "That's what Sammy needs the money for? Beer?" I slam my hand against the dash-board. "Are you an idiot? You know Mama and Daddy would help you with diapers. You don't need to make money this way!"

Whitney's hands grip the steering wheel. "Lay off, Amber. There's more to it than that."

"Then *what*? Explain it to me. We weren't raised this way, Whitney."

She doesn't talk, just drives. Her lips are set and her fingers drum on the steering wheel. After she picks up what she needs at the store, she pulls in to Eddie's Pawn. "Are you coming?" she asks.

"I'm coming." I pull Coby out of his seat and carry him with us inside.

A guy I'm guessing must be Eddie slides off the stool behind the counter. The display at the front of the store is an assortment of DVDs, jewelry, power equipment—and musical instruments. I can't believe I've never been in here before. My hands brush over a beautiful black mandolin, inlaid with mother-of-pearl.

"That's a nice one," he says.

I flip over the tag. Nine hundred dollars. I put my hands in my pockets.

Whitney hands him a ticket. "I need to get this out."

He gives her a hard look. "You were about out of time."

"I've got the money," she snaps. "We took out a loan, didn't pawn it to you."

Eddie disappears behind a mirrored wall. I'm guessing he can see us from the other side. As Whitney pulls bills out of her bra, I jostle Coby on my hip and look at all the guitars on the wall. I'll have to tell Sean about this place.

Eddie comes back and I recognize Sammy's Strat.

"That's what the money's for?" I ask.

Whitney nods and I see her, seventeen, beaming from the front of the stage at a younger, guitar-playing Sammy. I feel a pang of guilt. Maybe he is going to try and clean up his act.

Coby starts crying and Whitney takes him. I grab Sammy's guitar and start to follow her, but I turn around.

Eddie's stuffing Whitney's drug money into one of those zip bags from the bank.

"Excuse me?" I say.

"Yeah?"

"Is one of those guitars a Gibson? Les Paul?"

When Sean and I had eaten lunch together that first day, he'd told me what kind of guitar he'd played. Before I knew his mom had sold it.

Eddie looks up and stares at me. When I don't lose eye contact, he grunts and points toward a reddish orange guitar hanging above his head. "Got a Studio. Six hundred fifty dollars. Cash."

"Thanks," I say and walk out to the car.

CHAPTER FOURTEEN

- -

Friday afternoon, C.A. and I leave school together to initiate Operation Convince Mama Vaughn. Devon's on his way home to get ready for the party. It's not really going to be much of a party—just Kush, Sean, me, Devon, Will, Amber-o-zia, and C.A.—but it's more exciting than our usual Friday night.

I follow C.A. out to the parking lot to her battered old Subaru. The first time I saw her car, I was surprised. C.A. carries herself like one of the county's have-a-lots, but even though we'd gone to school together since kindergarten, I didn't know much about her life off campus.

"Don't diss the Sue-Bee," she says, like she can hear my thoughts. "My mother pays for my insurance so I had to have liability-only, which meant a beater car." She throws herself across the hood and hugs the dull gray metal. "My darling Sue-Bee cost me five hundred dollars' worth of baby-sitting money."

"At least you have a car."

She breaks into a grin and flips over, looking at the sky. "I know. Freedom. I love it."

"So what do your parents do?" I ask.

"Mom's a dental hygienist." C.A. flashes her pearly white teeth. "My dad left us when I was nine."

I remember a different C.A., one who would sit next to Mrs. Rafferty at every recess and cry if anyone picked on her, in fourth grade. At least Daddy never left us.

We climb in the car. C.A. follows my directions and pulls in behind Mama's rarely used minivan.

"I *love* your house." Amber looks up at the big maples in the yard. "It's like something out of a book."

"It's just an old farmhouse." I try to see what she does, but all I notice is the paint peeling off the clapboards.

"But it's two stories, and I bet it has an attic, a big one. Are there ghosts?" C.A.'s face is bright with questions.

"Come on." I get out. "I'll take you to the attic and you can see if the spiders tell you anything."

Her face goes pale. "Spiders."

"Spiders live in attics."

"Maybe I'll skip the attic today."

I shake my head. "So you're not afraid of ghosts, but you're afraid of spiders?"

Amber shuts her car door and follows me. "Girlfriend, have you not been reading all those new paranormal romances in the library? There are some *really* hot ghosts."

Mama pulls the door open. I'm glad to see she's put on pants and a blouse for company, instead of wearing her normal housecoat. "Hello, girls, how was school?"

I kiss Mama on the cheek and smell spice cake.

"Great, Mama. This is Amber Douglas, well, C.A."

C.A. holds out her hand and smiles big. "Hi, Mrs. Vaughn."

"Another Amber. And a pretty one, too. You girls put your things down and come on back to the kitchen. I made a cake. You can have a piece now and then you can take it on over to Devon's house."

"Thanks, Mama."

I lead C.A. up the stairs to my room. "Holy princess!" C.A. shouts as she walks in.

"Really?" Again, I try to see my room through her eyes. "You think?"

"Um. Yes. Look at this cool, old antique furniture, and your room is so light and sunny. Hardwood floors." She throws herself on my quilted double bed. "All I've got is a teensy apartment box bedroom with a window to the parking lot." She points to the mountains. "You, you've got infinity."

"Yeah, I guess it's pretty nice." I lean against the wall.

C.A.'s off the bed and heads straight for the thumb-tacked map on the wall opposite me. "What's this?" Her finger bounces from point to point.

"Hometowns of people I've met. Cities where there are supposed to be cool music festivals. Places I want to go."

"Do you have a color coding system or something?"

If I tell her yes—blue for hiker boys, green for music festivals, red for the afternoon with Will—she's sure to ask me to explain it.

"No, it's random." My palms start to sweat as C.A. studies the thumbtacks.

"Where are *your* tacks?" C.A. holds her hand out.

"What?"

"You're missing one."

I hand her the clear plastic box of thumbtacks and watch as she fishes one out. Red.

"Here." C.A. sticks the tack directly on Winston-Salem. "Let's go talk to your mama."

One whole piece of spice cake in, and C.A. and I still haven't convinced Mama of anything.

Mama settles deeper into her kitchen chair and sighs. "I don't understand why in the world you would want to bother with an audition. Amber, sugar, you know I'd be irresponsible if I let you run off to school in some big city. You're only sixteen."

C.A. smiles and says, "Mrs. Vaughn, this is the best cake I've ever eaten in my life. May I please have another slice?"

Mama eases the knife through the moist cake, creamy frosting wrinkling on the blade.

C.A. starts talking fast. "Mrs. Vaughn, an audition is great for self-esteem, and Amber, you know with her joining chorus and all, may just earn a solo. And then she'll have to sing in front of all of Sevenmile, because you know how everyone comes out for those things. If she can get through the pressure of a closed-door audition in front of people who really know their stuff, well, she'll be able to sing in front of anyone. Even Sevenmile's finest."

Mama looks at her hands. "You say it's in Boone?"

"Yes, ma'am," C.A. garbles through a mouthful of cake, licking her lips and moaning for effect.

Mama's smile is nervous, but it's something else that spills from her eyes as she turns in my direction. "Well, I reckon I can take you, even though I'm not much of a driver." She looks at C.A. again. "You think it will help my Amber shine?"

C.A. chews, smiling with her mouth closed, and nods.

I'm lost in Mama's hopeful expression.

Mama looks at the ceiling. "Oh Lord, help me drive to Boone." Then she looks at me. "I'm only agreeing to the audition, sugar. Nothing more."

"Yes, ma'am. I know."

And I know something else now, too. That my singing, my asking about this audition, lit something up inside my mama. Something I haven't seen on her face since Whitney was married, and Coby was born. Her face, for half a second, was proud. And it was because of me.

I picture that second red tack on my map. Maybe red isn't what I thought it had to be for at all. Maybe red is for love.

C.A. goes crazy digging through Whitney's old clothes and helps me pull together an outfit for the dance.

Soft corduroy miniskirt, purple shirt with a draping neckline, perfectly worn cowboy boots. It's not as sexy as some of the getups C.A. first suggested, but it's more form-fitting than the overalls and T-shirts I normally wear.

C.A. steps back. "You dress up good, girl."

I look in the mirror and turn from side to side. Maybe I should give Whitney's wardrobe another chance.

C.A. has applied pink blush to my cheeks and lipstick

to my puckered lips and black eyeliner to the tops of my eyes. I look like a lazy cat. A lazy, sexy cat.

Whitney's sitting at the kitchen table with Coby when we go downstairs. It looks like she's been crying, but I don't have time to stay to ask why. Her tears are usually about Sammy.

I kiss Coby on the top of his head. "Bye, Mama, we're going."

"Let me look at you." Mama stands up from beside Whitney and holds me an arm's length away from her, a hand on each shoulder. I see a flash of something like *Oh, my baby's growing up* cross her face. "Simply beautiful."

"Thanks, Mama."

"Hey, nice clothes. Glad somebody can fit in them." Whitney's definitely upset about something.

I stiffen and decide not to say anything. I look over at C.A.

"What, you got your rich friend and now you're too good for me?"

I cringe, noticing the glaze over Whitney's eyes. *Please don't let her make a scene.*

"Sorry, C.A. Come on." I start walking toward the front door, torn between bursting into tears and shouting something ugly at my sister.

"You can't run away from me. Why the hell is everyone

running away from me?" Whitney's voice cracks. I hear one last comment before we're out of the house. "You got a condom, Amber? You look like you might need one."

Mama fusses as the door shuts behind us. *Oh my God.* I can't believe Whitney. Why would she do that to me?

C.A. opens her car door and whispers at me over the roof of the Subaru. "Are you going to hook up with Sean?"

"No!" I yank the passenger door open, wishing she hadn't heard Whitney's last barb.

"Sorry."

"It's okay." I take a deep breath, willing my hands to stop shaking.

C.A. has seven Hello Kitty charms hanging off her key ring. They jumble against one another as she starts the car.

"Sorry about Whitney." I hesitate. "I think she was high." Might as well put it out there. It's not like the whole town doesn't know anyway.

"Oh." C.A. looks over at me, her eyes wide and head tilted in empathy.

"That stuff she said, she didn't really mean it. She used to be so fun. You would have liked her." Something hollow settles in my chest when I think about how my memories of the old Whitney are getting as dull as the gray on C.A.'s car.

"Yeah, I remember her from our freshman year. So, she got pregnant, huh?"

"Yeah."

"Well, I won't let that happen."

"Me neither." I start to relax.

"So . . . are you going to hook up with Sean?" C.A. asks again as the car hits the pothole and we both rocket forward in our seats.

"Watch out," I say, too late, then, "I don't think so."

"Why not?" C.A. asks me.

I could share my secret, tell someone else about what happened with Will.

But instead I say, "He's just a friend, that's all. Are you dating anybody?" I check my lipstick in the mirror.

"There are a few senior guys I wouldn't say no to." She rattles off their names and I see their faces in my mind. Out of curiosity I ask her about Will.

"Will McKinney? No. I'm not into the whole cooler-than-thou thing. And, he's taken."

I'm torn between relief that C.A.'s not into him, the instinct to defend him, and the hard reality of Amber-o-zia.

"What about Kush?" I ask. I need to get my mind off Will, and back to Devon's favor.

"*Please*. That guy is so insecure and out of his element. I mean, yeah, he's gorgeous, but I think he may be like Devon."

I freeze. "What do you mean, like Devon?"

"Devon's totally gay." C.A. smiles as we turn into the McKinneys' driveway.

She pushes my shoulder when we stop. "What? Did you think I didn't know? Oh, don't worry about it. I don't care. Come on, let's go inside."

"Wait." I grab her arm.

"Yeah?"

"Devon asked me to ask you for a favor."

C.A. cocks her head and her long ponytail flips over her shoulder. "*Now* I'm curious."

"Devon wants you to kiss Kush to see if he's straight." Knowing C.A. is wise to Devon makes explaining easy.

C.A.'s mouth slowly falls open. "He wants me to *what*?"

"I know, I told him it was stupid, and you wouldn't do it."

She flips down the rearview mirror and reapplies her lipstick. "It *is* stupid. But I'll try, I guess." She caps the lipstick. "But it's only for Devon. Not because I'm into Kush. And only if it works out."

"Fair enough," I say.

CHAPTER FIFTEEN

Will opens the door. "Look who's here. Gorgeous junior girls!" He gives me a careful once-over and holds out his hand as if he wants to shake mine. "I don't believe I know *you*."

"Stop it, Will McKinney." C.A. pushes him aside.

But he's still checking me out, from my boots to my lined eyes. "I like ogling the Ambers," he says, smiling.

C.A. rolls her eyes and pushes past him. I follow her, so I'm on her heels and Will's on mine. I can feel the tension, an invisible cord tugging my body, Will on the other end. Even though I don't want to like it, even though I shouldn't like it, I do.

The hall opens into the large family room at the back

of the house. Kush and Devon are dancing in front of the big-screen TV, their hands above their heads doing some kind of cobra dance. Women in saris and men in turbans twirl in perfect Indian show-tune synchronicity to loud Bollywood music as the boys try to match their steps.

C.A. whispers to me, "Um? I'm supposed to kiss that? Like *that's* going to work."

She has got a point.

Kush and Devon turn around at the same time. Kush immediately drops his hands, but Devon cobras over and dances around me in a circle. "Hey, Amber. Bollywood, baby! You look *hot*."

Kush is looking everywhere but at me or C.A.

"You think?" I cobra my hands and bob my head back at Devon, handing him the pint jar of brandy I snuck out of the barn.

He drops his hands and grabs my waist, jumping me around in a circle, before taking the jar. "Kush brought over all of his mom's old Bollywood movies. They are freaking amazing!"

C.A. interrupts us by placing her hands on our shoulders. "I'll see y'all after the game, 'kay?"

"Wait, you're leaving?"

She nods. "I told you, I could only stay for a minute. I meant that literally."

She leaves with a wave. I glance into the kitchen, but don't see Sean.

"Where's Sean?" I ask Kush.

"Helping my dad. He'll be at the dance later."

Will throws himself across the couch. "Amber-o-zia ditched me for *shopping*." He makes tear fists against his eyes.

"And Kush and I aren't going to the game," Devon announces.

I look from Will to Devon to Kush and back to Devon. "What? I thought this would be our Friday night."

"Amber. You know I hate football. I only like *fútbol*." His accent would be cute if he weren't trying to sound all sophisticated for Kush.

Kush adds, "Yeah, I'm not that into it either."

"Are y'all at least coming to the dance later?" I hear the whine in my voice.

"Sean and C.A. will be there. You won't need us." Devon's face is sending me a million signals that all say the same thing. *Just go and leave me and this cute boy alone.*

Fine, then. It's not like we've spent almost *every* Friday night together since the beginning of high school. "Whatever."

Devon pouts.

"I said fine. It's okay." I pat the pout off his cheeks.

Then, when I think it can't get any worse, Devon turns to his brother and asks,

"Will, you can give Amber a ride, can't you?"

"So . . ." Will's voice draws out the *o* as he turns his key in the ignition, the sports car roaring to life.

"So?" I smooth my hands down the sides of my skirt, which is shorter than I remember it being when I got dressed.

He turns on the stereo, and casually loops his arm over the back of my seat.

"Will."

"Yes."

"Stop it."

"Haven't started. Besides, I need to back down the driveway." He pulls his hand away and shifts the car into reverse. "Seriously, though." He glances at me, returning his arm to the back of my seat, his eyes wicked with mischief. "Don't you want to kiss me?"

"Will!"

I may act outraged, but he's right. I decide to not say anything else.

Will's voice breaks into my thoughts. "Going to be a wet night." Fat raindrops hit the windshield, picking up time with the speed of the car. It's already getting dark.

"You think they'll still play?"

"Oh, they'll play."

Great. I don't have a raincoat or an umbrella.

Will whistles a birdsong, then sighs. "I hate football games in the rain."

"Me, too. Actually, I pretty much hate them no matter what." Against my better judgment, I ask, "Do you think people will be hanging out somewhere else?"

Will's face splits into a wide smile. "I thought you'd *never* ask." He pulls over in the Self Suds car wash parking lot and turns to look at me. "Listen, don't say no until you hear me out."

My stomach jumps.

I watch a man pull into the wash bay. The end of his cigarette glows red through the windshield as he fumbles around, I guess looking for change.

Will clears his throat. "Let's go over the state line to Erwin and see some friends of mine for a couple of hours."

The burning end of the cigarette leaves red in my vision as I turn my head sharply toward Will's face. "Erwin? Tennessee? Tonight?"

When I said let's go somewhere else, I was thinking Dash-n-Burger, somewhere other MHHS kids would be. People that would keep me from kissing Will or Will from kissing me. There are so many things wrong with this alternative. Mama, most of all. If she knew I was thinking of crossing the state line to go to some party, she'd have my hide. Rather, she'd have the audition I just got hold of.

"Will, I can't."

He pouts his full lips. "Oh, come on, please. Erwin. Forty minutes up. An hour there. Forty minutes back. We'll be right in time for the dance. Nobody will know. And you'll be doing me a favor, because I want you to come with me. Sean and C.A. won't care if we miss the game."

Something dangerous streaks through my gut. Going to Erwin right now is bound to be an Even Worse Idea than just catching a ride with Will.

The rain drums on the car roof. Football games are never canceled. But seriously, who wants to sit out in this?

I watch the guy get out of his car and put quarters into the wash controller.

"We'll be back for the dance?" I ask, my eyes unmoving.

"Cross my heart," Will says.

The hose surges to life and jumps out of the guy's hand, dancing across the concrete. He races after it, doing a funny little hop and jump till he gets it in his hands. He turns toward our idling car, laughing, and then gives us the thumbs-up, like everything's under control.

I blow out a deep breath. "Well, I guess we better get going."

Will grins wide and turns the car onto the dark highway.

CHAPTER SIXTEEN

Will drives over the mountain. At the top, we pass the old WELCOME TO TENNESSEE sign. I'm humming along to the southern rock he has playing on the radio and wondering what it would be like to have a car and the freedom to go wherever you wanted. I close my eyes and imagine it's me driving, not stopping, and going far away from Mama and Daddy, from Whitney and Sammy and the whole congregation of Evermore Fundamental.

Will is probably headed to Chapel Hill next fall. He'll find friends from all over, maybe pledge a fraternity, and probably end up in law school and be a lawyer or a judge like his dad. I open my eyes when I feel his hand on the gearshift hovering near my leg. "So, Not So Plain and Small, have you thought about me at all?"

I push his hand away, but the warmth lingers. "Not at all."

"Not once?" He sounds incredulous.

"Not once." I cross my arms over my lap.

"I don't believe you."

I scoot toward the door. "Believe what you want, Will McKinney."

He grabs the gearshift. "Okay, then. I believe that you, Amber Vaughn, are an enlightened woman, far above the petty gossip of Mountain High and small mindedness, and that if you'd allow yourself, we might have fun together."

I let his words settle in. No rumors have gotten back to me. It doesn't seem like Will's talked to anybody. It would be nice to have his help for my audition, actually. Especially since he's in chorus, too.

I glance over. "Okay. Maybe I thought about you once."

He laughs and reaches over me, pulling his pipe out of the glove box. "Friday night lights?"

"Will, that's what you did last time. Got me stoned and . . ."

Will shakes his head and squeezes his eyes shut for just a second. "Fine then, put it away. I shouldn't have it anyway. But if my memory serves me, you seemed to be enjoying yourself quite a bit that day."

I uncross my arms, confused by the hurt in Will's voice. "Where are we going?"

"To see friends."

He pulls onto the interstate and we drive past a few exits before winding into one of the trashed rental neighborhoods occupied by university students. In front of a brick ranch house surrounded by vacant wooded lots, Will parks his car behind an old Ford Explorer plastered with bumper stickers. A few other vans and cars are parked along the street. The sound of electric guitars and guys shouting escapes from the shaded windows.

Will bangs on the front door and I stand behind him. The night is getting chilly. I wrap my arms around myself in a hug.

A bearded guy a little older than us pulls the door open. "Dude." He clobbers Will on the shoulder and gives me the once-over. "Is she cool?"

"Yeah, man." Will introduces me. "Amber, this is Sizz."

"Hi." I raise my hand in a shy wave and peer past Will.

There's a band set up in the den. A bunch of college-aged guys and a couple of girls are gathered in small groups on couches and chairs or standing around a plywood stage. I hang back.

Will steps behind me and puts a hand on each of my

hips, steering me inside. When he loops one hand around my waist, I let it stay, nervous and excited in this room full of people I don't know.

Will leans in. "You want something to drink?"

"Sure." I let him guide me to the kitchen.

He rummages in the fridge and emerges with two beers. If anyone smells alcohol on our breaths at the dance later, we'll be suspended for sure, but one beer won't hurt. I take the cold can from him.

"What is this place?" I ask, looking around.

"My friend Sizz's house."

A tall, thin brunette around Whitney's age slides into the kitchen and gives Will a look I'm not sure what to make of. "You singing tonight, baby boy?" She looks over at me. "Who's your friend?"

"Nicole. Amber. Amber, this is Sizz's girlfriend."

She smiles and instead of a handshake, offers the glowing red joint pinched between her fingers. "You the girl he told us about?"

I wave it off. "No thanks, and no, I don't think so."

Will rests his hand back on my waist. "Yeah, she's the one. I'm hoping I can convince her to sing with me."

"What?" My body goes rigid, and I turn to him. "What are you talking about, Will?"

Will's eyes snap with excitement. "Remember that day

in the car, when I told you any band would kill to have you sing with them?"

I step out of Will's loose hold. "Yeah."

"Well, a couple of the guys from Flat Trucker come over on Fridays, when they're not gigging, to hang out and play with Sizz. I've been trying to figure out a way to get you over here, ever since that . . . well, ever since that day we sang together for the first time. I tried to talk to you about it after chorus, but you keep running off before I can ask you."

Terror teases its way into my legs and arms. The songbird I've thought was so trapped goes still inside her cage, the open door more frightening than the cage itself. I whisper, "Will, I can't. I don't know these people and there are like . . ." I look around. "Twenty of them or something."

Nicole puts her arm around my shoulder, all warm and friendly like Whitney used to be. "Sure you can, honey. You look amazing. Don't you want to feel that rush of being onstage? It's not like an audition or anything, we're just hanging out, having a good time." She takes another hit.

"Come on." Will grabs my hand. "We'll just go watch for a while, then you can decide. No pressure."

In the den, Will sits in the last chair and pulls me toward his lap. I pull away, looking for another chair, but my only other option is an open spot on the couch between two guys wearing camouflage.

Will grins as I give in and perch lightly on his knees, trying hard not to mold into him like I want to. But Will wraps his arms around my waist and pulls me closer, despite my attempt to be proper. In a conspiratorial whisper, he says, "See, isn't this nice? You. Me. A rock-and-roll band." He makes a game-show gesture to the room at large.

This makes me laugh, and I turn around to look at his face. "Yeah, a mother's worst nightmare."

Will's face goes still. And I feel mine go still, because right now, right here, there is nothing more I want to do than put my lips on his.

Then, the band wraps up its jam and Sizz hauls Will out from under me and onto the makeshift stage.

They take a few minutes to tune guitars and adjust microphones. Will rubs his hands on his jeans and gives me a thumbs-up. I curl my legs underneath me and take a sip of the cold beer. Then the guitar and bass player start with the opening chords, and Will steps onto center stage. He puts both hands on the microphone stand and closes his eyes as the guitars come to life behind him. Then, Will steps closer, his mouth barely brushing the silver of the microphone. *"From the bright lights of Memphis . . ."*

His voice, deepened to a low growl, is perfect for the

song they're playing. He hangs onto the stand with his foot, letting it pivot on the floor when he pulls his shoulders to his ears or leans forward on a phrase. Every now and then he reaches out sideways with his hand and grabs some invisible note, or pushes his bangs off his forehead only to have them flop over his eyes again.

Onstage, Will is completely transformed.

I always thought music was a deep hobby for Will, something for Friday nights on the front porch. But looking at him up there, hanging on to the microphone, letting his voice play with the song, I know I was dead wrong. Will McKinney loves this as much as I do.

I glance around the room, feeling braver as the beer goes down. Twenty or so people. How hard would it be to get up in front of them and sing? I could pretend I'm at church like I did at the campfire this summer. I notice two girls whispering and looking at Will, batting their eyes. I glance back at him. He's oblivious, howling into the microphone. When the music stops, one of the girls unfolds her long college legs and slithers up to the stage. I hold my breath. But Will doesn't even see her, and jumps off the stage in front of where I'm sitting.

"What'd ya think?" he asks, settling on the arm of the chair, before tugging on a strand of my short hair.

"I think you may have a music career, Will McKinney,"

I say, poking him in the ribs, even though what I really want to do is pull him into my lap.

Will grimaces and pulls his hand away from my hair, before pushing his own sticky mop off his forehead. "Yeah, right."

"Why not?" I look at him, noticing once again, like I always do, Will's perfect, kissable lips, the scar, the veins running down his tanned, masculine hands, the way his dark lashes tilt up over his eyes just so.

"The judge," Will says quickly.

Judge McKinney? "What do you mean?"

"Don't worry about it. Come on, they're playing one just for you." Will leads me onstage and adjusts the microphone to my height. A few of the boys catcall me, and I start to sweat, but I notice Nicole giving me a wink from behind them. Will whispers, "Don't be scared. Just close your eyes and feel the music."

I grab his arm, panic beating in my chest. "Wait, don't go. What am I singing?"

Will grins. "A song you know, but we're going to play it like you've never heard it. I'll be standing right over there with my banjo."

He leaves me standing there and walks a few feet away to the edge of the small stage. I feel like a geek, my arms slack and nervous by my side, my eyes not knowing where to land, my feet twisting in my boots. I wonder if all these people can see my heart pumping under my suddenly too-tight shirt. Then, the drummer picks up a beat, and a bass joins in. The electric strains of the guitar break into a faster "I'll Fly Away." Somebody's brought Will's banjo in for him, and I hear his unmistakable style.

I know this song. I could sing it in my sleep, we sing it so often in church. My hands move away from my sides and find the microphone. I pull it closer and wait, closing my eyes so the only senses I have are the sound of the music and the smells of smoke and sweat swirling in the air. My feet start to tap in rhythm to the beat. Someone whistles.

When I open my mouth, the bird surprises me. She's not scared one little bit. It's like she knows she's been waiting for this moment her whole life. She opens her wings and heads for the sky, soaring higher and higher with each note, and I forget that I'm in front of people. I forget about Will. I forget about Daddy and Whitney. I am free. Nothing is holding me to the earth but the sound of the song, the music, and my voice pouring out of me.

When the music stops, I'm breathless. Exhilarated. Transformed. I am not Herman and Donna Vaughn's daughter, Whitney Vaughn's sister. I am all Amber. I am somebody and these people like me. I hear the drummer mumble behind me, "Damn, that girl can sing."

I open my eyes, and Will, his eyes bright with something I think looks like pride, is in front of me, holding his arms out.

I jump into them and wrap my hands around his neck, then throw my head back laughing. When I catch my breath we both take half steps back to look at each other. He starts to say something but I stop him with my lips before he can ruin this gift of a moment. I feel him start to pull away, but I want Will, and I want this. It's *my* turn. I press my hands to his hips and walk him backward into the kitchen, the band cranking up into the next song.

"Amber, wait, what . . ."

"Shut up, Will," I say, and let my tongue slip into his mouth when we reach a dark corner of the kitchen.

Will's hands slide from my shoulders down my back, as he leans against the counter, pulling me with him. I don't want the feeling of exhilaration to end, and besides singing, there's only one way I know. I don't say a word as Will's hand slips under my skirt, just relish the feeling of his skin on mine. I press my lips harder, pushing against him, feeling him want me the way the crowd did before, just a minute ago.

It's like this, Will and I slung up against a stranger's kitchen counter, when I hear a horrible, familiar voice.

"Well, look what we have here."

I freeze and then turn toward the voice as Will's hand slides out from underneath my skirt.

Sammy's leaning in the door frame, fingers hooked in his belt loops, grinning all bright-eyed, like he just won the lottery.

"Your mama know you're here?" he asks, lifting one eyebrow.

I step away from Will. From the other room, I hear the band starting up again.

Sammy laughs, a sound sort of like a bark, and sidles up next to us at the counter. "Yeah, that's what I figured." He claps Will on the shoulder. "What's up, judge's boy?"

Will looks at me. "You *know* him?"

Sammy drapes his arm over Will's shoulder. "Of course she *knows* me. I'm her big brother."

I interrupt. "Brother-in-law."

Will knocks Sammy's hand off his shoulder.

Sammy chuckles. "Come on now, man, you're not still mad at me, are you?"

Now it's my turn. I look at Will. "*You* know *Sammy*?"

Sammy grabs a beer out of the fridge. "Of course he knows me. We did a little business and he's still pouting because his name got mixed up with mine, scared his daddy would take away his toys."

The sound of the beer tab opening cracks through the

kitchen. Sammy chugs the beer. He looks at me. "So, little sister, first practice is this Wednesday at five o'clock. Bring that other fella of yours."

I open my mouth to protest. Sammy twitches his forefinger back and forth like an elementary schoolteacher. "Ah-ah-ah. I wouldn't say a word, little darling." He grins wide before hooking the beer can into the garbage bin. He whispers in my ear, loud enough for Will to hear. "That way, I won't say a word to your mama about where you've been."

As he strolls out of the kitchen, whistling, the band breaks into "Runnin' with the Devil."

Just great.

CHAPTER SEVENTEEN

- -

Will is silent as we walk back to his car. The gravel crunching beneath our feet is the only sound. On the short stretch of interstate before we take the exit to the drive back across the mountain, he turns the music up too loud to talk over. He doesn't even sing along, just stares ahead at the road.

Finally I crack. I can't take his cold shoulder, especially since I'm not sure what happened. "Did I do something wrong? Is it because I kissed you?"

He sighs and pushes his fingers through his dark hair. "No, Amber. I mean, yeah, we shouldn't have done that. Technically, I'm dating a different Amber."

Technically? An hour ago, my heart might have done

a backflip for "technically." But now, unlike when Will suggested going to Sizz's in the first place, unlike the way we were together onstage, unlike when we kissed, Will is distant.

"What did Sammy mean about your other 'fella'?" Will looks at me for the first time since he started the car. It's a quick glance, then his eyes are back on the road.

"Well, *technically*, I have *no* 'fellas.' But I believe he was talking about Sean. He gave me a ride home the other night, and Sammy met him."

Will turns onto the access road to our school. "Look, Amber. If you don't mind, I'm going to just drop you off. I'm not so into football game dance nights, and I think I'd rather go home."

My pulse gets faster. Just because Sean gave me a ride home one time, and my sister is married to Sammy, Will wants to go home? There's some stupid irony.

"Sean's only a friend, Will." Does he think all of my rides home end up like the one he gave me on the first day of school?

Will pulls up to the curb, his hands locked on the steering wheel. He slumps forward and lets out a breath. "No, not because of Sean. I mean, who am I to say if you like the guy or not? Remember?" He points to himself. "Girlfriend."

"I don't . . ." I realize my voice is uneven, so I breathe in and repeat myself. "I don't like him."

"It's not about Sean, Amber. It's about me. And my dad."

"Your dad?"

"My dad will crucify me if he finds out I've been hanging out with dealers. Tonight was fun, and you're a great singer. Really great." He pauses and looks at his hands.

I feel my face getting hot. "But I didn't invite Sammy! He showed up at Sizz's on his own. He would've showed up, whether or not you took me."

Will stills his hands. "I know that. But things are complicated."

A couple of girls walk past the car toward the cafeteria doors. They look excited, grabbing on to each other's arms and giggling. I recognize one of them from Amber-o-zia's table at lunch.

I reach for the handle, open the door wide, and step out onto the curb, watching them disappear inside the school. "Yeah, I got it," I say. "Complicated."

He starts to say something else, but I shut the door and walk away.

When I hear him drive off, I turn around and follow the side of the building until I slip into a window alcove. Inside the cafeteria, colored lights refract off a tiny disco ball hanging from the ceiling. Blue, green, hot pink, and white beams bounce around the silhouettes of awkward dancers. I slide down the wall, pulling my knees to my chest.

I press my forehead against them and sit for a while. The music shifts and I stand up to watch the dance through the window. We must have won the game because I can see burgundy bobcat stickers on everybody's cheeks. I spot C.A. laughing, dragging Sean out onto the dance floor. He's dressed in his normal T-shirt and jeans, hair flying everywhere, but there's the shyest smile flickering around his lips.

C.A. bounces on the balls of her toes, egging him on, and when she finally gets him moving, I can tell he's not a half-bad dancer. I watch them. C.A.'s dancing around him, and Sean's keeping up. There's no sense in me going in there. My dance rhythm is nonexistent and my mood would only bring them down. I pull out my cell phone and call Daddy's phone. It goes to voice mail.

I sit for another second, staring off at the black mountains. Some asshole's defied the ridgetop laws and built a house right on top of one. The lights look unnatural shining out from the black.

My phone rings. Daddy.

"Can you come and pick me up?" I ask him.

"Now?" Daddy asks. There's country music playing in

the background and I hear a sudden, sharp sound, like ice hitting glass.

"Yeah. I'm ready to go home."

I hear Daddy whispering. He never whispers to Mama. Then he gets back on the line. "Give me about thirty minutes."

"Okay." I hang up and stare at the lights near the ridge again. It's bound to be a vacation home. I wonder what those people think of us. The wife probably stood in the middle of a tangle of rhododendrons, a wild wind at her back, and held her hands out in a tiny square. "Oh look, honey," she might have said. "We can put a picture window right here." Because that's the thing. The folks that move in, they don't care so much about the actual view. Life looks too real back in the holler.

The rumble of Daddy's diesel, followed by a quick blow on the horn, draws me out of my hiding place.

Daddy grins as I climb into the truck. "Evening, Amber girl."

He's whistling Rosanne Cash's "My Baby Thinks He's a Train" with a big smile.

"What? Did you get a promotion? Win something from a scratch-off ticket?" Daddy's good mood is infectious, but I'm skeptical.

"Nah, just a good day, baby girl, just a good day." He stretches his arm over and gives my shoulder a squeeze.

Gross. Lilac.

"Did you get a new air freshener?"

If he knows I've figured out he smells like perfume, maybe it will knock some sense into him. But Daddy doesn't even blink before answering.

"Might've, I pick those things up so often, I forget what's what. Hey, look down there, I got an old farmer's almanac calendar in the mail today from eBay."

I pull the yellowed, musty calendar out of the padded envelope—1932. There's a picture of the Clinchfield Railroad engine on the upper part. "Cool, Daddy."

"Yep, I thought so. Going to frame it for the train room."

I'm struck with an urge to be Daddy's little girl again. To act like Mama and just blind myself to the obvious. While Whitney was my daddy's princess, I was his train girl, always up for heading to the tracks to lay pennies down or count the cars. I used to love going with him to the depot and listening to the engineers tell ghost stories. But now that I know how he really is, how can I ever be that girl again?

Like with so many other revelations in my adolescent years, Whitney made the Daddy situation crystal clear.

About three years ago, we'd gone to eat at the Fish House, just Daddy and his little girls. The hostess had flushed and looked everywhere but at Whitney or me. Daddy called her sugar and put his hand on her arm, and the lady had gone all red and silly. I remember asking Whitney why the lady acted that way, and she'd said, "That's Daddy's girlfriend." At first I didn't understand. Boys could have friends who were girls. Couldn't grown men?

Whitney had stood up, glaring down at me. "Grow up, Amber," she'd said. "It means they're screwing." I sat for a long time that night, just staring, watching the bats swoop in and out from the barn through the maple leaves, wondering if this meant Daddy didn't love us anymore.

The next morning, later on, when I'm sure she'll be awake, I walk the acre back to Whitney's trailer. Giant barks and jumps behind the chain-link fence Daddy put up for Whitney's ever-rotating foster animals.

"Hey, big man," I say to the tiny dog. It's Sammy's only redeeming quality, his acceptance of Whitney's animal obsession. Left to his own devices, he'd probably be as neglectful as the folks she rescues them from. I slip in through the gate and knock on the door. Nothing. I knock louder.

Sammy pulls it open. "Amber." He hangs on the door frame, bare chested with his Strat strapped across his shoulders.

I want to scratch his eyeballs out, but I can't. And if I renege on his stupid practice, he'll tell Mama I was at a college party in Tennessee. And if she gets wind of it, the speech will go exactly like this: "If I can't trust you at home, how can I trust you in some far-off city?"

I hug my arms closer. "Where's Whitney?"

"In the shower. Come on in. She'll be out in a minute."

"I'll wait outside."

"I said come inside. Wouldn't want my wife thinking I'd left her sister out on the porch, would I?"

I step in, but stand near the door.

Sammy cranks up the amp and starts tweaking his guitar strings. I look around. No matter how Whitney tries to add nice touches to their trailer, Sammy takes over. Electronics magazines, speaker parts, half-filled cans of Mountain Dew, which you have to be careful not to ever pick up because they double as spit cups. Even Coby's colorful toys look dull in here.

"Hey." He breaks for a second. "You ever got any friends that get sports injuries or surgery, whatever, and have leftover pain meds, hook me up. I'll pay for leftover scrips. I'm trying to buy a van for the band."

"Sammy, didn't you just get arrested? What the hell's the matter with you?"

"Ain't no big thing, it'll blow over. Once I start gigging again, legit money will be rolling in. But I've got to get there first." He goes back to playing, and I press against the wall.

Whitney walks out of the back, toweling off her hair, holding Coby on her hip.

"BerBer!" Coby reaches out his hands and I take him.

Whitney glances at Sammy, then at me. "What's up, Amber? Does Mama need something? She could have just called."

"No, you got a minute?"

We leave Sammy to his solo and go out and sit on the stoop. Fall swirls around under the air of fading summer. A soft breeze rustles the leaves on the trees. In the pasture, one of Daddy's cows lows soft and melodious. Coby toddles off to chase Giant.

"So?" Whitney pulls a comb through her long, wet hair. "You pissed off at me for last night?"

"It wouldn't kill you to apologize."

Whitney stops breathing for a second, then blows a big breath out. "I'm sorry. Tell your friend I'm not usually a bitch like that. It's just . . ." She hesitates. "I think Sammy's running around on me."

"Really?" Sammy is six or seven kinds of bad news, but I've never questioned his loyalty to Whit.

She stretches her legs out in front of her. "Maybe. I don't know. It's just this music thing again." She looks down at her body. "I'm not really looking like a hot groupie anymore."

"Sammy wouldn't cheat on you." Then I remember why I walked back here in the first place. "But I think Daddy's got a new girlfriend."

She doesn't even flinch. "I figured. You're a fool to think he'd ever quit. I doubt it's even a new girlfriend."

"I'm not a fool, I just . . ."

"Oh, get over yourself, Amber. Not one of us is perfect. Not even you, anymore."

"What are you talking about?"

"How arrogant you're getting. Running around with that judge's kid. He's just using you, you know."

She can't be talking about Will. Unless Sammy told her.

"What do you mean?"

"He's swishy, isn't he? You two have been hanging out for years and he's yet to make a move."

"Don't say that, Whitney. It's rude. It's like somebody calling you and me poor white trash."

She shrugs. "If it fits."

"Besides, he's not using me. We're actually friends."

But her words let in a ghost of doubt. I know it's not right, but I can't help but think that Devon might've been waiting for someone more interesting to move to town. Someone like Kush.

Coby bounds across the yard, then falls. Giant moves in and licks his ears until Coby's giggles are louder than Sammy's guitar. Whitney and I smile, watching them. After a second, she whistles and Giant moves away.

"Mama's perfect," I say. Even though I know it's not entirely true, she's the closest we've got.

"No, she's not. She hides behind God. Figures if she prays enough all of her problems will go away, but it doesn't work that way." Whitney talks like she's holding back a deep hurt.

"What do you mean?"

"Life. Just. Is. I've got Sammy, Daddy's got Mama, and Mama's got Daddy. And you, you've got a wild dream that's going to do nothing but disappoint you."

Coby crawls into Whitney's lap and snuggles against her. She strokes his back and stares off at the mountains.

"You think I'm stupid for dreaming?" It shouldn't matter what Whitney thinks, but it does. She's still my big sister.

Whitney's quiet for a while. "No." She looks at me.

"I don't want you getting hurt, that's all. Do me a favor, okay?"

"What?"

She inclines her chin toward Coby and throws her head back toward the door and Sammy behind it. "Don't be in the kind of hurry to grow up that I was."

It's the first time I've ever heard Whitney admit that her life might not be turning out exactly as she'd planned.

"You don't regret having Coby, do you?" I grab his chubby fingers and wiggle them.

"Of course not. And I can't wish that I'd waited. What's done is done. But I wish I'd figured out a way to still go to vet tech school."

"It's not too late," I say. "If you'd stop selling . . ." And using.

The door pulls open. Sammy looks down at us. He's pulled his pale blond hair into a bun and his jeans are slung low, exposing that slice of skin and hip bone Whitney once told me was her own personal heaven. "Hey, Whit, I just got a call. You coming?"

Whitney looks at me, her smile resigned. "It is too late." She lays her comb on the stoop and stands up, tugging her T-shirt in place over her faded sweats. "Watch Coby for an hour?"

I take Coby from Whitney, but can't help but turn

around and look at Sammy. "Go yourself. Don't get my sister into this."

"It might be hard for you to realize, Amber." Sammy's eyes dance, mocking me. "But your sister would do anything for me."

Whitney slides her arm around his waist and gives me a weary smile.

I hate him.

But I know he's right.

CHAPTER EIGHTEEN

Mama takes Coby from me while I make turkey sandwiches. Outside, the maples are hinting at the fall show to come. Tiny patches of orange. Red. Yellows so bright you'd swear they were an illusion. I snag a bread-and-butter pickle out of the jar. It's crunchy, sweet, a little sour, with mustard seeds that pop open in your mouth.

The need to hike to the top of the mountain tickles up my legs as we eat. If I can get where I can see out to the horizon, maybe things won't seem so desperate.

"I'm going to take a walk, Mama. Do you mind watching Coby till Whitney comes back?"

"Go on. He can help me sweep."

Coby puts his bread crust down and scuttles over to his

play broom. He's a good helper. "Weep?" I hear him say as I grab my hiking boots out of the hall closet.

I walk across our backyard and open my mouth. "Come All Ye Fair and Tender Ladies," an old ballad, tumbles out, and I hike up to the wood line.

"Come all ye fair and tender ladies,
Take warning how you court your men,
They'll tell to you some loving story,
And they'll make you think they love you well,
And away they'll go and court some other,
And leave you there in grief to dwell."

It feels fitting, after last night, and I kick at some leaves like they're Will.

I keep singing to drown out my thoughts. My eyes go soft and through the haze of green, I imagine the settlers who brought the old songs I love from Scotland and Ireland and England. They weren't afraid to leave their whole lives behind in search of something better. Like me, thinking about that school in Winston-Salem.

Whitney's probably right, though. It's a far-fetched dream. I've poked around on the internet, trying to figure out exactly what the songs *were* on that audition list. All the ballads I know, even our chorus song, "Shenandoah," work for the folk category. I'd found some of the English art songs on YouTube. They tended toward girls singing from way down deep in their toes, a way I don't know how to sing. And the lieder and the arias, the real opera? I should have signed up for chorus two years ago. Even with Mrs. Early's help, I doubt I can pull it off in time.

When I reach the logging road, the air cools. It's only been a couple of weeks since school started, but already the thick humidity of summer is giving way to drier days. I haven't been up here since that last night before school with Devon.

The barn is unchanged. I'm tempted to duck inside to see if I recognize any of the hikers' names left carved in the gray wood, but the trail calls. Up there, on the ridges, the world stills. It's just me and the loamy smell of rich Carolina dirt, the bite of pine, and the chatter of squirrels gathering stores for the coming winter. The woods, they don't judge.

I hike until sweat runs down my temples. At a gray rock outcropping, I stop and sit down. To the east, blue-gray ridges overlap each other into the distance. I tear a rhododendron leaf into pieces, letting the deep green fragments flutter to the ground.

I stand up and wipe the dirt off my pants. Maybe I'll see if Sean is around, and tell him about Sammy's band

and the practice on Wednesday. It won't be so bad if he's there. One of Sammy's friends is bound to have a guitar Sean can play, at least until he figures out how to get his own. With the audition seeming more and more out of my reach, maybe being in Sammy's band won't be the worst thing. At least I'll be onstage again. And maybe C.A.'s right. Maybe hanging out with Sean would be fun. And help me get my mind off Will.

Going down trail is always faster than going up, and I'm at the hiker barn before I know it. I trot around the corner of the trees and see movement. I speed up, hoping it's Sean and I can catch him. I don't notice the gnarled root at the edge of the trail. My foot snags in the crook and I go sprawling in the dirt.

Shards of pain shoot up my ankle. I roll over, pulling my knee to my chest. My ankle is pushing hard against my hiking boot. "Damn," I whisper.

"Hey, now. No need for that." A tall man jogs to where I sit in the logging road. He squats down, and I know from the shape of his face and the clay-spattered clothing that this is none other than Eric Whitson, Kush's father.

"Let's take a look at that." He helps me into a sitting position. "I'm Eric Whitson. This is my land, in case you're wondering who I am."

"I figured." I grimace as he loosens the laces on my boot.

"I'm friends with Sean. And Kush," I add. "I'm Amber."

He applies some pressure to my ankle.

"Ow!"

"Well, Amber, let's pray you haven't broken it." He pokes again. "Or a break might be better, in this case. Are you an athlete?"

I shake my head.

"Good thing rifle season's around the corner to keep you off the trail. Soft tissue injuries can be worse than a break. And that's my unofficial diagnosis. Sprained ankle." He stands. "Stay here. I'll run and get the four-wheeler to drive you back to the house and we can call your folks. You're probably going to want to get X-rays."

He's gone, then back in a flash, helping me onto the wooden box bed he's built on the back of his ATV. My ankle pulses as we bounce away from the barn toward the old Whitson house.

At the house, Mrs. Whitson stands at the back screen door, holding it open. She, like Mama, is squishy. But unlike Mama, she's got herself fixed up on a Saturday morning.

"Oh, poor girl. Here, let me help you. I'm Aneeta." She comes to my other side and they help me limp into the house.

I don't know what I was expecting, but it isn't this. The

house is just a regular house. Sofas, chairs, a maple kitchen table. But there are no framed prints of *The Last Supper* or pictures of cats with yarn for the Whitsons. They have real art and loads of it. Shelves separating the kitchen from the living room are filled with gorgeous pottery.

"Are those your pieces?" I ask Mr. Whitson.

"Some, others are friends' work."

Mrs. Whitson, Aneeta, pushes pillows under my ankle, then hands me an ice pack.

"Are you interested in clay?" Mr. Whitson asks as he holds out the phone.

Before I can answer him, Sean appears in the doorway. "Hey, Amber. What are you doing here?"

I point to my propped-up ankle. "Hiking injury. Your uncle saved me."

He walks over and sits down next to me on the couch, and nudges me with his elbow. I smile at him, and his permanent bed-head hair. Then Kush shows up from somewhere in the back. He looks like he just crawled out of bed, too. His hair's tousled and he's showing off a Devon-worthy display of abs.

Mrs. Whitson follows my stare. "Kushad. We have company. Go get dressed."

Then Kush sees me, and glances at Sean. "What? Y'all got a thing now?"

At the same time we blurt out, "No."

Kush looks at his mother and raises his eyebrows. She shoos him toward the back with her hands.

I remember the phone in my hand and dial home.

Mama picks up on the first ring. "Amber, is that you?"

"Hi, Mama. I'm down at the Whitson place. Can you come and pick me up?"

"Amber, you know what I've told you about going out into the woods without your phone. What were you thinking?"

"I know. I forgot. But I need you to come and get me."

"Are you in that family's house?"

"Yes, ma'am. I tripped and hurt my ankle."

"We don't know those people, Amber."

"Mama." I try to make my tone even, but it comes out irritated. "I go to school with their kids. Just come pick me up."

Mr. Whitson interrupts. "If there's a problem, I can give you a ride."

I shake my head. "She's coming," I say.

"What?" Mama says.

"I said you're coming."

I hear her sigh and the sound of the kitchen chair legs creaking as she clicks the receiver.

Kush reappears in an old T-shirt and jeans.

He pours two glasses of orange juice and brings one to me. He doesn't bring anything to Sean. "How was the dance?" he asks me.

I can tell he's only making small talk to be polite in front of his parents. "Pretty fun," I say with fake enthusiasm.

Sean shifts on the couch and stares at me. But I don't miss a beat and keep my face straight to cover the lie. "How was the Bollywood marathon?"

"All right I guess. Not like a Friday night in Atlanta, that's for sure."

If I hadn't seen Kush with his shirt off, I'd be struggling to understand Devon's fascination. The boy likes nothing about our town.

"So, Amber." Mrs. Whitson returns from the kitchen and puts a plate of fried bread on the coffee table in front of me. "What grade are you in?"

"I'm a junior." I take a bite of the flaky pastry and a whole chorus of spices hits my tongue. "This is amazing," I say before I finish chewing.

"Those are parathas, from Northern India." Her eyes flit from Sean to me and back like she's trying to figure out if we have something going on. Kush looks bored.

The doorbell rings.

"Oh, that must be your mother. Eric, go and invite her in."

Mr. Whitson disappears into the foyer, and then reappears with Mama. She's dressed in a pair of polyester pull-ons and a sweatshirt from Dollywood. She still has on her bedroom slippers.

"Oh, I . . ." Mama glances around at the light-filled room. "I'm sorry, my slippers."

Mrs. Whitson's laugh is musical. She grabs Mama's hands in greeting. "Oh, don't worry about that, we're just so happy to meet a neighbor."

"Amber had quite a spill." Mr. Whitson nods in my general direction. "Glad I was out in the rear of the property when it happened."

Mama's grown more comfortable now. "I swear, child." She shakes her head at me and looks at Mrs. Whitson. "Can you believe her, running off without her cell phone?"

"Yes, parenting teenagers is a constant struggle."

Sean, Kush, and I all do a simultaneous ceiling roll with our eyes. For once, we seem to be in agreement on something.

Mrs. Whitson says, "I would love for you to stay and have some parathas with us, but we're concerned Amber may need X-rays. Will you come another time?" She looks hopeful.

I hope Mama says yes. It would be nice for her to have a friend other than the church hens.

"Oh, well, yes. That'd be nice. Thank you." Mama smiles a little and presses her hands together.

Now the trick will be getting Mama to follow through.

When Sean gets up to help me to the car, he asks, "Why'd you say that?" His voice is low, so Mama won't hear. "About the dance."

I take a gulp of air. The sting of Will's blow-off burns fresh. "Long story. But thanks for covering for me. I didn't feel like getting into it with Kush." I also don't want Kush reporting back to Devon about me hightailing over the mountain with Will. "Hey." I slow when we reach the front steps. "Are you interested in going with me to this thing Wednesday? My brother-in-law is having a practice for his new band. He asked if you'd come."

Sean's voice rises. "Oh yeah?"

"Yeah." I pause and give weight to my words, testing them out. "And I'd *really* like it if you came, too."

Sean swallows nervously. "Uh, okay. Cool."

It gets awkward for a second before I blurt out, "But you'll have to drive us."

Sean lifts me down the stairs, then helps me hop toward the van. He won't meet my eyes. "No problem. Does your brother-in-law know I don't have a guitar?"

"Don't worry about it." I'm about to tell him I found a guitar like his old one at the pawn shop, but Mama starts the van behind us, her signal for *let's go*.

I backpedal a little. "I, you know. I'd really like you to come, so you can play again." I sneak a glance at Sean.

Sean opens the van door and helps me into the seat. "I'll see you at school."

I pull the door shut. Through the window, I see a tentative smile spread across his face before we pull away.

Mama drives silent and slow, like an eighty-year-old man on his way to church. She says the radio distracts her. A light drizzle starts to fall.

"Let me go change clothes then I'll take you to the hospital. Your daddy got called in for overtime." Mama's hands clutch the steering wheel and she peers over it. My height, or lack of it, came from her side.

"It's fine, Mama. We can't afford the deductible." I'm pretty sure there'll be no check that comes from Daddy's overtime.

"Amber Delaine. Our money concerns have nothing to do with keeping you healthy."

"Mama, I'm serious. It's only a sprain. Ice, rest, aspirin, and I'll be good as new."

She slows the minivan and turns in the driveway. The rain comes harder. Mama hates to drive in the rain. "Well, are you sure? It won't take anything for me to run in there and change clothes."

"No, Mama, I'll be fine. I might need those old crutches for a few days, though."

Mama goes into the house and Whitney comes out bringing me the crutches from when she broke her leg in middle school. Her eyes are red again. "What'd you do?" she asks.

"Fell. What's wrong with you?" I have to work to keep the irritation out of my voice. It's Saturday afternoon and she looks stoned.

"Department of Social Services called. Ever since we got arrested, they're spewing some crap about how I'm not fit to parent Coby." She helps me out of the van.

I hold on to my two cents about the social worker maybe having a point. "What do you think Social Services is going to do?"

"Nothing now. But they opened a case file on Sammy and me and assigned us a caseworker."

She crosses her arms and looks up through the dapple of leaves.

I reach out and touch her elbow. "Whit, I'm sorry."

She drops her face in her hands. I angle over on my crutches and lean against her back, hugging her awkwardly.

"I'm worried, Amber." Her shoulders shake and I hug her harder.

"You can get help, you know," I whisper.

She shrugs her shoulder and steps out of my embrace, wiping her cheeks. "I don't need help. I'm worried about Sammy."

I guess it's time to tell her. "That's why I'm going to sing with his band."

"You're what?" Whitney whips her head up and stares at me.

"Yeah. He asked me to sing backup. Actually, he blackmailed me to sing backup."

"What are you talking about?"

A truck drives by and bounces in the pothole. The back end rattles like it's going to fall off. I balance on the crutches and take a deep breath. "You can't tell Mama."

Whitney's eyes stay focused on my face. "Spill, Amber."

"I went to a party over in Tennessee when I was supposed to be at the football game. Sammy showed up and saw me making out with this guy. He swore he wouldn't tell Mama if I helped with his new band."

"Why didn't you tell me before?" Whitney's face gets all mottled like Mama's does when she's mad.

"Chill out, Whit. I didn't say anything because I wasn't sure I was going to do it. But I thought about it and it seems okay. If nothing else I can keep an eye on him for you. Besides, my friend Sean's going to play, too."

Whitney's breathing through her nose like a rhino.

"Are you okay?" I ask.

She gets up in my face. "Who was he with at that party?"

"Nobody, Whitney. He was probably dealing or something."

She drums her fingers against her arms. "I'm not sure about this, Amber. You don't need to be hanging out with him."

"I thought you'd be happy."

"I don't need you being my watchdog." She mumbles and I swear it sounds like she says, "Or Sammy watching you," but that's crazy talk. She paces back and forth.

I've got to convince her. "Whit, listen. It's a three-way win. Sammy won't tell Mama. I get to build my confidence onstage, help my friend out, and you know Sammy won't do anything stupid with me around."

Whitney stops. "That's the part I'm worried about."

"You think I can't handle myself?"

She pushes her palms against her temples. "Promise me."

"Promise you what?"

"You won't go along with any of his or his friends'

harebrained ideas. That you won't let him get you in trouble, too."

I plant the crutches firmly beneath me. "Whitney," I say. "I'm not you."

As soon as the words are out, I know I've tipped the scale too far.

Whitney drops her hands and snaps her head up. "Screw you, Amber."

She turns and I watch my sister storm across the yard to her trailer.

CHAPTER NINETEEN

Monday morning, my ankle is the entire range of purple and blues and swollen like an eggplant. I'm beginning to suspect it might be more than a sprain, but I don't want to cause a fuss for Mama and Daddy.

I swallow three aspirin and wrap it in an old Ace bandage.

Daddy drops me at school. "Bye, caboose, have a good day." He squeezes my shoulder. "Love you."

I don't respond. Besides, Coby's the caboose now anyway. I swing out to the sidewalk on my crutches. I glance at him before walking in. He's smiling at me from the cab and waves before driving away. He's my daddy. Right or wrong. Good or bad. I'm stuck loving him. Just like Mama.

The bell rings as I walk through the door. I rush to the art room, trying not to mow anybody over with my crutches as I go.

C.A. pats my chair and whispers, "Those crutches are the only reason I'm still speaking to you."

"I told you I was sorry." It was easier to let her, Kush, and Devon think I bailed from the dance, rather than explain what Will and I were up to that night. She'd pouted on the phone but I guess she was over it now.

Ms. Thomas passes out worksheets on facial features and takes us through a diagram of where to place the eyes, the nose, and the mouth within the oval of the face.

"How's your ankle?" Kush asks me, once Ms. Thomas sets us on task to draw our table partners. "My parents are all worried about you."

Devon reaches across the table for a kneaded eraser from the supply box. He has to lean across Kush to get it. Kush leans backward, away from Devon's arm.

"It's okay. Still really swollen, but it's only been a day and a half." I pull a bottle of ibuprofen out of my pocket and shake it. "Mama hooked me up, though."

We settle into positions. Me holding still while Kush draws. Devon holding still for C.A. It's silent for a few minutes while they sketch.

Kush stares at my nose, his pencil scratching across the

paper. "Well, my dad said to remind you and your mom to stop by one day. He was serious about it. So was my mom." He pauses, then looks at C.A. "You should come, too." He bends down to his paper again, his hair swinging forward, covering his face.

Devon inhales sharply and raises an eyebrow at me. I know what he's thinking. Kush said nothing about Devon coming over.

"Stop by for what?" C.A. asks.

I answer, hoping to calm the churn I know is rising inside Devon. "Kush's dad helped me on Saturday when I fell on his property. He offered to let me come do pottery if I wanted. And I think Kush's mom got really excited about meeting Mama. She might be a little lonely, being new in town."

"Aw, that's so great for your mom. She's awesome." C.A. holds her pencil out toward Devon's face, measuring the space between his eyes.

Devon holds his head still so C.A. can sketch. He pokes my thigh. "Tell them about the band thing."

"What band thing?" C.A. asks.

"My brother-in-law asked if Sean and I would come to his first practice. He wants me to sing backup and Sean to play guitar."

"Oh really?" C.A. tightens her ponytail and clears her

throat, then starts erasing all the smudges off her page. Even ones I can't see.

I try to make light of it. "Yeah, it's no big deal."

Kush's pencil pushes harder against the paper. "Sean's going to be in a band? With you?" He lifts his eyes from under his curtain of glossy hair, studying me.

"Seriously, y'all, it's no big deal." I glance across the table and try to get a glimpse of Kush's drawing of my face. "We'll probably just be practicing in somebody's garage and I doubt we'll actually ever play anywhere."

C.A.'s pencil starts moving again. "I think it's great. You and Sean will have a great time together. You have so much in common."

Kush erases, then uses his finger to smudge. He looks at me, then looks down again at the paper. "Interesting," he says.

"What?" I ask.

He holds his drawing of me up for all of us. Big eyes. Long eyelashes. He's even added shoulders, a neckline, and my chest. Kush drew me beautiful.

Devon leans over to look. His Adam's apple bobs twice as he studies the sketch.

C.A. grabs it. "Wow, Kush! This is great." She holds it up next to me. "This could be your album cover." Then she pauses. "But wait a minute. What about your audition?

You're still trying out, aren't you?"

I shrug. All of their attention, especially Kush's, is making me uncomfortable. "Yeah, I guess so."

"You guess so?" she says. "There's no guessing. You're doing it."

"Yeah." Kush leans back in his chair and stretches his legs out long, bumping my good leg. "Don't you want to get the hell out of here?"

I move my leg away. "Well, yeah."

Devon huffs. "She doesn't think she's good enough."

Kush raises his hands back behind his head and locks his eyes on mine. "I have a hunch she's really good." Then he whispers loud as he hands me his finished sketch, "I don't know why Devon calls you Plain and Small."

Devon's mouth falls open.

I look away.

Finally, the end-of-day bell rings and it's time for chorus. Mrs. Early smiles as I hobble into the room. "How's your ankle, dear? We missed you at church yesterday."

"Thanks. It still hurts some but I'm okay." My eyes dart toward Will's chair but it's vacant.

"I have something for you." Mrs. Early rummages through a basket of CDs on the shelf next to her piano. "Ah. Here it is."

She hands me a CD with my name written on it in Sharpie.

"What's this?" The CD is plain silver in a clear case, with no clue to what it holds.

"You were asking me about arias. And through a bit of deductive reasoning, *and* because your mother mentioned it yesterday, I'm guessing you're going to need some help with your NC-Arts audition."

"She told you about it?" I ask.

Mrs. Early steps aside as two other students brush past. "She did, honey. And she was lit up as bright as a Christmas tree talking about you." She smiles. "I made you a CD of some songs that I think might fit their requirements and your voice. Take a listen and see if anything suits you."

Another group of kids comes in and I see Will, walking in with his head down and his banjo case in his hand. I follow him with my eyes as he walks to his seat.

I may be singing backup for Sammy, but who says I can't learn some opera at the same time? I may be small-town, but I'm not stupid. I look back at Mrs. Early. "Do you think I have enough time?"

"We'll do our best, dear. But it's going to take dedication and hard work. Can you meet me in the mornings for extra sessions?"

I nod.

"Good." She smiles and points me to my seat.

Mrs. Early sits at the piano and without introducing anything, plays the opening notes for "Shenandoah." We're working on an arrangement where the whole chorus hums the opening bars, then the boys come in, followed by the girls. I watch Mrs. Early as she directs us, but I'm hyperaware of Will. He stands tall and serious. When he opens his mouth, I hear his rich bass circle the room. I know other people are singing, but it's his voice that fills my ears. I'm so intent on listening to him that I almost miss my own cue.

When we finish the third run-through of the song, Mrs. Early claps. "Beautiful. Now let's have some fun. I'm going to let you show off a bit."

The room rustles to life and the other chorus students whisper to each other. Obviously, the members who've been with Mrs. Early for a while know what's happening, but I don't have a clue. I glance over at Will. He's looking right at me, dark eyes unreadable. He raises his palms skyward with a shrug of his shoulders, like he's clueless, too.

Is acknowledging my existence again an apology?

Mrs. Early walks toward a girl in the front row. "Okay, Becca, pull out three names."

The girl, a senior I vaguely know, pulls out three slips of paper from a glass bowl. She reads them off one by one. "Destiny Miller, Brandon Davenport, Amber Vaughn."

"Delightful." Mrs. Early smiles. "Now remember, pick a song that best represents you."

I lean over to the girl sitting next to me. "What are we doing?"

"Show-off Solos," the girl replies. "You got picked, right?"

I nod.

"Choose a song you sing really well and show off."

I feel a knot swell in my gut. "You're kidding."

"Nope." The girl smiles wide. "But you'll do great."

Because my name got drawn last, I go last. The first girl, Destiny, sings a new country song I keep hearing on the radio. When she gets to the beer-drinking and hell-raising part, she pumps her fist in the air and the chorus room erupts in laughter. Even Mrs. Early allows it to slip with only a disapproving twist to her lips. Brandon, a quiet boy who's been in school with me since kindergarten, sings a sweeping love song I've never heard a man sing before. I notice a few of the girls wiping their eyes at the end.

When he sits down, I panic.

"Amber, you want to sing where you are?" Mrs. Early points toward my ankle.

I glance at Will and stand. "It's okay," I say. "I'll come down."

"What are you going to sing?" Mrs. Early asks.

"'The Cuckoo'?" I ask tentatively.

She nods.

I look at the case by Will's feet. "Can Will McKinney play his banjo while I sing?"

"Will?" Mrs. Early asks.

But Will's hand is already reaching for the latches on his case. That simple movement washes a wave of memory over me. Birds calling. The wind swirling. The smell of fading summer, and the feeling of his lips on mine. I clear my throat and give my head a shake.

I nod and Will starts picking the notes on his banjo. The sweet plink of notes surrounds me and I draw my voice, pure as mountain air, up and out into the room. *"Gonna build me a log cabin, on a mountain so high."* I tell the story of "The Cuckoo," letting my voice linger on the high notes. Will fills in the spaces with his own music. Our eyes never meet, but our music is seamless, like water flowing and filling a negative space.

On the final lines, *"There's one thing that's been a puzzle, since the day that time began. A man's love for, for his woman, and her sweet love for her man,"* I find myself doing exactly that. Puzzling.

Devon is waiting for me outside the chorus room. He takes my book bag and hoists it onto his shoulder. "Was that you singing?"

"Yeah. And your brother playing with me."

"Sounded really good." Devon's voice is distant, and he's not making eye contact.

Will pushes through the door. He hesitates when he sees us. "What's up, bro?" he says, slapping Devon on the back.

"The lovely Plain and Small is helping me spend Aunt Sue's birthday gift today."

Will glances in my direction. "Cool. See you later. Tell Mom I'll be home for supper."

We watch him walk out the glass doors at the front of the school and after a minute, we start to walk that way, too.

Will might be able to avoid me, but I can't avoid Devon.

"Devon. About art class . . ."

He cuts me off. "That was a *gorgeous* drawing, wasn't it?"

"Devon."

He sighs. "Just drop it, okay? I get it." He's already pulled his Jeep up to the doors for me and helps me climb in.

"What do you get?" I ask.

Devon starts the car and pulls out of the parking lot. "Kush isn't hiding anything. I was wrong about him."

"Maybe you can change him?" I stick my good foot on the dashboard.

"Please. The last thing I want is a straight boy for a boyfriend." We stop talking in reverence of a mini-Aretha marathon that comes on the radio. When they cut to commercial, and we catch our breath from singing, Devon looks over at me. "But you could have him, Plain and Small."

Devon pulls into his driveway as I start snort laughing.

CHAPTER TWENTY

Wednesday rolls around quick. Sean finds me at lunch and we firm up our plans to meet and play after school. Practice is being held in some guy's old tobacco barn way out on Honeysuckle Road. Sammy said we didn't have to be there till five, so I figure I've got time to take Sean by the pawn shop.

We pull into Eddie's and Sean lets the truck idle. "I don't know, Amber. There's no point in me even going in there."

"Don't you want to see it? I swear it's the kind of guitar you were talking about. Maybe they have a layaway plan."

That gets him to turn the truck off.

"Come on," I say and limp out the door before he can

say no. I'd tried to ditch my crutches in the morning, but my stupid ankle still hurts if I put pressure on it.

The door chimes as we push in and Eddie looks briefly away from the TV in the corner of the shop. "Can I help you?"

I point to the reddish Gibson. "Can my friend see that guitar?"

Sean is staring at the guitar, behind me.

Eddie must sense a certain amount of reverence because he holds the guitar out like it's a piece of glass. "Here you go." He points to a corner of the room. "There's an amp over there you can plug in to, if you want."

Sean is stroking the guitar with a musician's touch. He flips it to his body and holds it, cradling it. "I can play it?" he asks. His voice sounds young. Eager.

Eddie actually smiles. "Yeah, man. Give her a go."

While Sean plugs in the guitar, I ask Eddie about how a layaway plan works.

"Yeah, thirty percent down to hold it. Then two more payments."

Sean starts playing, and Eddie and I watch him for a minute. Eddie nods his head and hits the mute button on his TV remote. "The kid's good. Tell you two what. He can have the cash price of six fifty for layaway. I usually ask list. And instead of one ninety-five, I'll let you do a hundred and fifty down with four more payments instead of two. That guitar deserves him."

I've got fifty dollars in my savings account. If I tell C.A., I bet she'd give me some money, too. I could ask Kush, too, or his parents. We can surprise him with the layaway ticket, then figure out how to come up with the rest later. Mrs. Early is always talking about paying it forward, and Sean is the perfect candidate. He's got a real gift. Why not find a way to let him share it with the rest of us?

"Will you hold it until tomorrow? I can bring you fifty dollars then and we'll get the other hundred to you by next week."

Eddie frowns, but his eyes follow Sean's fingers flying across the strings. "Okay." He pulls out a ticket. "Write his information on here and I'll hold her for your fifty until four tomorrow."

I pick up the pen and start filling it out.

"But," he adds. "If I don't have that other hundred by same time next week, you're going to lose your fifty dollars, and the guitar."

The tobacco barn is way the hell out, at the end of a mile-long rutted gravel drive. Sammy and two other guys are smoking cigarettes at a half-rotted picnic table.

I get out of the truck. "Is there even electricity out here?"

"Yeah, baby sister, we've got the orange cord." Sammy points to an extension cord running to a run-down cabin hidden by the barn. "Hey, man." He nods at Sean. "What's up?"

"Hey," Sean says, stepping next to me.

Sammy hops off the bench. "Come on, then. We're burning daylight."

Inside the barn, locust logs crisscross above our heads. A few dusty, ancient tobacco leaves hang like bats from them, a testament to days gone by. The late afternoon sun sends shafts of light between the slats. In the corner, Sammy and his friends have set up a small stage, of sorts. A blue tarp covers the ground and on it is a drum kit, some mikes, a couple of amps, and assorted rickety chairs.

"Careful." I grab Sean's arm as he starts to lean back against the wall.

He looks behind him.

"Poison ivy," I say. Fuzzy brownish red vines crawl up the walls. The leaves are high, but the vine is more toxic.

"Thanks." Sean is looking smaller by the minute. It's like he's folding into himself and if he keeps going, we'll hear a pop as he disappears.

I loop my hand around Sean's arm. "You're going to be fine."

"What's the matter, man?" Sammy's plugging in his guitar and directing the other two guys.

"Um, I, um . . ."

"Spit it out, man."

"He doesn't have a guitar, Sammy." I squeeze Sean's arm.

Sammy stops for a second, thinking. "We got that acoustic you can play for now. But here." Sammy takes the Strat off and hands it to Sean. "You play this for the first song and I'll play the acoustic."

Sean takes the guitar and it's like watching one of those Mylar balloons inflate at the grocery store. He grows bigger with an instrument in his hands.

"First song is that song Amber sang for you in the truck the other night. But Amber, this time you only come in on the chorus."

"Whatever, Sammy."

"All right. Let's get this thing down."

Sammy starts with the acoustic guitar. After the first stanza, the drummer starts tapping his cymbal, slightly out of rhythm. I glance at Sean. He puts a finger to his lips, then motions toward Sammy, whose eyes are closed, head thrown back. When Sammy gets to the chorus, I try to ignore that the drummer's off beat and step into the microphone next to him.

Sammy holds up a hand. "Wait. Stop."

Finally, he's going to say something to the drummer.

But instead he turns to me.

"Baby sister, this is not your microphone."

"What?" I step away from him.

Sammy points to the rear of the tarp, next to the drum kit. "Your microphone is back there." I follow his finger and see that off to the side, in the corner, is a dinky microphone with a bent stand. I feel my face turning red.

Sammy grabs my shoulders. "Ah, sugar, don't get your panties in a twist. You're backup, remember?" He doesn't give me time to answer, just pushes in me in the direction of my time-out corner. He starts the song again.

This time, I come in on the chorus and blast my voice through the yard-sale microphone. Sammy glares back at me and makes the hand signal for lowering the volume, but he doesn't call for us to stop.

When we get to the part where the electric guitar goes wild, Sean's ready. He practically blows the roof off the barn. From where I'm standing I can see the drummer's smile, the bassist's approving head nod, and Sammy's scowl. I almost laugh out loud.

When the song's over, Sammy's quick to take back his Strat. "That was all right, man. But let's stick you with the acoustic."

Sammy swaps guitars with Sean, then slaps him on the back. Hard. "Let's play."

After Sean drops me at home, I pop in the CD Mrs. Early burned for me. It's kind of like what I heard on the internet. Girls with voices pulled from way deep inside, their notes hanging and rolling and bucking. It seems so complicated. So unlike me and the simple way I enjoy singing. I clip through the songs, immediately scratching a few off the list, knowing my voice doesn't have the training to even attempt them.

My phone lights up and I take off my headphones. It's a local number, but one I don't recognize.

"Hello?"

"Amber?" It's a guy.

"Yeah."

"It's Will."

I sit up fast against my headboard. "Hey, Will."

"I hope you don't mind me calling. I found your number on Devon's phone."

"No. It's fine." I stare out the window, like maybe he's out there under my maples, but all I see is the dark of a new moon.

"Um." He mutters. "I wanted to apologize."

"For what?"

"For being so abrupt the other night. Things have been sort of complicated with my dad for the last few years, and now he's finally listening to me. *Really* listening. And the less I do to screw things up, the happier we'll both be. I was just sort of surprised by your brother-in-law showing up, that's all."

"Yeah. I got that." I take a breath. "And I kissed you, again, and you have a girlfriend who probably wouldn't have been too happy hearing we'd showed up to the dance together."

He's quiet on the other end of the line. In the background, I hear the sound of the local radio station turned low. He clears his throat. "Yeah, so the other reason I called."

I start to cut him off, but he says, "Let me talk, okay?"

"I'm listening." I pull my good leg to my chest and prop my swollen ankle on a pillow.

"I want to help you."

What is he talking about? "Help me?"

"Come on, Not So Plain and Small, don't make this tough on me."

I blow out the thing that's been building in my chest. "Will, all I know is we have something when we make music. *And* when we're together. To you, what happened between us might mean nothing. But it was a big deal to me." I take a breath, then add, "And I can't even talk to my best friend about it. I can't talk to anybody about it."

"Shit." Will's voice is low. "I was only going to offer to help you with your audition."

"You want to help me?"

"Forget it," he says. "I shouldn't expect you to want to hang out with me."

"No. You shouldn't." It'd be easy to get worked up and give him a piece of my mind, but something in his voice makes me forget any anger, and I know we sound good together. "Actually, I could use your help."

"You could?"

I scoot down on the pillows and push aside everything other than the music that hangs between us. "Yeah. I was listening to the CD Mrs. Early gave me when you called. It has a bunch of selections for the different categories that they require. It's all so lofty-sounding. I wish I could sing something like we did the other day in chorus."

"That was pretty sweet," he says.

He grows quiet again and so do I. The sound of his breath on the phone is rhythmic, like a lullaby.

We speak at the same time.

"Maybe I could . . ."

"I'll let you . . ."

We laugh. He lets me finish.

"I'll let you borrow the CD tomorrow. I'll tell you my favorites so far and you can tell me which ones you think would be good."

"Sounds good. And Amber?"

"Yeah."

Will's voice is even, and entirely sincere, when he says, "I'm sorry."

When I hang up, I stare at the red tack on Sevenmile.

I'm not sorry. If nothing ever happens again, at least I said what I needed to say. And at least Will listened.

CHAPTER TWENTY-ONE

The sky is a killer blue and at lunch everyone heads outdoors.

I lie with my head on Devon's stomach, C.A. lies with her head on mine, and Kush and a few other soccer players sit to the side. Sean's missing. Kush says it's the stomach bug.

"How was band practice?" C.A. asks. Her head feels weird bouncing against my belly when she talks. "Did Sean like it? Do y'all sound good together?"

"She sounds better with my brother," Devon says.

I feel myself freezing against him.

"I thought Will had a girlfriend," C.A. says from my stomach.

Devon picks up his head from the ground. "I'm talking about music. What are *you* talking about?"

C.A. rolls off my stomach and sits up. "*I'm* talking about Amber and Sean."

I sit up. "God, y'all, we're only friends."

C.A. flushes then pokes me. "Oh, come on. You have everything in common."

"That doesn't mean he likes me." I figure it's as good a time as any to tell them about the guitar. "I do have an idea, though."

Kush is suddenly interested in our conversation and leans in. "Oh yeah, you've got plans with Sean?"

I have to tread carefully. It's not my place to spill Sean's story. "I think we should help him get this guitar he saw at the pawn shop yesterday."

"Why?" Devon asks.

"Yeah, is it his birthday or something?" C.A. says.

Kush scoots closer.

"No, it's just, he doesn't have one, and he's really good. If we all chipped in together, we could surprise him."

"Right, and I need a new laptop," one of the soccer players by Kush's side says. "Y'all want to chip in for that?"

It's all I can do not to blurt out the whole story, but I don't. I understand what it's like to want to keep some family issues close.

"So you *do* like him." C.A. pulls her ponytail over her shoulder and starts braiding it, focusing intently on her hair.

"Forget it," I say. "Y'all don't understand, at all."

Everybody lies back down in the sun. I watch the clouds shift as their shadows cross my face. Sean and I might be good together. Maybe. But that's not why I want to get him the guitar. To me, the guitar is the thing that will set him free from his past. The thing that will set him apart. And buying a guitar is tangible. It's solid. It's not some silly dream that's about as hard to pin down as one of those cumulous clouds floating overhead. It's not like my dream. This dream is something I can make happen—if I can find a way to collect the rest of the money.

After school, Whitney picks me up. I convince her to take me to the bank and to the pawnshop for Sean.

"So, are you in love with this boy or something?" she asks me.

"Or something," I answer.

"Does Mama know you're wiping out your savings account?"

"Does Mama know you love Vicodin?" That shuts her up.

When we get there, Eddie takes my money and grunts.

"Remember, I need the other hundred no later than next Thursday. And then a hundred and twenty five for the next four months."

"When can he have the guitar?"

Eddie raises the magnifying visor from his eyes. "Have the guitar?"

"Yeah, like next Friday?"

Eddie chuckles, but it isn't kind. "Girlie. I'm doing y'all a favor here. And that boy can flat play. But nobody, I don't care if you're Eddie Goddamn Van Halen, walks out of my pawn shop with an instrument until it's paid in full."

"Oh, right." I grab the ticket and receipt off the counter and shove them in my pocket. "Sorry." I'm in such a hurry to get out of the door that I don't notice the generator sitting on the floor until I've banged it with my ankle. "Crap." I lean over and rub the soft pad below my anklebone, but the pulsing has already started. I wish the thing would go ahead and heal already.

"Do you have any aspirin?" I ask Whitney when I get back into the car.

She rummages around in her bag and fishes out a blue prescription bottle. Inside are a bunch of different pills. She pours them into her hand and separates them. "You can't have these. But you can have this." She holds out a white tablet.

"I don't want that, Whitney. Just an aspirin."

She fishes in her purse and hands me a bottle of Advil. "Here." As she's dropping it in my palm, Whitney spills the handful of pills she'd been holding. "Shit." She jams her hand down between the seats, frantically looking for the lost pills. "Shit, shit, shit."

"What's *wrong* with you?"

"*Those* are oxys. Sammy sells them for like forty bucks each. And I just gave this girl two hundred bucks for them for him to sell. He'll kill me if I lose the profit. Will you help me look, please?"

There's a panic on my sister's face I haven't seen before. I dig between the seats and find a couple of the tablets. "Here." I hold them out to her and watch her face regain calm.

"Thanks." She puts everything back in her bag.

I keep staring at her.

"Stop," she says.

"Whitney."

Tears well up in her big eyes. "I know what you're going to say, but don't, okay?"

"Why don't you go back to school, Whit?"

She wipes her cheeks with the back of her hand. "For your information, I showed Sammy those brochures you brought me from school and he said for me to apply."

"Can't you make that decision for yourself?"

She stiffens, then turns the key in the ignition.

I want to slug myself. "Sorry, Whit."

That song, "Stand by Your Man," sneaks into my brain. I love singing it. My voice gets all twangy and melodramatic on the chorus, but right now all I can think is why? I take a breath. "Don't get mad, okay, but I need to ask you something."

She sighs. "What?"

"How come you're sticking by Sammy and this business? Aren't you worried about Coby?"

Whitney hesitates. "You know why."

I think I do. It's the words. The "for better or for worse" that Mama's always quoting when she reacts to the news of someone's divorce. To her those words are God's gospel. But I wonder, how worse does worse have to get before it's too far gone?

"Do you love him so much you're willing to risk going to jail?" I rub at the throb in my ankle.

"We're not going to jail, Amber." Whitney backs out of the parking lot.

"How can you be sure?"

"How are you so naive? You know, there are powers that be that want people on the ground to do the legwork."

"So, you're saying Sammy's working for the sheriff?"

It's common knowledge that our sheriff's department is as crooked as a broken-backed snake.

She shrugs.

I turn to look at my sister, hard. "They still arrest people, Whit. They make examples of people. And Social Services is quick to take kids. You know that."

"I'm going to stop, okay? As soon as we get Sammy his van. But seriously, don't worry. Sammy won't go to jail. They won't take Coby."

She turns on our road. We pass the Whitsons' house and I think, maybe I'll stop by soon and ask Sean's aunt and uncle about the guitar. Surely they'd want to help.

Whitney nudges me with her elbow. "I didn't say thanks."

"For what?"

"For those pamphlets from the tech school. If they hadn't been lying on the kitchen counter, Sammy probably wouldn't have gone for it. But the caseworker saw them and suggested one of us working toward a degree would look good in our file." She laughs. "Sammy thought it was his idea."

"That's great."

"Isn't it?" She grins, and everything between us feels right again. "Hey."

"Yeah."

"I missed hearing you sing Sunday. And I'm going to miss you next year when you're gone off to that fancy high school."

"Mama told you she said yes to the audition?"

"Mama's told everybody. In her mind, you're already onstage at the Carter Family Fold and buying us all a Cadillac. Gold. Like Elvis." She reaches over and grabs my hand to squeeze it.

This time I'm grinning—and even more determined not to let Sammy wipe the Cadillac out of my mama's mind.

CHAPTER TWENTY-TWO

- - - - - - - - - - - - - - - - - - - -

Devon and I are doing our Friday night hangout early, because Judge and Mrs. McKinney got tickets for the whole family for some chamber orchestra concert up in Banner Elk.

We slide our shoes off and curl up on the couch. Devon pulls his guitar into his lap and starts noodling on the strings.

"So, have you talked to C.A. much lately?" he asks.

I take a handful of the popcorn he popped and pick it up from my hand one kernel at a time. "Just at school. How come?"

He shrugs. Then I realize what he's asking. "*Oh, the thing.*"

Devon rolls his eyes. "Please, I've given up on that."

"Yeah, right," I say, but my attention gets drawn away from him when Will comes walking in from school.

Devon nods at his brother.

Will walks over and snags a handful of popcorn. "Do you mind if I borrow Amber for a sec? I want to show her what I found." He's got his laptop and the CD I gave him earlier in the day in his other hand.

Devon shoos us away. "Go somewhere in the back where I can't hear the twang." He riffs on his guitar.

Will motions for me to follow him and I trail him down the hallway to his bedroom. Will walks in and sets the laptop on his desk, plopping down in his chair. It's the first time I've ever really been in his room. I peek around. There's a double bed with a thick wool plaid comforter. Framed photographs of different Blue Ridge Parkway vistas line his walls. A hiking backpack and walking poles lean in a dusty corner. There's even a fish tank with bright guppies flagging their tails on his bureau. There aren't any photos of Amber-o-zia.

The sound of the computer turning on draws my attention back to Will. "What'd you think of the CD?" I ask.

"Let me show you something." He pulls up a video channel and there's a grainy seventies video of a banjo player in a tuxedo. He hits play.

Within a few bars I realize the guy's picking "Ave Maria," one of my potential choices, on the banjo. Joy rises inside like the notes the musician is playing.

Will looks up at me. "Right?" he says when he sees the giddy expression I can't contain. "But that's not all. Here's the 'Red, Red Rose' song you liked."

Another video, of some cute, young Irish guy sitting in front of a computer, plucking it on a banjo. It looks like he's reading the lyrics as he sings.

"You could do those arrangements?" I ask.

"Yeah, sure," Will says. "I mean, we can learn together. Would it be too weird if you hung out with me, though?"

I raise one eyebrow in a question.

"To practice. Instead of hanging out with Devon."

"We've played together before at your house. Remember? Nirvana?"

Will grins. "Right. You want to start tonight? Now?"

I feel the blood rush to my face but I manage to say, "Yeah. That'd be good."

Will unlatches the banjo case and pulls the banjo onto his lap. He gestures for me to sit down on his bed and he swivels the chair around to face me.

We start with "Ave Maria" and Will butchers the banjo part. I get more relaxed and pull my feet up onto his bed, then lie flat on my stomach to face him as he tries and tries again. When he finally gets a good semblance of the notes, I sit back up and try singing along.

"Sorry about that," he says when we've worked through it once. "I promise I'll get it."

"I'm not worried," I say and scoot back against his headboard, pulling my good leg to my chest.

Will moves to the other end of the bed and leans back against the footboard facing me. He starts picking the tune to "Red, Red Rose" and it flows easier for him. I hum along the first couple of times he plays through, and when it's fluid, I test out my voice.

"I wish I was a butterfly, I'd light on my love's breast. I wish I was a blue cuckoo, I'd sing my love to rest." As I sing, I realize the lyrics are pretty weighted. I can't look at Will, even though I can feel him watching me. But I let myself imagine our time together and pull the emotion out of the song.

He finishes off with a trill of simple notes and we sit silently for a minute. "You want to practice that again?" he asks, clearing his throat.

"Sure." I tug at the collar of my shirt, trying to let in some air.

Will starts to play again. This time, I can't help but look straight in his eyes when I sing, and it's Will who ends up looking away. When he gets to the end, I look down at my hands, feeling the flush of the song, and even a bit of power, from the way I sang it.

I'm fighting the urge to grab Will's shirt and pull him to me when I hear a slow clap from the open door of Will's bedroom.

"Very sweet." It's Amber-o-zia, leaning against the door, giving me a long look.

"Hey." Will jumps up. Even though he was nowhere near to touching me, he looks guilty as hell. He goes to her. "What time is it?"

She crosses her arms and Devon appears behind her, his eyes growing wide when he sees me sitting on Will's bed.

Amber-o-zia's still looking at me, her green eye-shadowed lids sparkling under the track lighting. "It's six o'clock. When you told me to be here. For the concert." Her eyes never leave me.

I try to break the awkwardness and slide off Will's bed. "Did you both hear?" I look between Amber-o-zia and Devon. "It sounded good, right?"

Devon's Adam's apple bobs. "It sounded great. Perfect. You're going to kill them."

"When you leave," Amber-o-zia says and she slides her arms around Will's waist.

I take the hint and slip past them into the hall, following

Devon. I can hear them whispering as I walk away, but I can't make out the words, only the tension.

"You stirring the pot, Plain and Small?" Devon asks me, his head cocked.

"No." My answer is fast.

"Come with me." He grabs my hand. "Help me figure out how to use Skype before your brother-in-law picks you up."

"What for?" I ask.

"No reason. C.A. was telling me it's cool. She uses it all the time to talk to her cousins."

We get on the family computer and mess around setting up Devon's account. I try not to think about Amber-o-zia in Will's room, sitting where I just was. I try to block out the sound of the stereo that just got turned on. But someone's playing music that's bluesy and slow and sounds an awful lot like sex.

For the first time ever, I find myself wishing Sammy would hurry up.

CHAPTER TWENTY-THREE

When he does show up, Sammy's in high spirits.

"Hey, baby sister. You want to practice?"

As much as I'd convinced myself I couldn't be upset about Will, I was. And strangely enough, screaming some rock and roll seemed like a really good idea.

"Yeah, all right. Let's stop by and see if Sean's feeling better."

"Dude doesn't have a guitar." Sammy's cheek flinches.

"Dude plays awesome," I say.

"Yeah, but if he doesn't have an ax, what good's he going to do? We don't need an acoustic."

"Sammy, you need two guitars to play that one song."

"Fine. But I'm lead guitar. And if he doesn't get a real guitar soon, I'm going to find somebody else."

"Nobody said anything about Sean being lead. But come on, how are you going to find somebody else as good as him?"

Sammy's cheek flinches again and I know he knows Sean is the more talented guitar player. But I also know he knows what having a guitarist like Sean could mean for the band's chances.

We drive through town and head out on the old highway. Sammy's always into driving the scenic route. As he drives, my mind blurs with the image of Will and Amber-o-zia doing who knows what to that thick, liquid music.

My phone rings. Mama.

"Hey, Mama."

"Tell Sammy to take you by the store. We need coffee for the morning."

"Yes, ma'am. Would it be all right with you and Daddy if I go play some music with Sammy and his friends?"

I hear Mama's suck of breath on the other end of the line. "Mama?" I say.

"Sugar, that's fine. Your daddy's working late. Does your sister know Sammy's out and about?"

I look at Sammy. "Mama wants to know if Whitney knows you're practicing tonight."

"She does. And if we had that van, she'd be driving out to watch us."

"We could pick her up," I say. "We've got to get Sean anyway."

Sammy nods.

"Mama, we'll bring you the coffee and we're going to pick up Whitney if you'll watch Coby."

We wind our way back toward the highway when I see a familiar flash of red. "Hold up, Sammy."

He slows down the car. Behind a small one-level ranch house, I see Daddy's truck. It's parked almost hidden in the backyard.

"Right. Overtime," I mutter.

Sammy leans over, looking out my window. "Must be his sugar shack."

"Don't talk about him like that."

Sammy shrugs and pulls the car away. "Whatever. But truth tells."

At the store, Sammy goes in for coffee and comes out lugging a case of beer and a Coke for me. He throws it in my lap. "For the minor."

From the Whitsons' front door, I can hear the stereo blasting hip-hop. I ring the doorbell once. When nobody comes, I knock. The music dims and footsteps fall on the other side of the door.

Kush is shirtless, with nothing on but a pair of Fila shorts.

"Um, is Sean here?" I ask him.

Kush hangs on the door frame and looks at me. "No, my parents took him to the doctor. Why? Did y'all have plans?"

I motion toward Sammy in the car. "We're going to go practice. We wanted to see if Sean might come."

"Can I come?" Kush asks.

I blink. Twice. "What?"

"Let me hang out. I'm bored as shit."

"All right. I guess."

"Cool," Kush says. "Let me grab a shirt."

The Coke hits my bladder. "Hey, can I use your bathroom?"

"Yeah, sure. Follow me."

I limp down the hall after him.

"In there." Kush points to a door. "Use my parents'."

The Whitsons' master bedroom smells like Fire and Rain, the perfume Daddy bought Mama one Christmas that she never wears. After I pee, I wash my hands and rinse my face. When I'm done, my reflection stares back at me in the mirror. I look like me, regular old Amber Vaughn. Not nearly as pretty as Amber-o-zia. Maybe Mrs.

Whitson has some lipstick I can use. I open up a drawer quietly. I shouldn't be snooping, but I don't carry around makeup, and I feel self-conscious all of a sudden, like I want to look good tonight.

The first drawer is nothing but brushes and a straightening iron. I open the second drawer. It's filled with department store makeup, like Clinique and Estée Lauder. No Revlon for Mrs. Whitson. I open tubes till I find a shade of metallic light pink that will look pretty on me. After I apply it carefully, and smack my lips, and put it back, I notice that there are a few prescription bottles rolling around at the very back of the drawer. I pull it open a bit farther.

Reverend Early's nasal voice sounds in my head. "*Young lady.*"

I ignore the voice and pull out the first bottle. It has Mrs. Whitson's name on it and it's a medicine I don't recognize. I dig a little farther. The bottles are dusty and covered with a fine layer of powder like they've lived in the drawer for a while. The third bottle makes my fingers tingle. It's Oxycontin. The pills Whitney was talking about. Kush's name is on the label. Probably left over from some old break or sprain. The pharmacy has an Atlanta address and the date is from last spring.

Just yesterday, Whitney said Sammy couldn't really go

to jail, and that they'd stop selling as soon as Sammy got a van for the band. The bottle is practically full. Probably enough to buy a guitar.

A knock startles me. "Hey, you coming?" Kush calls through the door.

I shove the bottle in my pocket. I rationalize my snap decision by reasoning that it's quieter than putting it back in the drawer. "Yeah, sorry." I flush the toilet again and ease the drawer shut as the water rushes down the pipes.

Kush is waiting for me, this time with clothes on, his long hair combed back.

"Um, we're going to a barn." I keep my hand in my hoodie pocket so the bottle won't rattle.

He smiles. "But do you think I'm hot?" He says it like it's a joke, but I'm not sure he's kidding.

"I guess?" I say, smiling a little.

"Good enough," Kush says, walking out of the house. I follow him to the car.

I unzip my hoodie, slip out of it, and ball it up on the floor as I climb into the backseat next to him.

He grins at the sight of my bare arms in a tank top I think is too tight to wear alone.

But I don't grab for the jacket again. It was like I lost my mind for a minute and panicked when Kush knocked on the door. What a stupid impulse. Do I really think I'm going to give Sammy pills to sell? I'll have to find a way to sneak the bottle back into the Whitsons' bathroom, or just throw them away.

We pull up to my house.

"You look nice," Kush whispers in my ear as Whitney buckles herself in.

Whitney catches my eye in the rearview mirror and raises her brows. I can tell she thinks Kush is hot.

"Thanks," I say and rest my arms across my chest.

We drive farther out into the mountains and the road narrows. Sammy's blasting loud music and Whitney and I have our hands out the window. Whitney's relaxed and laughing, cracking jokes over the backseat. It feels like how it used to be, before she got married.

When we turn off on a gravel road, Kush looks backward once. "Where are we going?" he asks. He seems a little nervous, which gives me sort of a patronizing high. For once, I'm the one in the know.

"I told you," I say. "We're going to a barn. It's where Sammy's band practices."

We pull up and there are a few other cars already there. Somebody's started a fire in a metal trash barrel, and people have coolers and rickety lawn chairs pulled out near the picnic table. Two guys are out past the barn shooting . 22s at stacked beer cans lit up by Maglites next to an old shed.

"Come on," I say to Kush. "I'll show you where we're going to play." I grab a small cooler and carry it with us. He follows me into the barn. Just like Sean, he tries to lean back against the vine-covered wall, and even though I'm tempted to let him, I grab his elbow. "Don't." I point.

"Right," he says. "Thanks."

We open our beers and take our first sips, looking around the barn. It's quiet and awkward, so we drink fast. When we start in on our second beer we manage to make small talk about school and teachers. When I get halfway through my third can, the question I've been dying to ask comes flying out of my mouth. "So, how's it going with you and Devon?"

"What do you mean?" Kush pushes a piece of hair behind his ear. He takes a swallow from his can, and when he pulls it away a single shining droplet hangs from the curve of his lower lip. I watch the bead quiver. He reaches up and wipes the liquid away with the back of his hand.

I make sure my voice holds the weight of truth. "I was just wondering. I mean, y'all hang out a lot these days. And it seems like you're having fun." I can't believe I'm asking him this, but I'm doing it for Devon.

Kush leans away and looks at me. "Did Devon say something?"

I shrug.

"So, just because I'm friends with a gay guy, I'm queer, too?" He pauses, looks down at the ground, and then back up at me. "And just because some girl hooks up with a random hiker, she's a slut?"

"*Ha*." I say it harshly. "So you *do* think I'm a slut."

"I don't care what you did that night." Kush steps closer.

"Does Devon know you're not into guys?"

Kush tosses his head back in exasperation. "I'm sure."

"Then why did he ask me to get C.A. to kiss you as a test?" I clap my hand over my mouth.

Kush tosses his beer can into the corner of the barn. It lands with a *clink* and I turn, watching it roll under an old bush hog.

When I look back, Kush takes my empty can out of my hand and throws it, too. It arcs away from us.

Kush's mouth lifts at the edges. "Maybe you should administer the kiss test."

I laugh. "No way. I'm not kissing you."

Kush grabs my hands.

"Forget it." I try to wriggle my hands out of his.

"No, really. You'd be doing me a favor, and I'm a good kisser. Please. Just one kiss. Devon wants to know, right?"

I don't like Kush. But the boy I do like is back at home with his *girlfriend*, and my head is humming with three beers and Kush is looking at me so intently. And Devon did ask me, sort of. I tilt my chin up. "Fine," I say.

Kush wraps his arms around me and pulls me to him gently, his hands on the small of my back. My eyes close, and then our lips meet. He teases at my lower lip, then tries to open my mouth with his tongue.

"Whoa." I push him off.

Kush doesn't let go of me. "Why? Is it because of Sean?" he whispers.

Outside, the guns start firing one after the other after the other, and everybody's hooting.

"Jesus," I say and try to break free to see what the hell they're doing out there.

Kush barely even looks back at the door. "You didn't answer me."

I look up at him again. "What? Oh, Sean. No. That's not it."

"Then let me really kiss you, Amber." He's practically begging.

Curiosity, and maybe Bud Light, gets the better of me, and I let his lips explore mine. I can tell Devon pretty certainly that Kush likes girls. But I push him off when he pulls me tight against him. "Enough, Kush."

"Come on. Weren't we having fun?"

"It doesn't matter. I don't like you *like that*." I put air quotes around the last two words.

I lean back to see Kush's cocky smile. "No? Funny. This summer, I got the impression you had a kind of secret life. That you wanted out as much as I did. That maybe a . . ." He raises his fingers, imitating my air quotes, ". . . *friendship* of convenience could make life more tolerable for both of us."

"What?" Something deep and heavy vibrates around in my rib cage. I try to keep my face calm, but inside, I'm furious. Is *that* how Kush sees me?

"You and me, hanging out, at least it'd be something to do while we're stuck here. Because, come on. This is no place to fall. Once you're down, you'll never get up. Like your sister and brother-in-law." Kush nods toward the door. "Listen to them."

He may have a point. But he's also talking about my home, about my family. And it's one thing for me to tell him he doesn't want to hang out with them, but another thing for him to bad-mouth them without even knowing who they are.

Sammy and the other guys trickle into the barn to set up their instruments. "You about ready to sing?" Sammy asks me, before looking at Kush then back at me.

"Definitely," I say, relieved, and for the second time in the same night, I'm glad that Sammy is here.

CHAPTER TWENTY-FOUR

Kush is drunk and all over me in the backseat of Sammy's car. Whitney's laughing in the front seat.

"Come on, Amber. Kiss me again." His hand flails toward my face and I hold mine up, blocking him, and turn my head toward the window.

"Kush, no. You're a mess." I don't know what all he took. He drank a ton of beer, I could see that from where I stood in the back with my tinny little microphone. But one of the guys had out a pipe, and who knows what else was going on. It was a free-for-all for the spectators.

Kush reaches across my waist, trying to pull me toward him, and collapses his head in my lap. "Don't be like that." I meet Whitney's eyes in the rearview mirror and roll mine.

"Kush." I look down at him and almost laugh. His eyes are squeezed shut and his lips are pursed like he's waiting for a kiss. "Hey." I pat his cheek.

He opens his eyes halfway. "Hey." He grins up at me, then lets his eyes rest on my chest.

He's completely gone. I hold out my hand. "Give me your phone. I need to call Sean so we can get you inside your house without your parents seeing you."

Kush laughs and throws himself back against his side of the backseat. "I left them a note. Told them I went to the movies."

Kush moves to kiss me again, but I'm already dialing Sean.

"Hello?" Sean sounds groggy.

"Hey, Sean? It's Amber."

"Hey."

"Look, can you help sneak Kush into your house? We're about five minutes out."

Kush grabs the phone from me. "Guess what, cuz?" His voice is loud and obnoxious. There's a beat and then he slurs into the phone, "Your girlfriend let me kiss her."

I grab the phone back from him and glare at Kush. "What the hell?" I whisper.

Kush's head lolls and he stretches his arms out like a

cat. "That's right. I kissed you. He's going to be so pissed."

I manage to put the phone back to my ear. "Um, hi, Sean. You're going to meet us, right?"

"What was that about?" Sean asks.

"He thinks I'm your girlfriend, I guess."

"So he kissed you?"

"Yeah, but it was nothing."

Kush keeps mumbling. "Damn straight it was nothing. Like I would want to hook up with a country girl."

At that, even Sammy's rolling his eyes at the spectacle in the backseat.

"Sean." I feel the breath coming short in my chest and my brows hunching down over my eyes as I stare at Kush.

"Yeah?"

"We're on your street, and I suggest you come out to meet us." I pause and push away Kush's hand. "Because, if you don't, I'm going to kill your cousin."

When we cut the lights on the car and ease up to the edge of the Whitsons' property, Sean is waiting for us.

Kush stumbles out of the car and practically falls into Sean's arms. Then he flings his arm back toward me. "You can have her."

Sean shakes him, to knock some sense into him or to wake him up. "Kush, *stop*. You're being a dick and you're pulling Amber into our old business."

Kush sways unsteadily, then leans over to puke in the yard.

I shrug, kind of embarrassed about returning Kush home in the state he's in. "Sorry. It was a little wild. I think he tried everything they passed his way."

"It's okay." Sean helps Kush to his feet. "Hey, Amber?"

"Yeah?"

"He's not really as much of a dick as he can act like sometimes."

"Oh?" I cross my arms over my chest.

Sean turns Kush toward their house, locking his hands on Kush's shoulders to keep him upright, then grins at me over his shoulder. "Okay, maybe he's a little bit of a dick. But there's some history here. This really isn't about you."

I mouth "thank you" to Sean, then climb into the backseat of Sammy and Whitney's car.

When I get home, the first thing I do when I get to my bedroom is call Devon.

"Plain and Small." Devon sounds groggy.

"I woke you up."

"S'okay. What's up."

"I kissed Kush."

"Oh." I hear some rustling, and I imagine Devon

sitting up straight in bed, suddenly alert.

I sigh and let it out slowly. "He was . . . into it."

"Oh. That's . . . what I figured." Devon pauses. "Were *you* into it?"

I bark out a laugh, because it's the only thing I can do to not burst into tears. "God, no!" I tell him about the whole night. As I talk, I distract myself by rummaging in my hoodie pocket until I find the bottle of pills from Mrs. Whitson's drawer. I count them out into my hand, then slide them back in the bottle for safekeeping. There are twenty-two tablets left. Eight hundred and forty dollars. More than enough money for the guitar.

Kush's name is like an ugly scar staring up at me from the label. It would serve him right for me to help Sean get the guitar he wants so bad. Everybody else in this house does whatever they want to make themselves happy. Why shouldn't I?

"Listen," I say to Devon a little later. "Don't tell *anybody* I kissed him. I don't want it getting around."

"Of course not. It sounds like he was a total idiot. Can you forgive *me* for thinking this plan was sane?" Devon sounds as embarrassed as I felt earlier with Sean.

"Yeah. But, Devon, really. You're better off without this guy. I know you were hopeful, but there's somebody better out there for you."

"I love you, Plain and Small."

"I love you, too."

As soon as I hang up, I text Sammy. I don't want to think too long about what I'm about to do. I might chicken out. But Sean deserves it. Kush is an ass.

—Meet me out front.

I sneak down the staircase, careful to avoid the left side, which squeaks and cracks. Mama and Daddy are in bed and I don't want to risk getting caught.

When I get to the front porch, Sammy's already waiting, leaning back against the maple tree, one leg cocked.

"What's up?" He loops his thumbs in his jeans pocket. "You need something from me?" He glances back toward his trailer.

"Yes. I mean no. I mean . . ." I hold out the bottle of pills. They clatter against the plastic as my hand jerks.

He relaxes and straightens, taking the bottle, then lets out a low whistle.

"I need six hundred from that." I pull my shoulders back.

He counts out the pills in front of me. "Since you're kin, I'll give you four twenty. Half. Normally I only give a quarter of street value. The risk is all on me."

"It's important, Sammy." A shot of anger races into my fists as I close them tight.

"Fine, whatever. But only because you're family. It's my van fund you're cutting into, you know?"

The pawn shop opens at nine on Saturdays. I punch my fists toward the ground and lift my chin. "Can I have it tonight?"

Sammy shakes his head and pockets the bottle. "For real?"

"Yes. I told you, it's important." I should probably ask him to empty the bottle and give it back to me. But I'm too scared to push the issue. He might change his mind about paying me tonight.

"This is my seed money, kid."

"You've got more seeds in that bottle."

Sammy sighs and pulls a roll of bills out of his pocket. He counts off six hundreds. Before he hands them to me, he hesitates.

I snatch the bills before either of us can think about it too much. As I stuff them in my pocket, I ask him, "We won't get in trouble for this, will we?"

The trailer lights come on and I see Whitney peek her head out of the front door. "Sammy?" she calls softly into the night.

"Shit," he says. He leans over and tousles my hair before jogging back toward the trailer. "No worries, little sister."

. . .

The next morning I wake up with a raw throat from singing and a sick feeling in my stomach. I'd hoped to buy Sean's guitar today and talk Mama into going over to the Whitsons' with me to give it to him, but I can't make myself get up. I'm not sure if it's from the beer or last night's scene with Kush. From the window, I see Daddy backing the truck out of the driveway. He avoids the pothole and drives off in the direction of town. I roll over and stare at my wall. Maybe he's going to work.

Mama knocks on my door and pokes her head in my room. "You okay, sugar?"

I hold my hand to my stomach. "I think I'm getting a bug."

Mama puts her hand on my forehead and sets down the glass of apple juice she'd brought me. "Let me take your temperature. You are a might bit warm."

"Mama?"

"Yes, sugar?"

"Is Daddy going to work?"

"Yes. Mr. Ward called in sick."

I feel a little relieved, but know it may not be true. "Tell me about when you knew you were in love with Daddy."

"Sugar, you've heard that old story a hundred times."

"But I want to hear it again." And I do. I need to be reminded of the foundation of my family. I need to know why the two of them still sleep under the same roof every night.

Mama smiles big and squeezes my shoulder. "Your daddy was *such* a handsome man. Even more handsome than he is now. Girls from miles around heard tell of him. I never did figure why he settled on me."

I close my eyes a little. "Because he loved your laugh, your smile, and your spice cake."

Mama smiles and takes the now-empty glass from me. "See, you know this story inside out, I don't need to tell it again."

"Yes, you do. Tell me." I need to see my mama giggling in my daddy's arms. To hear the blush in her voice when she talks about him. I need to understand.

Mama settles next to me on the bed. "Well, his mama had finally got him coming back to church. I'd just turned seventeen. Your daddy was fresh home from a stint in the army. I'd heard his name, of course, because he'd been such a big football star for Mountain High."

"Did they have his picture in the trophy case then?"

"Why, yes. And I recognized him straightaway that first day in church. He came walking in wearing his army clothes, all pressed with stiff creases. His hair was cut short, and the set of his jaw was hard and soft all at once, like the lines of these mountains. I was standing near the receiving line and it was all I could do to keep from dropping my own jaw."

"What were you wearing?" I ask softly.

"Me? Well, let's see. I was wearing a pretty little white eyelet blouse and a green skirt that twirled when I turned. My hair had been set in curlers overnight so it was full of bounce. I even had a brand-new pair of green Mary Janes to match. Like you, I was blessed and filled out that eyelet shirt pretty well." Mama giggles.

"Mama!"

"So, after the service we're in the parish hall, and I'm standing behind the desserts and he walks right on up to me. That gold hair of his was thick, like yours, and his eyes, hazel green like your sister's. Lord, child, he made me nervous on the spot the way he kindly swallowed me with one look."

"What'd he say?"

"He said, 'I hear you make the best apple spice cake in all of Sevenmile and I intend to try a slice.' But the way he said it, I sure didn't think he was talking about cake."

"Then what happened?"

"Well, I served him up a piece of cake."

"Mama . . ."

"Your daddy asked me out on a date. He took me out

on a date every Sunday evening until he left again for the army and I made him a cake every week. That man loved my cooking. When he left, I was worried he'd find a prettier face, or a prettier figure, but he told me not to worry, that he aimed to marry a woman with a gorgeous smile and a steady hand in the kitchen and that he aimed to settle right back here in Sevenmile. I knew then I loved him and that I'd be that girl."

I work up the nerve to ask her something that's been nagging at me. "Do you ever regret marrying him?"

Mama gets real still. "Where's that question coming from, girl?"

I look down at my hands. "I don't know. You were just so young, and Daddy seemed like he was kind of wild back then."

"No. If I hadn't married your daddy, I wouldn't have had the two of you. Your daddy's made some mistakes, and so have I, but when I married, I swore for better or worse, richer or poorer, and I took those words seriously."

I suppose I should have seen her answer coming. So I ask another question. "How come you never got a job?"

Mama's lips purse. "I'm looking at the reason."

"Well, Devon's mom's an elementary schoolteacher and Sean's aunt does catering. She works with her cooking. You could do that. They get up every day and get dressed and look good." I think about that drawer full of department store makeup.

"Do you have something you're wanting to say to me, Amber Delaine? Are you saying that I'm not good enough for your daddy? That I don't do enough around this house looking after your sister and her baby and that husband of hers? That I don't work hard enough at being your mama? Now I need to get myself fixed up every day on top of it all?"

"Well, it might make Daddy love you more!" I realize I'm yelling.

Mama's eyes narrow and she stands. "Your daddy loves me just fine the way I am. The outside of a person don't make the insides any different. Jesus knows the real you, and that is all that matters. If there's something you need to tell me, you better spit it out."

I can't tell her what's really bothering me. "Nothing, Mama. I just think he talks mean to you sometimes. I guess you're right. It's only the inside that counts."

But I'm thinking it's not true. What I figure is that the outsides of a girl matter way more than anyone cares to admit.

CHAPTER TWENTY-FIVE

At church on Sunday, I want to tell Mrs. Early about the banjo arrangements Will found. I know she thinks I can sing like those girls on the CD she gave me, but even if I could stretch my voice out wide and deep like they do, I'm not sure I want to. My voice likes high and lonesome. But lonesome isn't feeling so good for me in real life. I can't shake the thought of Will and Amber-o-zia together, especially after singing "I Wish My Love Was a Red, Red Rose" to him on Friday.

Mrs. Early calls me to the front of the sanctuary and has me sing "I'll Fly Away." The same song Will had me sing that night at Sizz's. It's not as fun this morning as it was that night onstage with Will, but I do love it. Through the windows in the back of the church, I watch the colors shift over the congregation as the clouds cover and uncover the sun. I know the words are about going to meet your maker when you die, but I like to sing it like it's a song about leaving, and that I'm the bird escaping.

When I finish singing, Mrs. Early comes to my side and squeezes my hand. Normally I go sit down after I sing, but Pastor Early comes and stands on the other side of me. "Now, folks, we need some special prayers today. Our young Amber Vaughn has a big audition coming up soon. I'm sure you've heard about it from her mama, but let's give her some prayerful Evermore Fundamental support."

I stand there, shocked and still, as the entire congregation bows their heads. Daddy actually has his arm draped around Mama's shoulders, and he's grinning like his prize bull got a ribbon at the county fair.

As Pastor Early prays over me, I feel a simple strength enter through my fingers and my toes. All of these folks, the people of my childhood, are praying for my success. Success that means leaving them. Leaving my mountains.

But I'm not like Kush. I won't be leaving because I hate this place. I just want a bigger life somewhere, and I want to sing.

As that sinks in, I realize that just because Kush was an

asshole, it doesn't give me the excuse to be a criminal and sell those pills.

When I sit back down at our family's pew, I fish a pencil out of my purse. On a scrap of hymnal paper, I write, *I need those pills back*, and lay it on the gap of dark wood between me and Sammy.

Sammy looks down and puts his finger on the paper, turning it so he can read it.

Whitney glances over and I crumple the note. She looks at Sammy, then takes his hand, pulling it over onto her leg.

I sit against the pew and feel my heart beating, the hard oak pressing on my spine. When we stand up to sing a group hymn, Sammy tilts his head toward me.

"Too late," he whispers.

After the service, Whitney goes with Mama to set up the refreshments and I follow Sammy to the nursery. When we walk past a darkened Sunday school room, I push him through the door with the flat of my hand.

"Settle down, girl. What's got into you?"

"Sammy, I need those pills back. I need that bottle. I shouldn't have given them to you. It was late, and I was mad, and I don't know what I was thinking."

"I thought you had a big emergency, Amber." Sammy

looks at me sideways. "What, you're not pregnant?"

"Huh?"

He shrugs. "I don't know, after this summer, timing seemed right. I honestly figured you needed that much cash for an abortion."

I throw my head down into my hands and choke back a sob. "For your information, I wanted that money so we could buy Sean a guitar. So he could help your band get somewhere." I look up at him. "But I came about those pills in the wrong way."

Sammy considers me. "He give them to you?"

"No." I grab Sammy's arm. "Please, give them back. I need to fix this."

Sammy puts his hand on my shoulder. "I told you. It's too late. I needed to make my money back and I sold them last night. But nobody's going to trace it. I don't sell them in the bottle. It's gone. Don't worry."

And just then, the door to the Sunday school room swings open.

Whitney's framed in the hall light. It shines through her skirt, silhouetting her legs.

"What are y'all doing?" Her eyes cut between the two of us.

I drop my hand from Sammy's arm and he casually drops his from my shoulder, stuffing his fingers in his pockets.

I make up a story fast. "We came to get Coby, but I needed to ask Sammy something."

Whitney's eyes narrow and she looks at me, then at Sammy again. "Is that right?" she asks him.

"Of course, sugar." Sammy walks to her and drapes his arm over her shoulder. "What else would we be doing?"

She looks at me again. This time the look is different, like she's appraising me. "Is that my old dress?" she asks.

"Yeah," I say.

"You look like a cow in it." She turns and walks out, pulling Sammy with her.

In the nursery, getting Coby, I glance at the mirror on the wall.

"Hey, Deana May?" I ask.

"Yeah?"

"Does this dress make me look big?" I turn from side to side.

"Are you *crazy*? You're not big. You're curvy. The kind of curvy boys like." She grins and hands me Coby's bag with his emergency pants, pull-ups, and sippy cup. "In fact, you should wear dresses more to school. All you ever wear is those old overalls, and you look beautiful today."

I tug the fabric over my hips. "I guess," I say. "Thank you."

I wonder if my clothes are part of why Kush called me a redneck girl. If I get into NC-Arts, what will the other students think of me? I put my hands on my waist, cinching the dress tighter, and arch my back so my chest pokes out. I think about Amber-o-zia in that orange tank top and heels. And the hostess at the Fish House all those years ago. I suck in my cheeks a little and position myself at an angle to the glass. "You're probably right. I guess I need a change." I touch the hair where it skims the back of my neck. "Maybe I should let my hair grow out."

Deana May steps next to me and holds up her thick braid so it looks like it's attached to my head. "I don't know," she says. "I like your hair short. You pull it off. And it makes you stand out."

Coby reaches his hands up toward my waist. "Up, Ber."

"Okay, buddy, let's go. See you at school, Deana May."

She waves and I hesitate once more in the mirror. The girl looking back at me issues a challenge. Try it. For a week. Pull out Whitney's old clothes. Dress up for school. Find a new Amber.

After Sunday dinner, lunchtime at my house, I go up to my room. Whitney had been stony toward me through two helpings of squash casserole and a tender pot roast. Fortunately, Mama chattered through the silence.

In my bedside drawer, tucked underneath the Bible I got in sixth grade, is the money from Sammy. I lie back and fan it out in front of me.

I can't get the pills back.

The thought of sneaking the money into the Whitsons' house hovers somewhere, but that's just stupid. A random six hundred dollars would be way more suspicious than a missing bottle of Oxycontin. Thinking about how Kush acted the other night makes me want to punch my wall. And thinking about how Sean bent his head reverently over that guitar, the same way Whitney cradles Coby, makes me happy. The money's here. It might as well go to good use if I can't take back what I've done.

I hop off the bed and rummage through the closet and drawers, digging all of Whitney's hand-me-downs out from behind my T-shirts and jeans and overalls. There's even a few pairs of heels stuffed in the way back of the closet. My ankle's better, but I'm still careful as I slip on a pair of three-inch red spikes. I think about calling C.A. She'd get me fixed up in no time. But what would I tell her? I think I might really like Will McKinney, but I'm not pretty enough for him? Kush called me a redneck girl, so now I don't want to look like myself anymore?

I slip on a short black skirt and find a white tank with a built-in bra. Over that I put on a floral gauzy overshirt with an open collar. I grab my hairbrush and pretend it's a microphone, and practice flirting with an audience. I'm tossing my head when my cell phone rings.

It's Will.

"Hello?" I hold the phone tight to my ear, and keep posing, trying to look sophisticated.

"Hey, Amber." His voice is soft. "Sorry our practice got cut short Friday."

I sit on the bed and curl my legs up beneath me. "It's okay. I understand."

"Can we try again? Tomorrow after chorus? I've been working on 'Ave Maria.'"

I look down at the quilt on my bed, and bunch it in my fingers. "Are you sure you want to?"

"I told you I'd help."

"I know. I just don't want your girlfriend pissed off at you. Not that I'm a threat or anything, but—"

Will cuts me off. "Not So Plain and Small."

"Yeah?" I grab onto the heel of one of the pumps and wiggle it back and forth on my foot. How do people walk in these things?

Then Will says, "It doesn't matter what she thinks."

"It doesn't?"

"No."

We're quiet for a minute, and then I get nervous. "Hey,

would you help me with an errand after school, before practice?"

"Sure. What do you need?"

"I've got to go by the pawn shop to pay for a guitar."

"A guitar? Is it for you?"

I take a breath. "It's for Sean. I took up a collection and we got him a Gibson. Sean's really good. We should all play together sometime."

Will's silent.

"Will? Is that okay?"

"Oh. Yeah, sure." His voice sounds different than it did a second ago. Less certain. "Um, listen. I've got to run. I'll see you tomorrow, okay?"

When I hit the off button, I stare at the phone.

CHAPTER TWENTY-SIX

Monday at school, I am all kinds of nervous. I've got six hundred dollars of drug money in my purse and I don't feel comfortable *at all* in my clothes. A group of sophomore girls looks in my direction and starts whispering. I glance down. I tug on the skirt, suddenly self-conscious, but there are at least six other girls in the commons with skirts as short as mine.

"Oh, *wow*, Amber! Look at *you*!" C.A. bounces over and gives me a big smile. She reaches behind me and tucks in the tag poking out of the back of my shirt.

"Did I do okay?" I look down at myself. It feels completely weird to have my legs showing and to be three inches taller than usual.

C.A. looks me up and down and says, "You should wear something like *that* to my party."

"Party?" I ask.

"Party?" Devon walks up behind me. I turn around and give him a quick hug.

C.A. squeals and claps. "Yes! Party! I want y'all to come over and meet my cousin from Bristol. He is *the* best." She loops arms with both of us. "And we can celebrate your upcoming audition. *Plus* my mom's going to be gone for the night."

The three of us head toward the art room, arm in arm.

"You should totally ask Sean," C.A. says to me as we pass Frog and the other burnouts hanging out by the band room. They chin nod toward me as a group.

I nod back to Frog, then stop, turning toward C.A. "What is it with everybody thinking me and Sean are together?"

C.A. cocks her head. "You're not?"

"No." I wobble forward, working hard to keep my balance on the slick floor. "He's a super-nice guy and a great musician, but just because a girl hangs out with a guy, it doesn't mean they're hooking up."

"Feeling a little touchy, P & S?" Devon laughs, knowing I'm still sensitive about the incident with Kush.

I punch his arm. "Look," I say to C.A. "I think *you* should ask Sean."

We put our book bags down behind our chairs and sit at our art table. Kush is already in the room, sitting at a new table, chatting with a couple of senior girls. I notice they both look in my direction, then look at each other when I walk in.

C.A. arranges her sketchpad and pencils in front of her. Then arranges them a second time. "Do you think? I mean, I'm not sure. He probably thinks I'm too blonde or something."

I smile as I watch C.A. reorganize her stuff for the third time. If C.A. is worried about a boy not liking her, then who else worries? It must not matter what you look like.

"He would be crazy to say no. Right, Devon?"

Devon holds a self-portrait mirror up toward C.A. and points a gun finger at her image. "Sizzling shortie in the house."

I groan. "Oh God, Kush has rubbed off on you."

Devon crosses his arm, and sticks his nose in the air. "Humph. I gave him that offer, but he refused."

C.A. laughs and shakes his arm. I guess Devon knows his secret's safe with her, too.

Just then, Kush strolls over and picks up his book bag

from our table. I avoid looking at him.

"What's up, Amber?" he asks.

"Hey, Kush. Nothing," I say, staring at the table.

"I think I'm going to move." He turns and strolls away.

The three of us look at each other. It's C.A. who laughs first.

"Good riddance," I whisper.

Devon puts his forehead on the table. "And I had such high hopes." Then he sits up and looks at us, grinning.

After class, as I'm walking up the stairs to my English class, I start to think that something's wrong. I'm getting a lot of glances and whispers today, and it can't be just because of a short skirt and some new shoes. My phone buzzes in my pocket. I take a risk and pull it out. It's a text from Devon.

—Meet me by the library before lunch.

When the bell rings, I rush downstairs. My ankle is throbbing and I'm dying to go sit outside on the grass and take Whitney's shoes off. Dressing up is all right, I guess, but I think I'd be happier in my regular clothes.

Devon and C.A. are both waiting for me, and their expressions look like Pastor Early at a funeral.

"What is it?" I ask before I even get to them.

The same group of freshman girls that'd laughed when Whitney got arrested walks past, giggling. I hear one of them whisper, "*That's* her."

It's quickly followed by, "I heard she had sex with, like, everyone at the party."

A vacuum pulls all the air out of my lungs. Devon and C.A. reach for me from across the hall but I freeze, suspended in a bubble of disbelief. When it pops, I turn around and take off running, away from the cafeteria, away from everybody, and away from Kush and whatever vicious rumors he's started. Tears well up in my eyes. I don't see the book bag blocking my escape route, and I go sprawling.

I grab my ankle. It shoots pain and I'm sure I look like an idiot lying on the ground, tears in my eyes, skirt too short for school. Eight feet appear. Four faces stare down at me.

"Are you okay, Amber?" Mrs. Early asks me, her eyebrows drawn.

"Here, we'll take you to the nurse." Devon and C.A. squat down and pull me up, my arms around both of their shoulders.

Then I see Will. "Are you okay?" he asks me. His eyes are concerned.

I look away from him. There's no telling what he's heard.

"I'm okay." I put tentative pressure on my ankle and

buckle. I squeeze the tears tight in my eyes.

"Oh." C.A.'s hands go to her mouth as I crumple.

Will steps in for C.A. "Here, let me help." Will pulls my arm around his shoulder and presses my hand tight.

Devon and Will practically carry me to the nurse's office, Mrs. Early and C.A. right behind us.

Will helps me climb onto the examination table while Devon explains to Nurse Barb in her office how I'd sprained my ankle on a trail. Mrs. Early excuses herself, something about lunchroom duty, but promises to check in with me later.

"I've got a cheer meeting. I have to go," C.A. says, looking around, and then at me. "Text me, okay? Love you, girl."

I nod. She gives me a quick hug and it brings up a new round of tears.

"So what happened back there? Why were you running?" Will whispers, sliding onto the table next to me.

He hasn't heard. I look toward Devon, who's walking over to us again with the nurse. "Kush is talking trash about her."

"Why would he do that?" I ask, blowing into the Kleenex Will hands me.

Devon shrugs. "Maybe because you rejected him? Because he thinks you picked Sean instead?"

"Thinks?" Will asks, looking back and forth between the two of us.

Nurse Barb takes my ankle in her hands and presses along the side of it.

I start to answer, but Devon continues in a whisper to his brother, "Yeah. It's my fault. I asked for her or C.A. to kiss Kush. You know, as a test."

Then Nurse Barb hits a spot on my ankle and I inhale sharply—because of the sharp pain, and because of what Devon's just told Will.

"Did you?" Will asks me. "Kiss him?"

I look over at him. "Yes. I did. But it's not what you think."

"But you kissed him." Will's Adam's apple bobs, just like Devon's does when he's not saying everything he wants to.

I bristle. "It's not like I have a boyfriend, even if I *had* been into it. Which I wasn't." I glare at Will.

Devon starts to say something, but the nurse interrupts us. "You boys need to go to lunch."

Devon winks at me before he leaves, but Will just slides off the examination table and walks right out.

Nurse Barb shuts the door, and then starts pressing on my ankle again. "Hon, when did you do this?"

"A week ago, Saturday," I say. "It was getting better

until I fell just now."

"Have you had X-rays?"

"No, ma'am," I say.

She purses her lips and her brows knit into one deep furrow appearing behind her glasses' frames. "You need X-rays, dear. I'm pretty sure this is more than a sprain. You need to call one of your parents to take you to the doctor right now."

"Oh, they wanted to take me before," I say. "But, I told them not to, that I was fine."

"That's not really your decision, though, is it?"

"I guess not." I dial Mama while the nurse helps me prop up my ankle with an ice pack.

Mama shows up so fast she's still in her dollar store slacks and gardening sneakers when she lumbers into the nurse's office. I see the looks the other ladies on staff give each other when she walks in. Judging her like Kush's friends judge me. Like people judge Whitney.

Mama's rattling on about how sorry she is she didn't insist I go to the doctor earlier, but my phone buzzes. I glance at it. It's Will.

—Practice?

Will still wants to play music with me.

—Yes.

Then:

—That kiss wasn't real. I swear.

—You don't owe me an explanation.

Then a second text.

—But I believe you.

When I read those four words, the anxiety I'd had since seeing Devon's and C.A.'s faces before lunch vanishes. Will believes me. So does C.A., and so does Devon. Sean knows the truth, too. And they are the only ones who matter.

Mama pulls up to the emergency room entrance, where an attendant meets me with a wheelchair.

The doctor examines me and the results are in. My distal fibula has a hairline fracture. My ankle's broken.

The doctor gives my mother a stern speech. *Should have brought her in sooner. Will take longer to heal now. Important to get medical attention.*

Mama looks like a beaten dog and I realize it's my fault she's enduring this doctor's lecture. I try to tell the doctor it was because of me we didn't come in sooner, that the insurance was too expensive, but she waves me off and leaves to find a nurse to take me to get my cast.

Mama drops me off at the McKinneys' on the way home. She'd tried to argue, telling me I needed to rest, but I'd told her that this practice for my audition was way too important to miss.

When we pull up, Will's waiting for me on the front porch. I'm on crutches again, at the doctor's insistence, hobbling up the walk. When I reach the front steps, Will comes down to help me.

"Purple cast. I like it," he says. He gives me a once-over. "How come no overalls today?"

I'm still wearing my clothes from school. I tug at the skirt as I sit on one of the white wooden rockers. "Just felt like a change."

"You look nice. Not like you, but nice." He smiles sideways at me, then starts to flat-pick a tune on the banjo.

I could watch him play the banjo all day long. He starts into "Ave Maria," and his fingers fly across the strings.

When he finishes, he looks up. "Well?"

I let go of the rocking chair's arms and bring my hands to my face and press to keep from squealing. Finally, I spread my fingers and whisper, "Amazing."

Will sits back against another rocker. "Yeah, it's why I decided to go tell my dad that I'm going to East Tennessee State University instead of Carolina. I can actually minor in bluegrass there."

Tar Heel memorabilia lines their family room. Judge

McKinney is a proud alumnus and a huge basketball fan. "Is your dad upset?"

"He wasn't real happy. He worries that I won't study something serious, and I'll end up hanging out with an unsavory bunch." Will rolls his eyes and pulls his chair closer to mine. "If I get into big trouble again, like I did before, the Judge will force my hand. And that means Carolina. It's not like I have a big scholarship to either one."

"What happened?" I ask, curious. Devon had hinted about something earlier this fall, but I just figured Will got caught baking with alternative ingredients and that's why he'd quit being the brownie guy.

Will starts "Ave Maria" again, a little more slowly. "I traded Sammy an old prescription for some weed. Kind of a dumbass move, since my name was on the bottle. Somebody in the sheriff's department gave Dad the heads-up, so I didn't get in real trouble. It was stupid." He plinks a banjo string. "But at least getting caught helped me finally tell Dad the truth about next year and what I really want. I'm still on thin ice with him and Mom, but it's all good."

My stomach constricts. Sammy said there was no way anything could trace back to me, that the bottle was gone. I can't stand Kush, but it doesn't mean I want to get him in trouble for what I did. *Why did I give Sammy that bottle?*

Will looks at me and starts playing the song again from

the top. "Time to sing."

It's hard to let go of everything I'm holding inside. But eventually, the singing takes my mind and clears it of all I'm holding on to. Will plays his banjo so confidently, so sweetly, and I let my voice soar and mellow and soar again, following Will's song.

After a while, Mrs. McKinney and Devon come out and sit on the porch swing with a bowl of popcorn, watching me and Will like we're the latest film at the little theater in the next town over. We run through all three songs again and again until I don't think I can even open my mouth to speak.

"Won't you stay for dinner, Amber? We're having lasagna," Mrs. McKinney asks me.

"Thank you, but Daddy's picking me up soon. It was all I could do to talk Mama into letting me come over after we left the hospital." As I'm saying it, I hear the sound of my dad's truck coming down the long driveway.

When I get up to leave, after thanking Will and Mrs. McKinney, Devon follows me down the steps and to the truck. "So . . . what's going on with you and Will?"

I stop mid–crutch swing. "What do you mean?"

He rocks back on his heels and whistles, a smug look on his face.

My heart beats in a panic.

"Oh, only that he broke up with his girlfriend. And I might've noticed your number on his cell phone." Devon waggles his eyebrows. "Do you like my brother, Plain and Small?"

"He broke up with Amber-o-zia?"

"Last Friday night. That music was blasting to cover Amber-o-zia's hysterics. And I noticed that you *deftly* avoided answering my question." He puts his face near mine. "Plain and Small, is there something you're not telling me? Something to do with how you feel about my older brother?"

I blush to my toes. "We're just practicing together. That's all."

I reach for the door handle of Daddy's truck.

Before I get in, Devon meets my eyes and says quietly, "You and Will would be amazing together. You both love that music. You both love the woods." He winks. "And best of all, Plain and Small, he's like me, but straight."

I give Devon a quick hug. "I'll think about it," I whisper.

As we drive away, I turn around and watch Devon walking back to his house, where Will has his head down, playing the banjo on his front porch.

Will McKinney, who doesn't have a girlfriend anymore.

CHAPTER TWENTY-SEVEN

When I get home, Mama's got my purse on the kitchen table, the six hundred-dollar bills fanned out beside it.

"What's this?" I ask, trying to keep my face composed.

"I reckon that's my question to be asking, isn't it?" Mama's hands are on her hips, a wooden spoon sticking out from one side like an extra appendage.

Sammy and Whitney are already sitting around the kitchen table for supper. I glance over at them. Whitney is sizing me up and Sammy is sending a message with his eyes that says, "Please don't screw this up."

"Oh, that," I say. "That's the collection money for my friend Sean's guitar. Everybody put me in charge of buying it."

"Who's everybody?" Whitney asks me, her eyes suspicious.

But Mama already seems satisfied with my answer and starts to bustle over dinner. "Well, I'm sorry to doubt you, sugar, but I was looking for the prescription the doctor handed you and saw those bills. I didn't know how you'd come across so much money. Your sister thought I should be concerned."

I glare at Whitney.

"They, for your information, are my friends from school," I say.

Whitney sits back and crosses her arms. "Right. You managed to raise six hundred dollars from a bunch of high school kids."

Through this whole conversation, Sammy has been sitting with his arm slung across the back of Whitney's chair, not looking at anyone, but he's making me uneasy.

"So what if I did?" I reply, unable to come up with anything better.

"Enough of this," Daddy says, walking in the kitchen. "I'm hungry."

After Sammy and Whitney take Coby back to the trailer, Mama and I sit on the living room sofa and watch reruns of sitcoms together.

"You know," she says. "Mrs. Whitson invited us to stop back by sometime. Why don't I take you to pick up your friend's guitar, and then we'll have a reason to visit?" Mama's staring at the television, but there's a slight anticipation in her voice, like it's something she's given some thought to.

"I don't think you need a reason," I say. "She invited you, Mama. You could stop by anytime. You don't need me." I'm a ball of nerves. I've rummaged in Mrs. Whitson's makeup drawer, used her lipstick, and stolen from her. And I'd be happy to avoid Kush as much as possible until I can get the hell out of town.

"No," Mama says. "I guess not. But what you've done here makes me proud. I'd like to be there, to see their faces. I'll take you tomorrow."

There's no getting out of it. "Okay, Mama. If that's what you want."

She pulls me in next to her and runs her fingernails through my hair. "Sweetheart, what I want is for your dreams to come true."

I hope to goodness I don't ruin hers.

The next day, Mama keeps me home. I guess she's still reeling from the doctor's accusatory words, because I feel fine. But I was up late worrying, so I sleep through most of the morning and around lunchtime I hear her coming up the stairs.

Mama cracks open the door. "You up?"

I waggle my cell phone at her. C.A. has been stealth-texting me with Kush news. Apparently, he'd called me an addict, a whore, and a drug dealer, among other things. I'm embarrassed, but my friends know it's not true, and they're the ones that count.

"Brought you some soup. Think you can eat?" Ribbons of celeried and carroted steam drift across the room.

"Smells good," I say.

Mama hands me the bowl and a spoon, then lays her hand across my forehead. There's so much love in her eyes, it's painful. How can my daddy cheat on her? She may not be as pretty or as skinny as some other women, but I'm holding a bowl of fresh-made chicken soup. She did that for me. And she'd do it for Daddy and Whitney, and anybody else who was feeling down. She'd even do it for Daddy's lady if the whole truth was laid out on the table.

"I love you, Mama," I say, curling up next to her.

"I love you, too, sugar. Now eat up, that soup will chase away the germs."

"Mama, I've got a broken ankle, not a cold."

She pats my cast and starts to get up.

"Mama?"

She stops.

"What's going to happen with Whitney?"

Mama sighs and sits back down on the foot of my bed, creating a wave in my mattress. I hold the soup in two hands till she's settled. "Your sister's got herself into something, hasn't she?"

It's not so much a question for me as a question for the universe.

"It's Sammy's fault." The words fall out harsh and I realize he scares me a little.

"Your sister loves that boy. Like me and your daddy, she promised to love him through thick and thin. Right now's their thin. And don't forget, they have a child together."

I look down at my quilt. "Is that worker going to take Coby away from her?"

"Not if she keeps her nose clean from here on out. Her going back to school will help."

I mutter, "Like keeping clean is likely."

Mama reaches over to press my good foot underneath the covers. "Amber, if something happens, we'll all have to step up and take care of that baby boy. Your sister may just have to learn the hard way."

"Would you be upset if she got a divorce?"

Mama looks toward the ceiling and runs her hand through her graying brown hair. "My first choice would be for them two to work things out, make things right for that baby."

"And if they can't?" Because that's the reality. Sammy won't ever be the kind of man who makes a good daddy and husband. He's talking about his guitar and his future, but really, it seems like his band is just another excuse to party.

"Well, I suppose there are worse things that could happen in the world." She pats my legs. "But let's just keep saying prayers that those two will come to their senses and start behaving like grown-ups. Eat up, then get dressed so we can get your friend's guitar."

I can't eat the soup. My stomach's in knots. I should give the money back to Sammy and forget this whole thing, get out of it as much as I possibly can. But what would I say to Mama about it?

I drop my face in my hands and rub the blood up into my cheeks. Once the money has changed hands, it will be over. Eddie will have had a cash sale. Sean will have a guitar that he thinks is a gift from his friends, and nobody will know any better for it. Sammy promised me it wouldn't be traceable and he'd be stupid not to keep it that way.

I glance up at my map. Sevenmile, Winston, Wilkesboro, Bristol, Nashville, New Orleans, Telluride. Soon, with any luck, I'll be starting on the first leg of my journey.

.   .   .

The Gibson lies across my lap and, surprisingly, now that the money is out of my hands, some of the guilt is gone, too. Eddie didn't even bat an eye when I gave him the balance, just brought the guitar from the back, already closed up in its hard black case.

Mama looks nice. She's wearing her go-to-town slacks and a pretty floral shirt I hardly ever see her wear. Her hair's pulled back from her face in combs and she's even slicked on some lipstick. When we pull into the Whitsons' driveway, I hug the guitar closer.

Mr. Whitson strides out of the new building next to the house to greet us. A white sign, painted with simple script letters in black, hangs above the door. *Whitson's Pottery.*

"Hello, Donna, Amber! Aneeta is so excited you've come by for a visit." He eyes me balancing on my cast. "How's that ankle?"

I shrug. "Still hurts some."

"Go on up to the house. Aneeta and the boys are inside."

Mama runs her hand through her hair and presses her blouse down. She purses her lips. Mama doesn't have any good girlfriends. She's been all about Daddy and me and Whitney forever.

"You okay, Mama?" I ask.

She straightens her shoulders. "I'm fine, sugar. Let's go surprise your friend."

At the door, Mrs. Whitson greets us with a big, warm smile. "Come in, come in. I'm so glad you two stopped by." Behind her, across the bar dividing the kitchen from the foyer, I can see Sean filling up glasses with tea. I don't see Kush anywhere around.

"*Amber.*" Mama prods me forward with the guitar case.

"What's this?" Mrs. Whitson says, looking up at me with wide eyes.

Oh God. I can't even look her in the eyes. It's *your* pink lipstick. It's *your* pill bottle. It's *my* greedy fingers all over your things.

I look down. "Um, it's for Sean."

Sean walks into the foyer balancing a tray of drinks in his hands, smiling at me. His eyes fall to the case and he freezes. Mrs. Whitson takes the drink tray from him and sets it on the coffee table. "Sit, please," she says.

"Go on," Mama says to me, her face alive with pleasure.

"So, um, we, well, some friends who want to remain anonymous, and the band, we got together and got this for you." I hold the case out.

Sean hesitates and then his hand crawls forward, the

slow reach of a man sensing what he's seeing is a mirage, but hopeful that, perhaps, it's the real thing. When his hand connects with the hard plastic, he lets out a breath and he takes the guitar from me.

He sits on the closest chair and opens the case. Slowly. Like I used to open my jewelry box with the spinning ballerina. The one that played "Clair de lune."

"The Gibson," he says. His hand strokes the slick varnish and plucks the strings. He looks up at me, his blue eyes wide.

Mama's grin is so big now you'd think she might pop like an overripe plum. Mrs. Whitson's hand is on her heart. Sean's looking at me like I'm a field of inflatable bouncy games at a MHHS Field Day and he's about to bounce.

I feel conflicted. It's everything I'd hoped. Sean is happy. My mama is proud. But I feel like a low-life criminal.

CHAPTER TWENTY-EIGHT

Later that night, I practice my songs alone. When I tire of them, I sing ballads I know by heart. "Pretty Saro." "The House Carpenter." "Barbara Allen." I finish with "Amazing Grace." The chorus burrows into my bones.

I doubt I'll get a do-over, but at least I can start fresh from this moment. I'd promised Sean we'd go to band practice tomorrow with Sammy so he could try out his new guitar. But once that's over, I'm out. Maybe Sean, Devon, Will, and I can start our own band. We can figure out some eclectic mix of tunes so everybody's happy.

Sammy can go blow himself.

My phone beeps from my nightstand.

It's a photo text from Sean. Of C.A. holding his guitar.
I text back a smiley face.

After a minute, I punch in a different number. Will's.
Hey, I type.

—Hey.

—What do you want to do when you grow up?

—Don't laugh.

—I won't.

—I want to be a wilderness camp director and a weekend bluegrass player.

—Really? A camp director?

—Told you not to laugh. What about you?

—I want to be onstage at a big music festival. And I'd
like to hike the Appalachian Trail. All of it.

—Me, too. I knew you were cool, Not So P & S. Can't
sleep?

I wait to see if he'll mention anything about breaking
up with Amber-o-zia, but he doesn't.

—I heard Sean got his guitar.

—Yeah.

—So who all donated? You could have asked me, you
know.

I don't want to lie to Will McKinney. But I can't tell
him the truth either.

—I can't tell you. Anonymous donors and all.

—Practice again soon?

He's not going to say anything about Amber-o-zia.

If there were an emoticon for a sigh, I'd use it.

—Yeah. Audition's getting close. See you tomorrow.

I shut the phone and turn out my light.

But it takes a long time to find sleep.

Sean picks me up in his uncle's truck to go to band practice. Sammy's managed to get us practice space on the stage at the Bobcat Lodge, a private club that sometimes hosts bands. They're closed on Wednesday nights, so it's just us, and the owner, who might be checking us out for a gig.

On the way over, I ask Sean about Kush. "What's his deal anyway? What happened between y'all?"

Sean turns down the music, classic Zeppelin, and eases into the story. "I told you Kush has a hard time sharing."

"Right."

Sean sighs. "So there was this girl, Daya. I'd just moved in with Aunt Aneeta and Uncle Eric and I was feeling so lost. Daya was the daughter of an Indian friend of my aunt's. Everyone was trying hard to make me feel welcome, really bending over backward, so I'd forget the shit with my mom. Anyway, Daya and I sort of connected. She loved music and had this big, raucous laugh. I liked hanging out with her."

I point at the road we need to turn on. "That doesn't sound like a big deal."

Sean hangs the steering wheel to the right. "It was. What I didn't know was that Kush had been crushing on Daya for a year."

"Oh."

"Right."

"So, that's it?" I ask, peering over at Sean. He looks tired. "That was enough for him to attack me to get back at you?"

We pull into the parking lot of the Lodge. It's a nondescript cinder block building with tiny darkened windows and an enormous American flag hanging next to the door.

"No." Sean rests his arm on the open window and stares up at a crow sitting on a telephone line. "I pulled away from Daya. It was more than I could deal with then. And Kush swooped in. She was vulnerable, and pissed as hell at me. It was a way to get back at me, because I still liked her, even if I couldn't show it."

"And?"

Sean leans his head back against the headrest. "It got ugly. Kush took Daya to some big party. They got wasted. He snuck her into the house. I think she was getting back at me when she had sex with him."

I watch the drummer pull up in a black Camaro.

"What a jerk." I look over at Sean again. "I can see how that would suck for you, but why is Kush so broken up about it still?" I wrap my hand around my necklace and slide it along my neck.

"Because his mom walked in on them."

"*No. Way.*"

Sean cracks his knuckles. "Yep, it was pretty bad. Aunt Aneeta grew up in a superconservative Indian immigrant family. She was mortified not only that Kush brought a girl back to the house drunk, but that he did it with the daughter of an Indian friend of hers."

Mrs. Whitson reminds me a little of Mama, but I bet she's a real tiger when she's pissed.

"But how could he blame *you* that he got caught?"

"He blames me for us living here."

Sammy sticks his head out of the door of the Lodge and yells out to us. "Are y'all coming or what?"

I hold up a finger. "One minute, Sammy."

He slams the door.

I turn back to Sean. "I still don't understand."

"Uncle Eric and Aunt Aneeta made the decision to move us here not too long after it happened. They said it was because I needed a stable home environment, not in a big city. But I think it's because Aunt Aneeta can't face her friends in Atlanta. But it doesn't matter. Kush has found a way to connect it all in his head and now I'm the spawn of Satan to him. It doesn't help that I'm working in the pottery studio and really love it. It all boils down to jealousy."

"What a prick," I say.

Sean shrugs. "Nah. He's a good guy deep down. He'd been an only child forever. He went from being the only one to being the one in trouble."

"Is it okay if I don't like him? He said some crazy shit about me."

Sean rubs his wayward hair. "Yeah, sorry about that."

"It's not your fault," I say, and smile. "And I'll try and see him through your eyes."

Sean smiles and grabs his guitar from behind the seat.

After we're finished, the Lodge owner calls Sean to the bar.

"What are they talking about?" Sammy's wrapping up cords and watching the two of them talk. Sean's nodding in his shy way and the owner claps him on the back every so often.

My hunch is the Lodge owner is trying to book Sean in for a night, on his own.

"I don't know." I slide onto the table. "He's probably asking him where he's from or something. Small town and all."

"Is that Whit's old shirt?"

I look down. "What, I don't meet your approval in this either?"

"You look nice. I was only going to say I don't remember that shirt looking so good on Whitney." He sets the extension cord on the table and brushes his arm against mine. It's almost like he did it on purpose.

When it's time to go, he insists on driving me home.

"You sure?" Sean asks, looking between us.

"Yeah, we're going to the same place, it's fine. Besides . . ." I look at my phone. "A certain blonde friend of ours has been texting *me* wanting to know if *you* are finished with practice."

Sean grins at the floor.

"Uh-huh. So maybe Daya is fading into memory?"

Sean looks at me. "Do you think C.A. would go out with me? I mean, she's a junior and I'm only a sophomore."

I throw my hands up and slide off the table onto my good leg. "You two are ridiculous. And perfect for each other."

As I follow Sammy out the door, I notice Sean's typing into his phone.

On the way home, I'm about to tell Sammy my decision. But then I stop. Sure, I can confess the party to Mama, but I can't confess my theft. It's a spiral of lies. I know Sammy.

He'll trade one blackmail for a worse one.

We drive on the back roads, cutting across hollers and down gravel roads. Sammy's like a watchdog, or the neighborhood patrol of drug dealers, always wanting to know who's up to what. As he drives, commenting on who's hanging out where and what their particular brand of poison is, I fret. There's got to be a way to get out of singing with him. If I'd only told Mama the truth about the party before this mess, then I'd be in the clear. But then Sean wouldn't have his Gibson.

Ideas swarm in my brain like gum balls. It's like I'm cranking the silver dial, waiting for the right one to drop into the hole and spiral down the curved shaft into my hands.

Sammy hits the pothole in front of the house and my shoulder knocks against the glass.

"Damn." I rub the sting as we pull up to Sammy and Whitney's trailer. But no great scheme knocks loose from the others.

When we park, I get out of the car. Lights shine out from the house. Sammy opens the trunk and starts pulling out gear to take inside.

"Do you need my help?" I lean against the open trunk.

Sammy puts the amp down on the ground. "I was thinking."

"Yeah?"

"What would you say to sharing the front of the stage with me, and I let Sean go."

I look up at the night sky. "God, Sammy. Are you serious? He's an amazing guitar player. He might actually get you some gigs."

Sammy's mouth jumps at the corners. He reaches into the trunk for his guitar case and pauses. "Yeah, he's good enough, but I'm just thinking one lead guitar is plenty. And with you co-fronting the band, it'd be as good as two guitar players."

"I don't know, Sammy. Playing with you makes Sean happy." For some reason I can't fathom.

Sammy lets go of the guitar and stands, grabbing my hand. "C'mon, Amber. Tell him he's out. Be my lead singer." He plays with my fingertips and I pull my hand away. He puts his hand on my hip and steps closer, his eyes intense.

"What the hell, Sammy?" I push against his chest, but he doesn't let go.

He puts his hand on my cheek and strokes me with his thumb. "God, you are so beautiful, and you don't even know it. Don't you want to front the band with me? Think of the places we could go."

I pause for a second when Sammy steps in and mashes

his lips against mine. I try and wriggle free, but he wraps his arms tighter around my waist.

His mouth is all over me, one hand holds me to him, and the other climbs to the back of my head, locking me into his kiss.

I hear the screen door slam and try to push him off of me. "Sammy, stop. Whitney," I mumble.

Whitney rounds the corner of the raised trunk. "Sammy? Do you need help carrying . . ." My eyes are wide as I stare at her, staring at us.

Sammy jumps away from me. I stagger backward, wiping his spit off my mouth as I regain my balance.

"What the hell!" Whitney yells.

Sammy turns and holds out his hand to her but Whitney charges past him, knocking his hand sideways as she passes it. When she gets to me she takes her palms and smacks me backward toward Mama and Daddy's.

"I knew it. I knew it." Her voice is shrill and loud. She keeps coming at me, like she's going to push me to the ground and stomp me into oblivion, before she suddenly turns and goes after Sammy. "Both of you, you kept saying you were talking about the band."

Her voice cracks as her anger caves into a high-pitched grief, and then she wheels on me again. "The Sunday school room. The texts. I thought he was pulling you into the drug thing, but this . . ." She buckles and drops her face into her hands, then starts rocking and keening like a wild animal.

"Whitney." I look at Sammy. "Tell her, Sammy."

He only flicks his eyes in my direction before returning them to Whitney, who's still rocking and hiding her face in her hands. "What? I don't have to tell her anything. She already knows, Amber. She's known you've had a crush on me since you were thirteen."

I scream. "That's not true! Whitney, it's not true!"

"Just fucking go." Her words fall like ashes. When she moves her hands and looks at me, I take a step back. Her eyes burn with anger.

As I limp across the yard, Giant following on my heels, I hear Whitney laying into Sammy again before Sammy's car starts up and he guns out of the driveway. When the car bangs in the hole out front, I hope it sent Sammy sailing through his own windshield.

The pleasure doesn't last long, though. My sister accused me of going after her husband. How can she really think I would do something like that to her? Can't she see it's Sammy she should blame?

That night I dream about flying. I'm soaring above the trees and the horizons are spread in every direction. Endless. Possible. I'm a bird of happiness. But nearby, the timpani beat of heavy wings grows louder. The scream of a hawk cuts across the sky. Panic beats in my bird breast. The hawk dives and cuts into my flight. I roll, beating frantic soft wings, and turn. The hawk stares back at me. Its eyes are filled with rage.

I sit bolt upright in bed.

Outside the clouds have gone and pinpricks of starlight shine through the window. I clutch Giant to me and let him lick my cheek.

What has Sammy done?

CHAPTER TWENTY-NINE

- -

When I walk through the door of her chorus room on Monday afternoon, Mrs. Early gives me a big hug. "Are you getting excited, hon?"

My audition is this Saturday, and there's still so much I have to do to get ready. I've got to type up my paperwork and clean my shoes. Will and I need to practice more and I need to figure out a way to keep my nervous stomach calm.

"I'm more of a wreck," I say honestly.

Will walks in behind me and stands by my side. He looks at me with a big, wide smile. "You're going to be great. I know it."

Mrs. Early beams at him. Then she turns away from us and to the rest of the chorus. "Okay, places, everyone!"

After a couple of run-throughs of the songs we're preparing for the end of the year recital, Mrs. Early holds up the glass bowl for Show-off Solos. The first name she calls is Will McKinney's.

I hear him clear his throat. "Mrs. Early, may we sing a duet?"

My eyes skip to his seat and he's waiting with a wink. Inside I feel the flutter of that butterfly.

Mrs. Early looks up at Will. "What do you have in mind?"

"I'd like to play my banjo and sing one of Amber's audition songs with her. So she can practice."

Mrs. Early nods her approval and smiles a little.

Will looks at me from across the room and holds out his hand. Ladies first.

I clomp down the stands. My ankle doesn't hurt at all anymore, but the doctor says three more weeks in my cast.

We sit in the chairs Will's set up, slightly turned toward each other. There are only a few inches between my knee and his, but I don't scoot my chair back. Will doesn't look at me as he pulls the banjo into his lap and plucks the opening chords for "I Wish My Love Was a Red, Red Rose." We've never sung it together before. It's only me who's sung it, and he's played to accompany me.

Will starts picking the tune on his banjo and sings first.

"I wish my love was a red,
red rose growing in yon garden fair.
And I to be the gardener, of her
I would take care.
There's not a month throughout
the year, that my love I'd renew
I'd garnish her with flowers fine,
sweet William, Thyme, and Rue."

He doesn't look at me as he sings, but the energy between us is palpable, and draws me toward him. It's a wire, a cord, a ribbon binding us. It's more than song.

Will stops then, and it's my turn to sing.

"I wish I was a butterfly,
I'd light on my love's breast,
And if I was a blue cuckoo,
I'd sing my love to rest,
And if I was a nightingale,
I'd sing the daylight clear,
I'd sit and sing for you, my Will,
for once I loved you dear."

The song is really for someone named Molly, but just then, singing Will's name instead felt right. Out of the corner of my eye I glance at him, to see if he's noticed. I see him smile to himself, but he keeps his eyes focused on his banjo as he sings the last stanza.

"I wish I was up on the mountain
and seated on the grass.
In my right hand, a jug of punch,
and on my knee, a lass.
I'd call for liquor freely and I'd pay before I go,
I'd roll my Amber in my arms, let
the wind blow high or low."

There's a loud murmur coming from the chorus in front of us, but I am frozen to my chair. He's swapped "mountain" for Dublin Town, and my name for Molly's. Will and I are both looking at our feet but that doesn't stop me from feeling the way I'm feeling. Like we're in each other arms. Like we're connected. Like we just had song sex in front of the entire chorus.

Somebody whistles and yells. "Turn on the AC, Mrs. Early. It's hot in here."

She clears her throat. "Okay. Thank you, Will. Thank you, Amber." She hustles us back to our chairs.

When chorus is over, I walk as fast as I can, even in my cast, to get out of the door first. My face is red, and my heart is doing flip-flops. I won't be able to say one intelligent word if Will talks to me.

"Amber," he calls behind me.

I close my eyes for a second and slow down so he can catch up to me.

When he does, Will touches my arm. "That was good," he says, smiling.

I want to sling my arms around Will's neck and push him up against the brick wall and press the length of me against the length of him. But instead I manage to meet his gaze and whisper, "Thank you."

Mama honks the horn.

"I gotta go."

"Hey."

"Yeah?" I wait.

"Um. I was wondering . . ." He looks down, shifts his banjo case to his other hand. "Would you want me to come with you to your audition on Saturday? To be your accompanist?"

"You'd do that?"

"I want to," he says, and opens the car door for me.

I nod and climb into the passenger seat of the minivan.

He slides the door shut and grins before turning away.

It takes a second before I look over at my mother, but when I do, I gasp, "Mama! What'd you do?"

She holds up a hand to her hair, newly colored a rich auburn and styled in long, soft layers. "Do you like it?"

"It looks amazing!"

Her smile is girlish. "Aneeta did it for me." Since last Tuesday, Mama and Mrs. Whitson have traded recipes, cooked in each other's kitchens, talked on the phone, and Mrs. Whitson even came to church with us on Sunday. Being around Mrs. Whitson makes me a little nervous, still, but Mama's the happiest I've seen her in years.

"Daddy's going to be floored." I can't stop staring at her. "Hey, let's go shopping this afternoon. There's a new consignment shop in town. You need something pretty to match your new 'do."

"Oh, I couldn't do that." Mama shakes her head.

"For me?" I put the tips of my fingers together and bat my eyelids at her.

She pulls the rearview mirror toward her and checks her reflection. When she sees herself, she smiles. "No," she says, readjusting the mirror. She places her hands firm on the wheel. "I'm going to do it for me."

We find a parking spot in the town lot and walk the cracked sidewalk to the new shop, "A-Z Me to You Consignments. Quality Clothes at Reasonable Prices." A couple of ladies we pass on the sidewalk comment on Mama's hair.

"You sure do like nice, Donna."

"That color suits you."

Mama grins and I can tell she's working hard not to seem too proud, but I like seeing her carry some pride.

A bell chimes when we push through the door. From the back a muffled voice calls out, "Be right there. Y'all look around."

Sure enough, they have a whole section of larger lady clothes. Lots and lots of nice brands like Lane Bryant and Doncaster, not double-knit stretch-waist pants that Mama tends to wear.

I help look and soon we have an armful of things for Mama to try on. She disappears behind the yellow-curtained dressing room door.

I'm picking through a rack of blouses when a young saleswoman appears. "Y'all finding everything you need?"

"Yes, thank you," I say.

Mama steps through the curtain, her eyes shining. "Amber, would you look at this?" She's wearing a cowl-necked blue top and a full print skirt. They look great on her.

"You look gorgeous."

Mama does a side-to-side twirl. "You think so?"

"Absolutely." I want to tell her Daddy will think she looks beautiful, too. But I don't.

Mama tries on a few more outfits and she actually seems to enjoy it. By the time she's finished, she's piled up a purse, a couple of pairs of shoes, and four or five out-fits. I'm not sure where she's going to wear all these new clothes, but there's no way I'm stopping her.

As the young woman rings up Mama's purchases, she pulls a handful of small white bottles out from behind the counter. "Do you like lotions? Try some of these samplers. My mother sells Body Soft products, if you're interested."

Mama slowly flips the cap on a bottle. She raises it to her nose, but the lilac smell hits us both quick. The bottle drops from Mama's fingers.

It's the scent.

Daddy's other woman.

Lilac with a hint of vanilla and spice.

Mama shoves a handful of bills at the saleslady and grabs the bags. "Come on, sugar. Let's go."

The saleslady calls after us. "But your change. There's over three dollars here."

"You can keep it." Mama's mouth is set in a tight line, her expression a combination of resolve, anger, and sad-ness.

Mama knows. She knows about Daddy's girlfriend.

I stomp after her, the stupid cast slowing me down. "Mama?"

Mama turns. Her eyes meet mine and in them, pain flashes like the bright scales of a rainbow trout.

My heart breaks in two. "I love you, Mama."

She nods and takes a deep breath. "I love you, too, sugar." Her fists clench around her shopping bags before she whispers, "This family. You, your sister, Coby, your daddy. You are my world. You understand? And it is my fight, my job to keep us together."

I nod, fighting back tears. Knowing that she knows I know. I take the bags from her hand.

"Let's go home," I say.

"Home," Mama says.

In my room, I punch Will's number into my phone. He answers on the first ring.

"Amber." The way he says my name fills me up, and I fight the urge to cry into the speaker.

"I need to sing. Right this minute." My voice cracks even though I'm fighting to keep it strong.

"Go ahead."

I love him for not asking why.

I sing one to make me feel good, Dolly Parton's "Little Sparrow," and let the sweet notes surge down through me and around and I push out all the dark feelings on my exhales.

When I finish, he sighs, a sound sweeter than any music I could ever make.

We're silent for a minute.

"Will?"

"Yeah."

"Do you know if your dad has ever cheated on your mom?" I lie back on the bed and stare up at my ceiling, tears welling up.

"I don't think so."

"My daddy's cheating on my mama."

He doesn't try to fill in the space with small talk as he waits for me to say something else. Then he says, "That must hurt like hell."

After a minute, I wipe away the tears and spit out the other thing bothering me. "Can I ask you something else?"

"Anything."

"When you drove me up on the mountain that day after school, were you expecting what happened to happen?"

"You mean did I expect we'd hook up?"

"Yes." I curl up into a little ball, waiting.

He's quiet, then says, "I guess a part of me hoped we might."

His honesty silences me. "Is that what kind of girl you thought I was?"

"Of course not."

"Then how come you were so prepared?"

Will laughs. "I'm a teenage boy. With a mom who's been preaching at me for years. I've carried condoms in my wallet since the ninth grade, not that I needed them much."

"Oh." I pause. "Will?"

"Yeah?"

"Why did you cheat on Amber-o-zia?"

He sighs heavily. "Because I was a dick. To you and to her. Because I was on a mountain with an incredibly beautiful and interesting girl I've been stealing glances at for two years. Because I'm a boy, and it felt good." He pauses. "Amber, I'm sorry. It was way more than I expected and since then, I've wished I could take it back." He pauses. "Me and Amber-o-zia were never like that."

I close my eyes. "I don't want you to think it's always like that for me."

"I don't. Hey, Amber?"

"Yeah?"

"I've got to go. My dad's calling me."

"Oh. Okay. Bye."

What am I doing calling Will McKinney, expecting him to want to listen to me sing, to hear about my problems? What am I doing, thinking something real might be happening between us? Even if he did refer to Amber-o-zia in the past tense.

"I'll see you at school," he says, and then he's gone. I lay the phone back down on my nightstand and look at the red tacks on my map.

After a few minutes, I stand up and pull out the one stuck on Sevenmile and put it on the dresser. The only red tack left is the one for Winston-Salem. My future.

CHAPTER THIRTY

I'm dressing for school on Friday morning when Mama comes into my room. "What happened between you and your sister?"

I stop, one hand still on the zipper of my skirt. "What do you mean?"

"Amber Delaine, I'm not blind. She hasn't said a word to you in more than a week. That's not like the two of you."

I ache to tell Mama the truth. But nothing bad has come of what I did. Sean's got his guitar. Sean's aunt and uncle haven't discovered the missing pills. And even though Whitney thinks I'm a husband-stealing bitch, at least I'm out of the band. Sometimes what nobody knows doesn't hurt a thing.

But I can hit near the truth. "She thinks I was flirting with Sammy."

Mama's mouth drops. "She *what*?"

I finish zipping up my skirt and turn toward the big open window, then face my mama again. "She thinks I like him, God knows why, in an *unsisterly* way."

Mama fiddles with the strand of red beads hanging around her neck. "That beats anything I've heard all week. You'd as soon throw Sammy in a nest of rattlesnakes as say two kind words to him."

"Well, you asked. That's why she's not talking to me."

Mama shakes her head. "Crazy talk."

"Thanks, Mama."

"Don't thank me. You two need to work it out. This tension is wearing on my nerves."

Devon picks me up with a frozen coffee in his hand. "Mom McKinney daily special," he says, and hands it to me. "With toffee chips for luck."

I take a sip. I've lied to Mama and Daddy, to Whitney, to Sean, and even to Will about where the guitar money came from. But I've got to tell something true to Devon.

"Devon."

"Super-tasty, correct?" he asks, starting off down the driveway.

"Yes, it is. But I need to tell you something."

He slows the Jeep and looks at me. "Do I need to pull over?"

I shake my head. "No, keep driving. You need another focus."

He puts his hand to his chest between shifting gears. "Please tell me you didn't really sleep with Kush."

"*What?*" I roll my eyes. "He added that to his hit parade?"

Devon nods and pats my shoulder. "But don't fret. Everyone's catching on to him. And it isn't pretty." He mimics somebody stirring a pot.

I rub the condensation on the side of the plastic cup, worrying patterns into the wet surface. "No. I didn't hook up with Kush." I pause before getting out the next words quickly. "But I did have sex with Will."

Devon hits the brakes so hard we both fling forward. "Oh my god. *When?* What was it like?"

He seems completely unconcerned I named his brother. "You're not mad?"

He starts driving again and looks over at me. "*Mad?* I love my brother. I love you. It's the closest I can ever come to hooking up with you myself."

"Devon, I'm serious."

This time, Devon does pull the car over at the turn-in

to someone's vacation home. "Okay. I'm serious, too. Amber, I don't care. When did it happen? This week?"

I twirl the straw in my fingers and whisper, "The first day of school."

Devon's mouth drops open. "Shut the hell up."

I grimace. "Stop acting so shocked. It just happened. I've felt guilty for so long. About Amber-o-zia. About not telling you. About it happening at all."

Devon's quiet for a minute. "Has he been nice to you?"

"Will?" I ask.

Devon's hand clutches the gearshift, waiting on my answer. "Yeah."

"He has been nice. He never said anything to anybody. He never tried anything again." The memory of the kiss at Sizz's house flares in my brain. But that was me, not Will. "He's a good guy, Devon."

Devon lets go of the gearshift and grabs his cup out of the cup holder and takes a sip. "Yeah. He is. So . . . what now? Are you two dating?"

Devon's sweet concern and his question open something inside me. Big tears slide down onto my cheeks. Then my nose starts running. Devon pats my back and I blow my nose into a Kleenex.

I shake my head and finally manage to speak again. "No. He hasn't even told me that he broke up with

Amber-o-zia. I keep waiting. Hoping . . ." My voice trails off. Then I whisper. "I really like him, Devon."

Devon rubs my shoulder. "Oh, Plain and Small. Let's see what Devon can do."

He pulls back onto the road and drives us to school.

Mrs. Early calls me down to the floor during chorus to practice my audition pieces. This is it. My last practice before the moment when I will either fall or stand as tall as the hills I call home.

Will comes down to play his banjo and Mrs. Early joins him on the piano.

We go in the order I'll follow at the audition. I start with "Shenandoah," which everyone in the chorus knows. Then I move into "I Wish My Love Was a Red, Red Rose," though this time I sing the traditional lyrics. My last song is "Ave Maria." It hasn't been as hard as I'd thought it'd be to sing in Latin.

Will starts in on the banjo, a slow plinking of strings that ascends upward until I open my mouth.

"Ave Maria . . ."

I close my eyes and my arms lift slightly from my sides. I picture the song swirling inside of me, like butterflies. I draw the notes out. When I release the words, they fly around the room. The chorus is silent, listening, and all I hear is the sound Will and I make. When the final notes of my last "Maria" land, there's a collective inhale. It's a quiet I wouldn't mind living in for a while.

Slowly, my classmates start to clap. I open my eyes to see Mrs. Early clapping with them. "Amber, dear, I think you're ready."

The rest of the chorus murmurs in agreement. Will shouts, "Damn straight, she's ready!" and stands up next to me with a big smile on his face.

After chorus, I head out front and don't see anybody's car.

"Need a ride?" Will's by my side, his backpack slung over his shoulder, banjo case in his hand. Outside of the chorus room, Will's grin is wicked.

"I get in trouble when I go for rides with you, Will McKinney."

"Come on, it's only a ride."

Right then, Mama pulls up to the curb.

I look back at him and smile. "Maybe another time."

I start to get into the car but Will stops me with a hand on my arm. He looks down, then looks back up at me. He looks a little nervous. "Hey, I don't know if you heard about me and Amber-o-zia."

I shrug. "Maybe. But I don't put too much stock in gossip."

He drops his hand. "Fair enough." He shrugs. "But it's true. It took me longer than it should have—I kept hoping she'd say the words—but in the end I had to be honest with her about my feelings."

"Okay," I say. When Will doesn't say anything else right away, I reach for the door handle.

"You said maybe another time. For a ride. How about tomorrow?"

I furrow my brow. "To Boone? Mama's driving. She insisted, actually."

Will swings the banjo case, then stops. "I was thinking more about after. I was wondering if you'd want to go with me to C.A.'s party. You know, like a date."

"A date?" I take a breath. "Did Devon talk to you?"

Will eyes are questioning. "Devon? I haven't seen him since breakfast."

His words settle in. Devon didn't say anything. This is all coming from Will. An "Ave Maria" tries to burst its way past my lips, but I only smile. "Yeah. Okay. A date." I open the car door. "See you in the morning."

Will's rocking on his heels and swinging his banjo case, watching us pull away.

Mama glances behind us. "Is that Judge McKinney's older son?" she asks me.

"Uh-huh," I answer, a grin bursting like fireworks across my face.

"Uh-huh," she repeats, her face mama-wise, her voice shrewd. Then she pats my leg. "I'm so proud of you, sugar. A fellow like that would be a fool not to see it, too."

I whisper, "I think he does, Mama."

CHAPTER THIRTY-ONE

The next morning, the whole house is in an uproar. I'm tearing through my closet, worried that the outfit I've chosen is wrong. Mama's yelling at Daddy about going to work instead of coming with us. Whitney's yelling about who's going to watch Coby because she and Sammy have "things to do."

I pull Whitney into the stairwell. "Are you ever going to talk to me?"

She lowers her brows and then looks up at the ceiling.

"Listen to me," I whisper. "I didn't kiss Sammy! He kissed me. How could you not have seen me pushing him away? I was trying to get away from him."

Whitney crosses her arms and leans sideways against

the wall, but I catch her glancing at me first.

I talk fast while I know she's listening. "Maybe he thought I still had a crush on him and if he kissed me, I would agree about getting rid of Sean."

Whitney shifts slightly. She's almost facing me.

"C'mon, Whit. You know it wasn't real."

She looks away, then scuffs her foot on the hardwood floor.

"Whitney?" I whisper.

She drops her arms, and searches my face. "But he kissed you." There's something resigned in the way she says it.

"Nothing would have happened, Whitney. Not once he'd gotten me to do what he wanted."

She shrugs, then laughs, sadly. "Right, look at you. He'd have taken it as far as you would have let him."

Sammy bellows from the front porch. "Whitney, let's go. I've got to meet a friend."

"I've got to go," she whispers.

At the last second, she leans forward and hugs me hard. "Good luck. I hope you get in. I want you to get out of here."

When we finally load into the van, Mama, me, and Coby, I'm so frazzled I can't think. My audition is in two hours, which is plenty of time, except Mama's driving and she is a *careful* driver.

Once I calm down a little, I notice Mama looks great. Hair's fixed just so and she's got on her new pretty skirt and sweater combination. There's a light in her eyes I've missed seeing.

"Mama, you look gorgeous."

"Gook gorjuice," Coby mimics from the backseat.

Mama laughs. "Thank you, baby boy."

We swing by the McKinneys' first. Will's already waiting on the front porch, and when he walks down the drive, black button-down shirt tucked into dark jeans with a shiny pair of Sunday black shoes, it's like I'm seeing a young Johnny Cash, or at least the actor who played him in that movie, *Walk the Line*.

I start to climb out of the front seat and get in the back with Coby, but Will stops me.

"No, stay there. I don't mind hanging out in the back." He places his banjo case behind the second row of seats and climbs in next to Coby.

I'm too nervous to talk, so I sing scales softly and watch the scenery pass as we drive. What will my life be like, if I'm surrounded by concrete and city people? They may not judge me based on my family's history, but they won't know me either. They'll look at my clothes, they'll hear my accent, and they'll figure out where I'm from and come up with their own opinions of who I am. Damned if I do, and damned if I don't, that's what Daddy says sometimes.

Slowly we curve our way through Avery County into Watauga County, home of Appalachian State University in Boone. Mama's hands start to sweat as the traffic picks up on Highway 221.

"You're doing great, Mama."

"No talking, Amber."

"But you need to get over to the left lane."

Mama whimpers as she looks over her left shoulder, hits her signal, looks again, then finally starts to move. A car horn honks. Mama jerks.

"It's okay, Mama, you got it."

Will speaks up. "You want me to drive, Mrs. Vaughn?"

Her hands are trembling. "No. I can do this. How am I ever going to help run a catering business if I can't drive?"

The red light gives us a break and I put my hand on Mama's arm, helping her steady its shaking.

"What?" I give her a curious look.

"Aneeta has asked me to go into business with her. She likes my desserts and thinks having a local cook will help make folks more confident about hiring a stranger. We even have a name, East-West Mamas' Cooking."

"Are you serious?"

"That's great," Will chimes in from the backseat.

She giggles, then grips the steering wheel, alert as the left-turn arrow flashes green. "No talking, I'll tell you later. Just tell me when to turn. With plenty of warning."

Looking down at my audition materials, I direct her to the music building and we find visitors' parking. Mama unlatches Coby and hoists him onto her hip.

Will sidles up next to me. We walk with our arms close. When we get to the stairs to the entrance, he slips his hand around mine.

I peek at our locked fingers. The idea of an us begins to take root and I feel it, warm and squiggly, burrowing into my center.

Mama walks ahead of us with Coby.

"So, does Daddy know?" I ask her. Mama, a business-woman. I like it.

"I told him Wednesday. He wasn't happy."

Good. Maybe it will knock some sense into him. "What did he say?"

"He said, Didn't I have enough to do at home in my own kitchen?"

"And what'd you say?"

"I said if I had a husband that cared more about his own kitchen, then his opinion might make a difference to me." She glances back at us. Her eyes flit to our hands and she smiles. "Excuse me, Will, if this sounds petty."

Will shakes his head in a quick no.

Mama keeps talking to me as we approach the front door. "So I told him, he'd made his own bed and now his wife was going to be a businesswoman and if he was lucky I might use some of my money for the phone bill. But I might use it all for salon appointments and new skirts."

I throw my head back and laugh. I'm happy to see this strong version of my mama. I like her. A lot. And I'm happy to have my hand tucked into Will's. Happy they're both here to help me chase my dreams. "I love you, Mama."

"I love you, too, Amber Delaine." She looks up at the sign on the door, NC-ARTS AUDITIONS. "It's time for you to shine, sugar."

In the auditorium, I try to keep my hands from shaking as I present the panel my paperwork. Other singers fidget in chairs near the sides of the stage waiting their turns. Families are settled into the very back rows sitting quietly. I watch a boy who looks sort of like Sean kill the songs from *West Side Story* for his drama department audition. Another girl sings arias from an opera. She's amazing. I can see the judges scribbling furiously on the papers in front of them. Each vocal applicant is accompanied by piano.

Maybe I've made a mistake. Maybe the banjo was a

bad idea. Its sound is unique, and not everybody likes it. I start jiggling my knee so hard, I shake the seats around me.

Will whispers, "You've got this."

I nod.

He puts a hand on my knee to calm me as another girl sings "Ave Maria" to piano.

Finally, it's my turn.

The male judge calls my name and I approach the stage. Slick wooden stairs lead up from the audience. My cast sounds like a hammer as I walk to the microphone set center stage. Will slips into a chair on the side.

One of the female judges looks down at my paperwork, then up at Will. "Banjo? For 'Ave Maria'?" She doesn't wait for an answer, but I hear her mumble, "Interesting."

I close my eyes for a minute and try to calm my beating heart. If I do this, I'll be someone special. Gone. Living a new life, away from Sevenmile. I look at Mama and Coby and my throat constricts. Mama smiles and nods. She waves Coby's little hand.

I put my palms over my stomach. Will takes his cue and starts moving his fingers on the strings, bringing his instrument to life. I open my mouth. For a split second, I think nothing's going to come out, but then the song soars from my center. I open the door and let the song-bird fly through. I imagine sitting out on the mountaintop with Will, sending my notes out to the sky. My voice wavers, but not enough to make a difference. I get through "Shenandoah" and "I Wish My Love Was a Red, Red Rose" without incident. Then it's time for "Ave Maria."

The judge who'd made the banjo comment leans back in her chair and crosses her arms.

I glance at Will and see that he's there, waiting on me. He winks and I almost start laughing. But then he starts playing that slow beautiful movement of strings that climbs like they're headed for heaven itself.

I open my mouth and allow all my high and lonesome to flow out in my song. If they want me, they're going to have to want to shape the raw voice I have. I can't sing arias like the girl with all the rounded notes and rolling crescendos. I can only sing like me.

When I finish, I take a huge gulp of air.

The skeptical judge uncrosses her arms and allows a small "humph," but from her raised eyebrows, I can tell she's been pleasantly surprised. Whether they'll want me or not, though, who knows.

I do notice all three of the judges on the review panel are making furious notes, almost as fast as they had after the opera singer.

"Thank you," I say. "Thank you so much."

I look for Mama to gauge her reaction, as I leave the

stage, but she's not in her seat.

Will and I find her in the hallway, her brow furrowed, talking on her cell phone and nodding. She looks up and holds up one finger. We stop and wait.

She hangs up.

"Who was that?" I ask.

"Your daddy." Her mouth is a straight, tense line.

"Is everything okay?" Will asks her.

She sighs and picks up Coby from the mess of bubble wrap he's found to pop. "Just a little issue at home," she says. "But let's not worry about that right now. Today's your day, Amber honey. Your daddy's going to take care of it." She looks between the two of us. "Well? What did they say?"

My grin spills over. "They were impressed by Will and his banjo."

"And by your amazing voice." He looks at me and grabs my hand again, right in front of Mama.

Mama's smile is guarded. "I never thought I'd say this, but this might be a real good thing for you." She kisses Coby's head. "A real good thing to get away."

"Mama?" I ask.

"Nothing, honey. I'm so proud of you."

CHAPTER THIRTY-TWO

When we get back to Sevenmile, Mama drops Will and me off at his car. We'd gone out to eat in Boone after the audition.

"Bye, Mama." I lean back across the seat and kiss Coby, then kiss her on the cheek. "I had a great time today. Thank you."

"You're welcome, sugar. I'm so glad things are okay with you." She turns to Will. "Bring her home by midnight, no later."

"Yes, ma'am."

Mama drives away.

Now it's already well past dark, and the party's gotten started when we get to C.A.'s condominium complex.

Through the brightly lit window, I can see Sean dancing with C.A.

Nerves pop up like dandelions. Will and I have been holding hands all day, but walking in holding hands in front of everybody is going to cause some kind of scene.

I look over at Will, and he's started to unlatch his banjo case.

"What are you doing?" I ask him.

He looks up, hands me the case, and straps the banjo around himself. "Surprise," he says, grinning.

We don't knock. The door opens onto a small alcove connected to the living room, where some people are dancing. We slip past them and head toward the kitchen.

When we get there, Devon shimmies over to us, a blue plastic cup in each hand. "Plain and Small." He kisses me on each cheek, *à la française*, he calls it.

"Will," he says, and looks over the rim of nonexistent glasses at his brother, who's right by my side.

Devon thrusts a cup into my hand. "Here. Liquid courage." As usual, Devon wants me to dance.

"Don't think I can tonight." I point down. "Ankle."

A tall, slightly awkward boy who doesn't look comfortable with his height yet joins us, walking up right next to Devon. He has big, curly brown hair and a gap-toothed grin. He puts out his hand and says, "Hi, y'all. I'm Gil, C.A.'s cousin from Bristol."

"Hey. I'm Amber," I say, smiling. "It's so nice to meet you."

There's a look that flashes from Devon to Gil to Devon. No wonder Devon hasn't been devastated by how things turned out with Kush. Judging by the bouncy excitement ricocheting between Gil and Devon, my guess is there's a real *thing* between them.

"Devon?" I cock my head, then glance at Gil.

Devon grins and pushes Gil toward me. "Gil, Amber here is my BFF. Amber, Gil is my . . ." Devon pulls Gil's elbow so they're both leaning in and whispers to just me and Will, "Well, I'm not sure what he is, but we've been Skyping every night. Poor thing's lonely up in Bristol."

Will and I laugh as Devon and Gil step back, their eyes sparking at each other.

"Poor thing, indeed," Will says as our hostess, C.A., bounces in, breathless and laughing, Sean right behind her.

"Hey, Amber, how'd it go today?" Sean asks me, his blue eyes big and bright.

He's the first person to mention my audition.

"Really good, Sean. Thank you."

Will starts playing his banjo then—and it's the bouncy theme to *The Beverly Hillbillies*, a tune I haven't heard since the first soccer game of the year. He croons,

> *"Now listen to a story 'bout this girl Amber,*
> *Who traveled up the road to sing a song for sure,*
> *And then one day she was sitting on a chair,*
> *When along came a letter said,*
> *Yes, we want you here!*
> *Winston-Salem, skyscrapers, shopping malls!"*

He finishes with a flourish on the strings and everybody bursts into laughter.

And that's when Will turns and kisses me. Square on the lips for all of our friends to see.

I feel the blood rise to my cheeks, but I kiss him right back.

I look back at our friends and see Devon let out a big, dramatic breath. "Well, now."

"How'd y'all like my song?" Will turns in a circle, threatening to wipe everybody out with the neck of his banjo.

C.A. pats our heads like we're children. "That's nice, Will, but I'm turning the music back on. It's time to dance!"

The music goes up and Sean, C.A., Gil, and Devon push each other into the living room. Even Deana May is there, about to dance with a boy I recognize from chorus. Will and I don't go anywhere. We stay in the kitchen, me sitting on a stool and Will moving to stand in front of me. I put my hands on his hips and he leans forward until his perfect lips meet mine. I breathe into his kisses and he runs his fingers across the back of my neck, up along my jawline, behind my earlobes. I feel like I'm going to burst with the rightness of it.

He murmurs against my ear, "I almost don't want you to get into that school."

I slip my thumbs into his waistband and pull him closer, locking him against me, between my legs. "They have a college."

Our tongues collide and—there's a banging on the door. Louder than the music.

Will and I break apart, give each other a questioning look, and walk to the living room, where everybody else is. Someone peeks out the window. "It's somebody's dad. And the cops!"

Cups and bottles disappear quick, and then C.A. opens the door. Someone turns off the stereo.

Mr. Whitson fills the door frame, one of the new county officers by his side, all dark blue uniform and shiny badge. Mr. Whitson looks angry. "Hello, young lady," he says to C.A. "I need to see Sean." His voice is harsh as it travels down the narrow hall.

Sean cuts through the crowd to meet his uncle. "What's up, Uncle Eric?"

Mr. Whitson's face is hard. Harder than I've ever seen it. "We'll talk about it outside. We've gotta go."

C.A. takes a step forward, then stops, thinking better of it, I guess.

Mr. Whitson and the officer separate, allowing Sean to move through the door between them. The cop hesitates and looks around the room. "I'd suggest you go ahead and break this party up. Unless you want me to call for backup."

"Yes, sir," C.A. says. Everybody's already grabbing purses and coats.

When the door shuts, the room erupts in speculation.

"What do you think Sean did?"

"Oh my God, C.A., the cops were here."

It sounds like the chattering of crows. Then, I think—

Today, after my audition. That phone call from Daddy. Something's happened. Something with my sister, and that means something with Sammy. A sinking suspicion settles into my bones, and I lean against the wall, wishing I were invisible.

Devon watches Sean, Mr. Whitson, and the police officer from the window. "Oh my God, what was that? Sean isn't the kind of guy the cops show up for. Do you know what he did?" he asks me.

I shake my head, but I can't talk.

Will's packing up his banjo. "Let's go to our house, have a porch party."

He leans in to kiss me again but I look away. "I need to go home," I say to no one. I look back at Will.

"Home?" A quick hurt flashes across his face.

"Yeah," I whisper.

On the car ride home, I stare mutely out the window. I can't stop thinking about Mama on the phone outside the audition. Her serious face. The flashes of disappointment that followed the rest of the day. And if it really is something with Sammy and Whitney, then is it possible they found that stupid bottle, and connected it to the Whitsons? To Sean? I close my eyes for a second and replay every conversation I've had with Sammy. No, it can't be. He swore the bottle was gone.

Will interrupts my thoughts. "I don't understand, Amber. Did I do something?"

I press my hands against my face, hoping to stop the shame I feel inside. "No, you didn't do anything, Will." I pause. "I did something. Something really, really bad."

I look out the window again, and my breath steams the glass. I feel it all. All of the anger I felt the night after I took the pills. Anger at Kush, yes, but an even deeper anger, too. At Mama, and at Whitney, for not fighting back. At Daddy. At Sammy. But all of that hot anger, and now, all I feel is chills.

Will pulls over into the car wash parking lot. It's the same spot we turned into before going to the party in Erwin earlier this fall. I almost laugh at the coincidence, but can't.

Will faces me and touches my hand. "I'm listening."

I rub my arms. "Remember how you said you needed to stay away from guys like Sammy, because of the stuff with your dad?"

"Yes."

"Well, the same thing's happened to Sean."

"Whoa." Will leans back against the seat. "Sucks for him."

"You don't understand," I say. "Sean didn't do anything. *I* did. I took pills from his aunt and uncle and Sammy gave me the money. It's how I bought Sean his guitar."

Will shifts in his seat again and turns back toward me, leaning close. "What are you talking about?"

I can't meet his eyes. "I stole pills. For Sammy."

"You *what*?"

"Don't make me say it again."

"Jesus, Amber. Please tell me you didn't take the prescription bottle."

I'm quiet, even as I talk. "Sammy took the bottle. I tried to get it back, but he promised me it would never link back to anyone. Besides, it had Kush's name on it, not Sean's." But of course the Whitsons would look at Sean. He's the one with the new guitar. He's the one with the past.

Will stares out at the road and rubs at the scar on his cheek. Then he starts the car without saying anything and starts driving again.

"Will, talk to me." How can I make him understand it made a horrible kind of sense in the moment? That I was so incredibly angry at Kush? That at the time, Sean having the thing he most wanted seemed to be the only sure bet. That if Sean got his dream because of me, then I might get mine, too.

Will shakes his head, and his voice is quiet. "I don't know what to say." He flicks the signal to turn onto my road.

When he pulls into my driveway, I say more to myself than him, "I made a stupid mistake."

Will takes my hand again. "Amber, it wasn't just stupid. It was illegal. The only reason I didn't end up in huge trouble is because of my dad." He leans against the window. "Look, I get that you were trying to do a good thing. But how you did it was crazy. Why didn't you go to your church? Or ask your friends?"

"I did ask . . ." But I drop it. I didn't ask enough. I didn't try hard enough. All I know was that Kush made me crazy and I acted impulsively. And when I had chances to fess up, I kept going. I did everything wrong.

And in that moment, I know I can't get Will involved in my mess. I can't risk the tender balance he's found with Judge McKinney.

I take a deep breath and pull my hand free from his. "Will."

"Yeah?" His hand rests on his thigh like he's waiting for mine to come back.

"I'm . . . not sure us dating is such a good idea."

"What are you talking about?" He tries to lock me down with his eyes but I look out the windshield.

"We're so different. I mean, don't you think this is sort of a fluke?"

"You're crazy," he says. "We're great together."

He's making this hard. "No, Will. We're not. We play great music together, but beyond that, we're nothing alike." I bite my lower lip to hold back the words I really want to say.

He rubs his hair off his forehead and I see the muscle in his jaw working, his eyebrows bunched like he's trying to figure me out. "I told you before, Amber. I don't think I'm better than people from here."

I plow on. I'm breaking my own heart, but I'm not going to kill Will's dream, too. Not like I think I've done to Sean's. "It's not that. I'm not ready for a relationship, Will. I want to focus on myself." I face him and look him square in the eyes, keeping mine free of emotion. It's not a complete lie. At least not till I work out whatever mess I've gotten Sean into. Besides, this is neater. And Judge McKinney won't fault him if I'm not around.

He stares back, searching for something in my face. After a long second, he straightens, then leans across me and opens the door, just barely brushing my arm. Cold air rushes in. "Good night, Amber," he says. Will's expression is awful, his jaw stiff.

I climb out and push the door shut.

Will drives away, and I watch. His taillights grow smaller and smaller until they're gone.

My hand opens and closes, feeling the ghost of his hand, the warmth trailing away like a dying campfire.

CHAPTER THIRTY-THREE

The house is dark except for the flickering light of the television.

I linger for a minute outside, under the maple trees. I watch bats dart across the cow field. A chant of *stupid, stupid, stupid* rushes through my head. I'd been ignoring it, but I always knew, somehow, I'd end up found out. That I wouldn't go unpunished for my sins. And now I've let Will go, too.

I hug my arms to myself and lean against the tree's wide trunk. I allow myself a moment to think about something good, something that should have made me happy. Will's kisses in C.A.'s kitchen, less than an hour ago. Will's wicked smile onstage, earlier today. His belief in me, always.

I wipe away the wet tears of regret rolling down my cheeks, then push myself back to standing and walk inside the house. I've got to be strong. I've got to trust my decision was the right one.

Inside, Mama is slumped in Daddy's recliner, a Kleenex wadded in one hand, her face red and swollen from crying.

I feel my stomach drop to my feet, but I knew something was going on. "Mama?"

She turns in the chair to face me.

"Mama, what's wrong?"

A strangled cry tears her throat. I go and crawl into the recliner with her, curling up on her lap like I'm six.

"Oh, baby." She sniffles in my hair. "They came for Coby."

I pick my head up and look at her. "*What?*"

She sighs and dabs at her eyes. "Your sister and Sammy got taken into custody. Again. Social Services came for Coby." A new sob escapes her lips. I hug her.

"But what about us? Wouldn't they have left Coby with you and Daddy?" Why on earth wouldn't they have left him with us?

Mama shakes her head as tears roll down her cheeks. "No, sugar, they say they have evidence that we might not be fit to take care of him." Her shoulders curl and uncurl with the shake of her breath. "He's in foster care."

Poor Coby. My sweet nephew in some stranger's house. He must be so confused. So lost.

"Where's Daddy?" I ask, nervous.

Mama folds her arms around me. "Down to the police station, trying to make heads or tails of this mess."

Panic jumps inside my chest. Daddy's going to find out what I've done, before I've had a chance to tell anyone myself. Sammy's probably being questioned as we speak.

For the first time in hours, I think about my audition, the faces of those judges and the way it made me feel to know I'd captured my audience. That I'd surprised them.

Mama and I sit for hours. I feel the confession bursting inside but I also hear Whitney's practical voice playing in my head. "You don't know for sure if that's why your friend's in trouble. Just play it cool. You've already lost your boyfriend. You want to lose Mama's trust, too?"

Daddy walks through the door around 1:00 a.m.

"Well?" Mama asks him.

"They won't let her go. Not yet."

Mama's chest rattles with a sob and Daddy comes over, scooping her into his arms like she's no bigger than a rag doll.

I watch them as they hold each other and I see the love. It may not look the way most people want it to look, but it's plain as daylight to me.

"Good night," I say and leave, holding tight to the image of the two of them in each other's arms.

The next morning Mama is in her house robe when I clatter down the stairs in my Sunday clothes.

"Church?" I ask.

Mama shakes her head and sips her coffee. Daddy's still in bed after staying up till the tiny hours of the morning. I can't remember the last time Mama skipped a Sunday service.

"Any news?"

Mama sets her cup down with a rattle on the kitchen table that had been her mother's. "Sammy had a lunch box full of cash and prescription drugs he'd gotten off other folks. Some they're pretty sure he stole, but some seems to have been sold to him by people looking to make a buck. Regardless, your brother-in-law is most likely going to end up with some jail time."

I swallow. "How do they know who the other people are?"

"Names on the pill bottles, I reckon."

This is *so* bad. It's not fair if Sean gets in trouble for what I've done.

"And Whitney?" I ask.

Mama shakes her head and drums her fingers on

the table. "Well, the magistrate knows the situation, and knows her as a friend of his daughter's from school. They didn't catch her selling, just in the vehicle with him. He's saying that he thinks they can sentence light. We're hoping she'll end up with a plea. Your daddy's trying to talk her into helping out the law, but for now they're keeping her in the county jail."

"Is she going to tell them the truth about Sammy?"

If she won't, I sure will.

"Yes, sugar. Her child is at stake." Mama's voice cracks as she raises her coffee cup to her lips. "And that husband of hers is a no-account SOB."

It's the closest I've ever heard my mama come to cursing.

I am going to break my mama's heart if she finds out what I've done, and how I've been an accessory to his crime this time. It's funny, I've been running so hard from my family's reputation, and here I am, about to ruin my own where it still counts. Right here at this kitchen table.

I call Devon.

"Well, well, well," he says. "Looks like you didn't need my help at all. My brother seems to find you not so plain and small."

I don't bother telling him Will already called me that. I

sigh, but it turns into a sob before I can get my breath out. "It's all screwed up, Devon. It's over."

"What are you talking about?"

I draw in a ragged breath. "I'm pretty sure I'm responsible for whatever's happening to Sean. My sister's in jail and Coby's been taken to foster care."

He's quiet on the other end of the line except for a soft, "Whoa."

I take another breath and tell him the worst part. "My brother-in-law sold some drugs for me, that I stole from the Whitsons' house. That's how I got the money for Sean's guitar. And now Will hates me and Sean's probably going to hate me, too. And Mrs. Whitson's probably going to decide she doesn't want to be in business with my mom." I run my fingers in the space between the top of my cast and my leg, picking at the frayed netting. "Do you hate me now, too?"

"Of course not! And I really don't think Will hates you either. But, girl, what were you thinking?"

I start crying again. "It made so much sense at the time. Sammy convinced me nobody would get in trouble. I didn't mean to hurt anybody."

Devon's quiet. "Did you really tell Will you wouldn't go out with him again?"

"Yes," I whisper.

"Did you really mean it?"

"Yes. No. But it's done, Devon. Leave it alone. Promise me."

Devon's quiet, but then he sighs and says, "I promise."

"You can do something for me, though." I grip the phone against my ear and avoid my blotched reflection staring back at me from the mirror.

"Anything, Plain and Small."

"Will you call the Whitsons' house? See if you can find out what really happened, so I know for sure?"

"I already tried," Devon says.

"And?"

"They're not home, and Kush wouldn't talk to me. He actually said, 'Quit stalking me.'"

"Ouch," I say.

"Look, are you sure I can't talk some sense into you about my brother? You were a total idiot, but we all know the real you. You lost your mind for a minute or two. Who in this world hasn't?"

I take a deep breath. "It's okay," I say. "I think Will knows that, but maybe this is for the best. I'd rather keep him out of it."

"You're the boss, Plain and Small. You going to be okay?"

I look at my map. "Yeah. I'm going to be okay."

CHAPTER THIRTY-FOUR

The first school bell is like a death knell. Daddy gave me a ride on his way to the police station to pick up Whitney and it's teacher-early. I'm the only student in the commons. The space echoes every tick of the clock, every scuff I make of my foot on the tile floor. The cafeteria doors are still closed and won't open for another fifteen minutes.

I decide to go to the library and, thankfully, the door is unlocked. I slip inside. There's a comfy chair squeezed in on the far side of the checkout desk. It's hidden from view and everyone's favorite spot during rainy-day lunch, so I never get to sit in it. I settle into the cushions.

Sean's in trouble. Will probably won't come near me. C.A. will, understandably, question becoming my friend.

Devon's been good to me, but he's got a boyfriend to spend his nights on Skype with now. But worst of all, Coby's gone, and my sister's in jail.

If I keep my mouth shut, I'll be gone. Sammy hasn't said anything yet, who knows why, so I could get to Winston-Salem with most people not even knowing I was a part of this. But I sure wouldn't want anyone to see me when I come back to visit, if I don't come clean.

I hear teachers' voices from the other side of the library.

"I heard their child was taken into DSS custody."

My ears perk up.

It's Nurse Barb. "Well, I had no choice but to make a report when Amber was hobbling around here with a broken ankle and only an Ace bandage. That was pure and simple neglect."

Nurse Barb reported my ankle to DSS? Could it be my fault Coby got taken away?

I wait till the voices fade and I walk out of the library, barely able to breathe.

Down the freshman hall, I look for room 119.

The door is cracked open, and I knock softly.

"Come in."

For the first time ever, I slip into Mrs. Early's guidance office.

She looks up at me from her papers. "Good morning,

Amber. We missed you at church yesterday. I've been waiting to find out how your audition went."

"Good," I say flatly. There's no enthusiasm in my voice. Only sadness.

Mrs. Early folds her hands. "But that's not why you're here."

I shake my head.

"Do you want to have a seat?"

I nod.

She gets up and shuts the door and I start talking.

For the next thirty minutes all she does is listen. And she does it really well.

When my entire story's been spun out, she takes a deep breath. "Amber, if what you're saying is what happened, you know what you need to do."

I appreciate she doesn't put it as a question. That she already knows my answer.

"I do." I nod.

"Go on to class. Finish out the day. I'll see if I can't help with Coby and get in touch with the Whitsons."

"Thank you," I say.

She hugs me. "You're welcome."

I've been walking with my head down all day, so it was only a matter of time before I collided with someone.

Kush. Great.

"Excuse you," I say.

"Me?" he asks, pointing a finger at himself. "You know, I need to thank you."

"Thank me?"

"Yeah, getting Sean involved with your drug dealer in your family was brilliant. My dad is so pissed Sean let him down." His eyes are alive with excitement. "Your brother-in-law nailed Sean's ass to the wall. Sean tried to act like he was so innocent and the guitar was a gift, but Sammy called foul."

"Sammy blamed Sean?"

"Yeah, isn't it great?"

I stare at him. "Kush? Why are you such a dick?"

"What are you talking about?" His eyes are trained on the group of cheerleaders congregating at the end of the hall.

"After you spread all that crap about me, Sean was the one who defended you. Kept insisting you were such a good guy and that I only had to see inside of you."

Kush turns to face me. "You don't know what it's like. Ever since he moved in it's all Sean this, and Sean that, and oh, poor Sean. He's the reason we moved here in the first place."

"That's bullshit," I say. "Sean told me about Daya. He

told me what happened. You need to own your crap."

Kush shrugs. "I was only kidding. I don't *really* want him to go to jail."

"Whatever," I say and walk toward the stairs.

"Hey, Amber."

I turn.

"Sorry about the shit I said."

"Hold your sorrys. You may feel differently tomorrow."

CHAPTER THIRTY-FIVE

- -

Mama's outside waiting for me in the van. I take a deep breath as I climb into the passenger seat. I still haven't sorted out why Sammy pointed the finger at Sean instead of me, but that doesn't matter.

"Mama." I watch Will cut across the parking lot toward his car. My muscles tighten across my chest. "We need to talk."

"What about, sugar?"

"Everything," I say. I turn toward her. "And you're probably not going to like it too much."

When I get to the part about giving Sammy the pills, Mama's cheeks are as mottled red as I've ever seen them. "Now Aneeta's going to think I'm as bad of a parent as the Social Services worker does. How could you *do* this, Amber? How *could* you?"

"I was trying to do a good thing. I know it was stupid. I lost my mind for a minute. I wanted to tell you. Every day I wanted to tell you."

Mama is somehow able to accept the truth. And then she starts in on Sammy. "I should have kicked him out a year ago. It's bad enough he dragged Whitney into it, but now you, too."

After she's wound it all out, she calms down and looks at me. "Let's fix this."

Mama makes some phone calls and then drives me straight to the courthouse. Her fingers drum furiously on the steering wheel, her fear of driving completely gone.

It's weird how I can feel so empty, so scared, but so full at the same time. Like I'm back in my own body. Like no matter what's about to happen, at least it's happening to the real me. The one I can respect.

Mama parks and makes me walk in ahead of her.

I count the stone steps as I climb.

Sixteen.

Seventeen.

Eighteen.

The tall oak doors are heavy as I pull them open and a rush of stale air swirls out to greet me.

The Whitsons and Sean are already waiting inside, standing near the watercooler outside the magistrate's office. Sean is looking down, kind of like he did on the first day of school. Mrs. Whitson smiles at Mama, a kindness I wasn't expecting. I look at the textured granite floor and want to crawl into it, knowing the things I'm going to have to say in front of everybody.

"Miss Vaughn?" A man in a pin-striped navy suit and red tie walks to me, a folder in his hand.

"Yes, sir."

"I'm Mr. Gunn, the magistrate."

I nod. I recognize him from the reelection billboards all over town.

"Why don't you folks follow me into my office so I can take a statement."

When we're settled onto the cold metal chairs, Sean between his aunt and uncle, me next to Mama, Mr. Gunn clears his throat. "Amber, why don't you tell me what happened?"

It's my moment of truth. My confession. All my hard work, all my time singing with Will, practicing with Mrs. Early's chorus—now, it's all going to be for this. I'm going to lose NC-Arts, because whether it's a sentence from the judge or a sentence from my mama, there will be consequences, and I deserve them.

I glance at Sean. His Carolina blue eyes are focused on an invisible spot above Mr. Gunn's head. He's willing to throw himself under the bus, to prove he's unlovable. I won't let that happen. I can't let that happen. I count down from five and open my fingers, letting the dream slip through.

"I took the pills from the Whitsons' house." My voice is barely a whisper. Sammy may never have brought the pill bottle into it, but I still need to confess.

Mrs. Whitson's eyes widen. Mama looks at her lap.

"I'm going to need you to be a little more specific." Mr. Gunn's pen hovers above the pad.

I take a deep breath and start when Sammy first told me that I could take drugs from my friends so Sammy could sell them. I swallow, working up the nerve to tell the rest, willing myself to keep looking right at the magistrate. I even confess to using Mrs. Whitson's pretty pink lipstick.

I hear Mama's feet move next to me. I don't want to look at her, to see her reaction, but it almost sounds like someone covers a laugh with a cough.

I can feel the Whitsons shifting next to us. Mr. Whitson speaks first. "Now, I feel worse than horrible. But, that young man, he confessed. He insisted Sean was involved."

I squeeze my fingers under the lip of my chair's seat. "I think my brother-in-law is jealous of Sean. I don't know, but Sammy might be trying to get Sean out of the way for his band."

Mrs. Whitson leans forward. "Amber, are you sure?"

I close my eyes. "The pills were at the very back of your drawer. They had Kush's name on them. You like Clinique and Estée Lauder makeup."

"Oh," she says and sits back.

"Aneeta," Mama says. "I'm so sorry. It's not like her."

"Please don't be mad at Mama, Mrs. Whitson. She didn't know."

Mr. Gunn clears his throat and addresses me. "So, your brother-in-law coerced you into stealing prescription drugs?"

I look at Mama. Her face is teary, but she nods and grabs my hand. "Go on, sugar."

I hang on to her as I say, "No, sir. He only suggested it. I did it all on my own."

"So I'm hearing you say that you, Amber Vaughn, are the one who stole and delivered the drugs from the Whitsons' house to Sammy Crowder?"

"Yes, sir. I did."

He scrawls something on a legal pad, then looks up at the Whitsons. "Are you interested in pressing charges for theft?"

My heart stops. I knew this was a possibility.

Silence hangs for a few long seconds.

Sean clears his throat.

Mrs. Whitson's laugh breaks the thickness in the air. "Press charges? Lord, no. We're the ones who need to say we're sorry." She reaches out and takes Sean's hand. "What I want to know is what to do about this blessed guitar."

Mr. Gunn thinks for a minute. "I suppose it should be part of court evidence."

Sean speaks up for the first time. "I don't want it."

"What?" I say.

"No." His aunt reaches her other arm around his shoulder.

Mr. Whitson reaches for his wallet. "How much is this court evidence worth? The boy needs his guitar. I've got to start making this up to him. Right now."

Mr. Gunn waves his hand at Mr. Whitson. "Put your wallet away. The guitar wasn't stolen. The origin of the money came from your home. Personally, I've never even seen the guitar or know where it is. As long as we keep it that way, I think we're fine."

I clear my throat. "Can I say something?"

Mr. Gunn holds out his hand, giving me the go ahead.

I turn to the Whitsons, and to Sean. "I am really sorry about what I did. It was like a train that started rolling downhill and I didn't know how to stop it." Then I look at Sean. "I'm sorry I lied to you about the guitar. It's just, when you talked about music, when you played it that day, I recognized something like myself in you. I guess I wanted the me in you to have it. Does that make sense?"

Sean's eyes meet mine for the first time all day. "It messed things up, but yeah, I get it." He cuts his eyes toward his aunt and uncle. "It is a really nice guitar."

Mr. Whitson looks like a man who's come out on the losing end of a street fight. "Sean, I . . ." He drops his face to his hands and starts crying. I don't think I've ever seen my daddy cry. He pulls himself together quickly and claps his hand on Sean's shoulder. "I love you, kid. I wish I'd had more trust." He pulls Sean to him and hugs him hard. "I promise, from here forward, no snap judgments."

Sean's face is buried in his uncle's shoulder until they pull apart.

Mrs. Whitson slips past them and holds out her hand. "Open your hand," she says to me. When I look down there's a silver tube of lipstick shining up at me. She pulls me toward her and kisses me on both cheeks. "I'm sure it looks better on you. Thank you for caring about Sean." She sighs. "And Kush. Most people would have left him that night you snuck him home." She hugs Mama. "What hurts us makes us stronger, yes?"

Now we're all crying.

Mr. Gunn scratches something down on his legal pad. "Well then, you folks are free to go."

Mama and I start to follow the Whitsons out the door, but Mr. Gunn calls us back.

"Not so fast, young lady. Judge McKinney is going to need to see you. The Whitsons might not be pressing charges for theft, but the state wants a little say in the matter of the narcotics."

Mr. Gunn leads me and Mama up a flight of polished stairs to a small office. Will and Devon's daddy is sitting in his shirtsleeves and slacks behind a wide mahogany desk that fills the room.

"Mrs. Vaughn, Amber, come in." He pauses, letting the resonance of his deep voice echo away.

Mama seems as nervous as I am in the judge's office. We perch on the leather chairs in front of him. He's got the same laughing brown eyes as Will and Devon, but today they're nothing but serious as he takes the paperwork Mr. Gunn hands him. I notice a framed photograph of Will and Devon on his desk. They're sitting on the front porch of their house with guitars in their hands. A familiar ache throbs in my chest when I think about Will.

"Amber."

"Yes, sir?" I grip the arms of the chair. My heart is

pounding a thousand times a minute.

He rolls a fountain pen across the desk's shiny surface as he finishes reading Mr. Gunn's notes.

I want to curl up into a little ball. Judge and Mrs. McKinney have been good to me over the years.

He stops the pen under his hand. "In light of this situation"—he pauses and looks at me under bunched brows—"I'm recommending six months of probation."

I can feel Mama stiffen next to me.

"You will report to your assigned officer once a month during that time. If you stay in school and stay out of trouble and comply with the rules, at the end of your probation period, your record will be clean." He looks up. "Is that clear?"

I nod. Out of nowhere, Johnny Cash's "Folsom Prison Blues" starts playing in my head, and then I remember standing in front of a different set of judges. Judges who thought I was talented. Ones who looked at me with delight, not disappointment. Panic beats in my small-bird breast.

"Judge McKinney?" I know the answer, but I still have to ask. To hear my sentence ring in my ears, like the note of a song tapering off in the wind. A note I won't be singing in Winston-Salem this year.

"Yes, Amber?"

"Can I leave the county, like if I got into a special school for the arts?"

"No, you'll have to stay here under your parents' guidance. I trust they'll help keep you on the straight and narrow. And away from Sammy Crowder."

I glance at Mama. She's nodding in agreement, her eyebrows furrowed.

"Mama, but . . ." I let the words trail away. It's me. I've done this to myself. I'm just lucky he didn't put me in custody.

"I understand, Your Honor," I say, hoping he hears the sincerity of my words, but unable to keep the tears and flush of failure from my face.

Judge McKinney stands up to show us out. "Now, now, no need for tears. Think of it as a favor. An enforced separation from evil forces." He opens the door and I swear he winks. "Besides, big city like Winston, young girl like you, better to stay home with your folks another year or two."

Mama beams at his words, hugging me close. I hold her tight.

"I'm not going to see you in here again, am I, young lady?"

I turn from the door. "No, sir."

Then he smiles. "Don't be a stranger, then. We miss seeing you around the house. All of us."

CHAPTER THIRTY-SIX

It's been a month since Whitney was arrested, and outside, the first snow of the season is falling. I sit in my window seat and open the creamy paper for the millionth time.

> *Dear Ms. Vaughn,*
> *We are pleased to inform you of your*
> *acceptance to the North Carolina School*
> *of the Arts for the spring term.*

I don't bother rereading the rest of the letter. None of it matters. I blew it. I'm not going anywhere.

There's a knock on my door.

"Can I come in?" Whitney peeks her head inside my room and waits.

I motion for her to come and sit next to me.

Whitney climbs onto the window seat. "I never said thank you," she whispers.

"For what?" I ask. It seems like all I did was peel back the layers of our family till each of us was raw and aching with the pain of our collected lies.

"For turning yourself in, for telling Mrs. Early, for giving that up," she points to the letter. "For me, for Coby."

Whitney pulls my striped socked feet into her lap. "I hate that I picked Sammy over you. I'm not sure I'll ever forgive myself."

"I've forgiven you," I say.

"You have?"

"Of course. You're my sister, but he's your husband. I know that."

She smiles and wiggles my toes. "How'd you get so wise?"

"Had a pretty good role model."

She sighs. "I hope I will be again." She flicks the letter. "What about going your senior year?"

I lean my temple against the cold glass. "Maybe." I fold the letter up. "The more I've thought about it, I'm not completely sure the kind of singing they teach is the kind of singer I want to be."

"You could learn. You've got the chops."

"Yeah, maybe, but there's more to it."

"Oh, yeah?"

I wiggle my feet in my sister's hands. "Don't laugh, okay?"

She grabs my little toe. "Pinkie swear."

"I've been so focused on getting out of here that I forgot about this." I point out the window to the mountains. "And this." I put my hand on my heart. "I want things to be right before I go off. Right with you, with Mama, with Daddy." I pause. "With me." With Will. "Besides," I add. "I've spent my whole life here. And as much as it drives me crazy, and as much as I screwed up, what's one more year? I need to fix things with my friends. Not just run away."

Whitney smiles. "I get that."

I stare at the map on the wall. The red tack C.A. put on Winston-Salem is still there, but I moved it back to Sevenmile. Because the thing is, even though I made pretty big mistakes, I found my something, the something that makes me unique. Wherever I go in my life, hiking the Appalachian Trail, off to college in some big city, singing with a local band, my voice is me. My voice. A gift from these mountains, from my parents, even from the folks at Evermore Fundamental who first paid attention to it. And Kush was right, even if he didn't know what the hell he was talking about. This is no place to fall. It's not possible. There are way too many people who love me.

I laugh. "You know, Mrs. Early would be happier than a bug in a cow patty if she knew I'm staying to sing in her chorus."

"That'd make Mama happy."

"Yep." I smile. "I think it'd make her real happy."

Whitney and I sit, watching as fat flakes of snow coat the maple trees and the yard. A truck pushing a plow blade approaches and my shoulders hunch for a second, waiting on the thud. I keep forgetting the county finally fixed the road. When it glides on past, I relax.

"You think Daddy's going to stay true?" I draw a heart in the steam on the window.

Whitney sighs. "I hope so. I think Mama's got him running a little scared now that her business with Mrs. Whitson is taking off."

I laugh thinking about my sweet mama giving him the what for, Daddy's head in his hands on the kitchen table. But Mama's a woman of her words, and whatever Whitney or I think of what our Daddy's done, Mama's not backing down from her vows. It's like what she said about Whitney and Sammy. Right now she and Daddy are in their thin. But I'm hopeful it's going to be thick again, real soon.

"And what about you?" I ask.

"I start classes January fifteenth."

She grabs my hands and I squeeze them. There's more she's not saying. I know she met with a lawyer about filing for a divorce. It's hard for her to give up what was once her dream. It's been hard for her to realize Sammy's never going to change.

"Whitney?"

"Yeah?"

The snow is gorgeous. "You want to go for a hike?"

"Now?"

I pull my feet back and cross them, excited by the idea.

"Yeah, now. It's beautiful. It will be like old times."

"Amber, hon, it's cold. Call a friend. You're not grounded anymore." She pats my foot and leaves the room.

I think about who I could call.

Devon's gone to Maine with Gil to ski.

C.A.'s in South Carolina with her dad.

The Whitsons are in India visiting relatives.

Sean was so excited when he left. He couldn't stop talking about this guy Ravi Shankar and his influence on the Beatles, and I'm pretty certain he'll be coming home with a sitar. All Kush was excited about were beautiful Indian girls.

That leaves Will.

He hasn't started dating anybody else. In chorus we

still sing together. Nothing like our Show-off Solos duet, but it's still our voices, singing together. But in the halls we don't talk, we don't hang out on his parents' front porch goofing on Nirvana songs, we don't have a friendship anymore. I miss him.

I text Devon instead.

—I wish you were here for a hike.

My phone buzzes almost immediately.

—Call Will.

Then another text.

—Gil here. Please call Will. You'd be doing us a huge favor. He always wants to hang out with us. We're in Maine to get away from him.

—Ha. I'll think about it.

I can't think about it long, or I know I'll chicken out. I take the coward's way and text him, too.

—Want to go for a hike? As friends?

I wait. The phone lies dormant. Lifeless. He's not going to text back. He can pretend like he never got it.

Then.

It buzzes.

—With me?

I count off one-one-thousand, two-one-thousand. When I get to five, I text him back.

—Yes.

Again with the silent pause. Is he counting seconds, too? Another buzz.

—I'll meet you at the hiker barn in fifteen.

I get dressed in a hurry and run downstairs. My family is gathered in the kitchen in all the usual places. Daddy in his recliner. Mama baking a cake for dinner. Coby rolling trains across the linoleum floor and Whitney, sitting at the table, nursing a sick baby kitten with a bottle. It's peaceful without Sammy.

The local news guy teases us with a story of hypothermia and avalanche.

Mama glances at the TV, then at me in my hiking boots and layers. She flaps her whisk at the television, "That won't happen around here. No avalanches in the Appalachians. And you're too smart for hypothermia. Go on, but be back an hour before dark." As I walk out the door, she yells at me, "But take your cell phone!"

I wave it at her as the screen door slams.

The snow swooshes under my feet as I walk the logging road behind the Earlys' farm. A flash of a red cardinal darts through the brush to my right. The silence of winter sings its quiet melody. I can tell by the lack of boot prints that I've gotten to the barn first. I slip inside and let my eyes adjust to the dim light after the bright snow. My fingers bump over the names carved in the wood. One day,

I'll earn the right to put my name here. And year after next, I'll go to college and study music. Maybe at ETSU, maybe in Winston. But for now, I just want to walk in the woods with a friend.

I peek through the boards to see if I can see Will coming.

Just then, the door cracks open, throwing a triangle of bright light across the dirt floor. Will's standing there in his winter coat, his smile hesitant.

"So, Not So Plain and Small."

"Will." A mild disturbance still kicks up in my chest when I say his name.

We stand there, awkward. Me in the darkness. Him in the light.

Will clears his throat. "Thanks for asking me to hike."

"No problem." I flex my toes in my boots and shove my hands in the pockets of my coat. "It was too pretty not to get outside." I clear my throat. "I've been trying to work up the nerve to call you."

Now Will puts his hands in his pockets, his shoulders lifting toward his ears. "Really?"

Hope floods my insides when I hear the possibility in his voice. "Yeah. I've thought a lot about what I said the night of the party."

"You know, you could have let me decide if it was

worth the risk to hang out with you. I know what you were trying to do."

Will looks at me, and I make myself meet his eyes. He's biting his lip in a cute, worried way. "I heard what my dad did. It sort of messed you up, didn't it?"

"I think your dad's idea was to keep me out of a mess," I say.

Will rocks back on his heels. "Yeah. He's a big fan of tough love."

We stand for another charged second, neither of us moving.

"So you want to go on a hike?" I ask him.

"In a sec," Will says. He clears his throat and starts singing, slow at first.

"Come and listen to a story 'bout a boy named Will,
He really liked this girl who made
a mistake by stealing pills,
But then one day Will was feeling bad and alone,
When a ring, ring, ring started
chirping on his phone.
Amber Vaughn. Beautiful."

He ends with a wicked smile and takes a step closer to me. The cupid bow of his upper lip quivers.

He drops his head so his forehead is touching mine. "Not So Plain and Small, can we be friends again? I miss you."

I nod, which causes a funny friction between our skin. "Will you forgive me for being an idiot?"

"I already have," he says.

My heart is racing like a girl who's never kissed a boy before. But I have. I've kissed this boy, and I want to kiss him again. I take my hands out of my pockets.

"Just friends, right?" He takes a step back, away from me.

What? No way.

I close the gap. "Would you be terribly disappointed if I said I didn't want to be *just* your friend?"

He thumps a hand over his heart. "What? You don't want to be my friend? Not again."

I step closer to him again. "Nope." I shake my head and crawl my fingers up the front of his coat. "I have a better idea."

"Oh yeah?" He catches my fingers and presses them against his chest. "What's your *better* idea?"

I grab his other hand and drag him outside so we're both standing in the light. Snow squeaks under my boots as I rise onto my tiptoes. I whisper in his ear. "*Just* friends don't kiss."

His brown eyes crinkle, laughing, as he tilts his head down. I wrap my hands around the slice of his shoulder blades and pull him forward. Will's hands wrap my waist. When our lips meet, I kiss him like I mean it, letting it strike me warm in all the appropriate places. He doesn't seem to mind.

When I'm breathless, I break away and touch the thin scar on his face.

He tucks a strand of hair behind my ear, letting his fingers slide along my neck. "I missed you, Amber Vaughn."

I look into his eyes and see myself reflected there, smiling up at him. I'm ready to hear all about it. In bass and soprano. In songs of longing and love. In our voices, braided like the strongest cord.

I take off running up the trail, Will on my heels, the whole world waiting for us at the top of the ridge.

I'm ready to fly through the door and back again.

I'm ready to sing to the wind.

ACKNOWLEDGMENTS

Now it's time for my own song of thanks. Your voices, rising together, are what made Amber sing as brightly as she did.

First I need to thank my editor, Sarah Dotts Barley. In her graceful, yet determined, way, Sarah pulled the heart of this story out of me. She was my Mrs. Early, believing in me, knowing the raw lump of words could be turned into something amazing. Thank you for loving Sevenmile and its people. Thank you for challenging me to be a better writer and allowing me to find my way, even when my voice cracked and my throat grew dry. Your guidance inspires me, and look, we made a book! (P.S.—Will thinks you're cute.)

Also first (because how can I put one before the other) is my indomitable agent, Alexandra Machinist. She's my very own C.A. She flings all caps and exclamation points and adjectives like ADORE, and AWE, and INCREDIBLE at the perfect moments. She believed in this story from the moment she read it and I'm lucky to have her in my corner.

To the team at HarperTeen, who took my cover thoughts and made them a reality and who have helped craft this novel into a symphony—you are the resounding twang of the rarest New York City banjo ensemble. (And I think that's pretty darn rare.)

To Pat Esden, Kip Wilson, Jen McConnel, and Samantha Vérant, my frontline readers who bravely listened to the tunings of lyrics in process and were always able to find the promise, I love you each. I couldn't have done this without you. This is your story, too.

To Joy Neaves and my classmates at the Great Smokies Writing Program—you are my mentors, the ones who taught me to give and take, to listen and make changes, and how beginnings are never where they seem to be.

To the original YA-MG Critter group, Pam Vickers, Tara Stivers, Jeanne Ryan, Meradeth Houston, and Erika David, thanks for being awesome.

To later readers, Lynne Matson, Marieke Nykamp, and Kristen-Lippert Martin, thank you for the fine-tuning and the kudos. To Ruth Stevens for the chance. To the sweet and spicy, message-bearing, candy-heart club known as the YA Valentines, "More sinkhole, yo!" And to the communities of Verla Kay's Blueboards, SCBWI-Carolinas, OneFour Kid Lit, #wipmadness, and #5amwritersclub—keep singing!

To the students and colleagues (Angie!) who suffered through endless conversations about the birth of this book, thanks for pretending to listen and making me feel famous. (Jake!) And Zach—Devon is not you, though his love of Gaga is all your fault.

Finally I thank my family. My parents, Lynn and Robbie, who taught me that books make excellent home decor, the library is better than Six Flags, and summer reading lists mean trips to the bookstore. Thank you for raising a challenging, creative kid and for teaching me to love the written word. To my brother, Ken, and his wife, Lorraine, and to my awesome-sauce nephew and nieces, Jack, Kathleen, and Susan, you are the coolest. You can show your friends at school I said so.

To Emily and Abel—the bravest people I know. I love you more than anything.

And to R. for the magic carpet ride. It's all because of you. Let's keep flying over the horizon, letting the music play loud, catching our dreams.